Two *Yellow* CABOOSES

Sometimes home in Alabama is not so sweet…

LEVI BRONZE

Black Rose Writing | Texas

ISBN: 978-1-68513-177-7
PUBLISHED BY BLACK ROSE WRITING
www.blackrosewriting.com

Printed in the United States of America
Suggested Retail Price (SRP) $21.95

Two Yellow Cabooses is printed in Garamond

*As a planet-friendly publisher, Black Rose Writing does its best to eliminate unnecessary waste to reduce paper usage and energy costs, while never compromising the reading experience. As a result, the final word count vs. page count may not meet common expectations.

To Jena, my Mississippi Queen,
and the one who always gives me shelter from the storm.

Two Yellow CABOOSES

PROLOGUE

March 1857

Feeding and foddering the horses were not burdens in and of themselves. Napoleon loved horses. He thought them to be the most magnificent of all the Creator's animals. His grandfather had told him of lions, leopards, elephants, and rhinos, as well as many of the other animals that populated the motherland. But he could not imagine one of them being comparable to the horse. Dignified. Loyal. Useful. Napoleon had a way with them that bordered on the supernatural. News of his gift with horses had reached Jack Johnson's ear all the way from Atlanta more than twelve years ago. It was said that Napoleon could green break a stallion simply by staring the animal in the eyes. Dead break it in three days. Bombproof it in a week. The talk of the negro horseman caused Jack Johnson to covet. And being a man accustomed to having what he desired, he made the long journey to Atlanta, intent on buying Napoleon. He'd never paid over $2000 for a slave, but he'd decided that Napoleon would be part of his stock even if he had to pay $3500. When the transaction was finalized, he'd paid the $3500 . . . plus an additional $1500 to boot. But be that as it was, he'd returned home with what he'd set out to possess—the famous horse whisperer.

Drafts knifed between the boards of the one-room shack, burglarizing some of the warmth. Napoleon placed three hickory logs on the fire. He hoped the remaining two pieces would suffice till he returned from the stable. He'd risen a half dozen times during the night and rekindled the flame to ensure the coals maintained their orange glow. It was the first day of spring, 1857. The forces of nature had come calling on the heart of Dixie the day before. Without warning, an uncanny cold snap poured freezing rain on the middle and northern portions of Alabama. The Farmer's Almanac notwithstanding. The icy plague cursed every structure, every tree, every shrub, every fence line, and every farm implement. Everything about the Johnson 600-acre plantation, all the way down to the wheat blades, looked as if they'd been petrified in glass. Icicles decorated the landscape like translucent skeleton fingers.

Apart from the house workers, every slave of Jack Johnson's was given a respite until the hazardous ice subsided. Except Napoleon.

"Be careful. It's bound to be slick as greased glass out there," came a female voice from behind.

Napoleon straightened himself and put his hands on his hips. "I bet Massa Jack and his family are doin' mighty fine this mornin'," he said, one side of his upper lip curled as he looked at the blazes dancing over the logs. "Bet they all warm and bout ready to sit down to breakfast. Bet they havin' hotcakes and bacon. Bet they got plenty of butter. And maple syrup too. They probly . . . "

Napoleon stopped mid-sentence at the touch of his wife's hand to his elbow. "Now, Napo, you know it ain't gone do no good to busy yo mind with what Massa and his family be doin'. It ain't gone put feed in troughs and water in buckets. The sooner it gets done the sooner you can get back here by the fire."

Napo turned and embraced her. He held her close, one side of her face against his broad chest. "I know, Baby. But I show wish the Good Lawd would come down here from heaven and free us from our Egypt. How much longer is He gonna let Pharaoh's foot be on our necks?" He stroked her hair with one hand. "Massa goes to church every Sunday. His preacher preaches out of the same Scriptures Reverend Turner preaches to us out of. But I guess white preachers looks over ALL them verses about love and kindness and doin' unto others and all God's people bein' His chillin' no matter what color they be."

She pushed back and looked up at him. "You wastin' time. Turn me loose now and get on. I'll be here when you get back. Isaac be awake by then. He'll be wantin' to hear some of his daddy's stories. So be thinkin' bout some good ones while you's out there." Napo gave her a kiss and reached for his coat and hat. "Here," she said. "You gone need these," and helped him put on two tattered gloves. He plunged his arms into the coat and buttoned it to his neck. With his hat pulled down low on his head, he grabbed the axe that leaned against the hearth and exited the shack.

Realizing the wisdom of his wife's counsel, Napo stepped across the frozen ground with the concentration of a man walking a ledge. A cracking sound from above interrupted the stillness of the frozen countryside. Napo cut a glance. A branch fell from the massive oak tree that grew next to the horse stable. It crashed against the barn's tin roof, spooking the horses. They snorted and nickered as they pawed the ground and kicked against the sides of their stalls. "Easy! Easy!" Napo called out.

When Napo reached the barn, he beat the ice from the hardware and hinges with the blunt side of the axe and broke the doors free. Once inside, he propped the axe against the wall and walked to the feed crib. The familiar screech of the crib door latch alerted the horses to the fact that food was inevitable. Their snorts and nickers reverberated throughout the barn, excited at Napo's presence and eager for the early morning feed. Napo began shoveling sweet feed into a wheelbarrow. He sang a spiritual as he worked. A sudden, loud crack from above halted his labor and his song. Napo looked up. His blood ran cool at the sound of the bough tearing away from the trunk of the oak tree. He dropped the shovel and bolted to flee the stable. But before he could even get out of the crib, the large limb crashed against the top of the structure. The roof caved. Napo fell to the crib floor with a thud, the blow to the back of his head erasing his thoughts. After several minutes, the daze loosened its foggy grip and Napo regained consciousness. The snorts and squeals of injured horses rang in his ears. He felt pressure against his entire body. Against his stomach. Against his head. Against his chest. Pain shot through the muscles in his back and legs as he pushed up on all fours. He managed to lift up his shoulders and plant a foot on the crib floor. Then, like a

Samson, the robust black man raised the load of boards and tin, stood to his feet and shrugged off their burden.

"Rose!" a familiar voice cried out.

Napo turned to see Jack Johnson straining to lift a ceiling joist, his face grimacing and red.

Like a machine, Napo climbed over the heap and made his way to his master. There she lay . . . Rose. Jack Johnson's only daughter. Pinned under a roof beam, blood dripping from the cut on her forehead. "Get out the way," Napo ordered, shoving the lean, older white man aside. A sharp, rusty nail gashed one side of Jack Johnson's face as he tumbled against the rubble. Napo squatted down as he had many times before. Sometimes it was to raise a side of one of Johnson's several wagons. More than a thousand times, it was to pick up a long sack of Johnson's cotton. Each time, his heart pumped a mixture of blood and bitterness through his veins. He performed each chore because he had to. It was his lot in life. This time, however, he had a single, undiluted motivation—love. That a slave could love his master's children was an affection born from the Almighty. And God did it more times than not, though many slave owners didn't realize it. The few that did took it for granted and seldom expressed appreciation. Napo loved Rose Johnson.

"She may be a white child, but they's a ray of light in Miss Rose," he'd often told his wife.

Now, Rose Johnson lay helpless. Her life in jeopardy . . . if she still had life. What she might become in life was a matter to be settled in the future between her and God. In this moment, she needed an angel. Napo put his shoulder under the beam and prayed that he might be just that angel. He inhaled through his nostrils and gritted his teeth. The veins in his thick, dark neck stood out like ropes under his skin as he endeavored to press the earth downward with his feet. Like being pulled by a chain from heaven, the beam lifted. Jack jerked Rose from under it and Napo dropped the timber. The slave owner cradled his daughter's limp body and wailed. Blood dripped from his grazed face staining the little girl's blonde locks. Without asking, Napo grabbed her from Jack's arms and lumbered over the wreckage. "Help me, Jesus," he whispered, laying her down gently on the frozen ground. He checked the pulse on her neck with an index and middle finger and slapped her cheeks the way he'd seen seasoned slave women slap the buttocks of newly delivered babies. But Rose didn't respond. Napo made a fist. He punched the iced-over soil. The impact of his calloused knuckles cracked the frozen layer like a hammer. His second punch broke the ice in pieces. Napo took one piece and held it to the young girl's forehead. "Come on, Miss Rose. You wakes up now! You be stubborn and strong like you always is. Gather yo-self and open dem blue eyes now." The girl lay unresponsive, immune to the touch of the ice, deaf to the powerful black man's words. With one hand Napo slid the frozen chunk inside the collar of her wool coat and rubbed it on the tender, warm flesh of her neck. With the other, he held her delicate chin. "You do as Uncle Napo is tellin' you now, you hear," he commanded, his words painful in his throat. Her limp body balked at his earnest commands. The slave looked up into the cloudless gray sky, large, sincere tears gliding down his dark jaws. "Sweet Jesus, I beg you. She be just a baby. Ain't never done no wrong to nobody. Please, Lawd, resurrect this child." Rose inhaled as if she'd surfaced from being held under water. Napo pulled her close to his chest and kissed the top of her head through her blonde locks. "The Lawd done went and did it, Massa Jack. She's alive. She's alive."

• • •

Three weeks later
Straddling the beam at the roof's peak, Napo hammered pencil-sized nails. The reconstruction of Jack Johnson's stable was well underway. Napo would miss the horses the destruction had claimed, especially Red Man. Johnson didn't work his slaves on Sundays. One of but a few evidences the man had a human soul. He'd allowed Napo to ride Red Man at will on the slaves' favorite day of the week. The Appaloosa stud stood 18 hands tall, his rich auburn coat accented by his dappled white hindquarters. His mane and tail shiny black. His turquoise eyes gleamed from his white face. Four white stockings reached from his blonde hoofs halfway up his legs.

Napo had often imagined himself on Red Man's back, holding his son in front of him. His wife mounted behind him, her arms holding tightly around her man's waist. Red Man galloping at full speed. All of them riding away to freedom.

"Napo! Massa wants to see you in the big house!"

Napo looked down. A black man with silver hair and a matching beard stood between two of the four back porch columns of the Johnson mansion. He stared up at Napo, one arm motioning. "Come on now. Don't be tarryin' none." He wore black pants, a white shirt and a black bowtie. William Mansfield had been the Johnson family's house negro for over thirty years. He had it better than the other slaves on the plantation. Nicer clothes. Better food. Sweeping floors instead of picking cotton. Polishing boots instead of mucking barns. Dusting furniture instead of plowing fields. Straightening framed pictures and stocking cabinets instead of chopping wheat and stacking hay. None of the other slaves despised him. It wasn't his decision or doing. Mansfield, like every other black who belonged to Jack Johnson, was playing his part. Living the life that life had dealt . . . if it could be called a life.

Napo tossed the hammer to the yard below. He shimmied down one truss and climbed down the ladder, his thoughts ricocheting. "My Lawd, what could Massa Jack want? And why not just come outside and talk to me in the stable? Why call me up to the big house?" He'd never been summoned to the big house before. Napo's heart beat like a drum. He tried to swallow the lump in his throat.

"Have I angered him? Is he about to sell me? My wife? My son?" Napo prayed, "Great God in heaven, no! Please Lawd, anything but don't let this man split up my family."

When Napo reached the steps to the house, Mansfield opened the door. "Massa Jack is waitin' fer you in his office. I'll shows you the way."

Napo removed his hat as he entered the house. Pleasant smells filled his nostrils. Pipe tobacco. Fresh baked bread. Cinnamon. And other smells that Napo couldn't identify. He'd often wondered what the inside of the big house was like. What sort of things did Massa Jack have in his house? What kind of pictures did he have hanging on the walls? The sound of a piano could often be heard in the nighttime. What did it look like? Now he had his chance to see, but his nerves were so on edge he couldn't even raise his head. He just followed Mansfield through the house, looking down at the floor as he walked. He clutched the brim of his hat in one hand as if he were wringing water out of a towel.

Mansfield stopped at a closed door and knocked. "Come in," came the voice of Jack Johnson. The house slave opened the door and leaned in. Napo remained where he stood. He shut his eyes and prayed some more.

"He's here, sir," Mansfield said.

"Good. You can go back to what you were doing."

Napo's heart ratcheted up at the sound of his master's emotionless words. His throat pained as he swallowed warm saliva. Mansfield pushed the door open further for Napo and walked away. Napo stood in place like a stone statue. He dared not make a move without Jack Johnson's command. This was Jack Johnson's house. Jack Johnson's office. The place where he made decisions—important decisions—decisions that affected his business—decisions that affected his slaves.

The heels of Johnson's boots tapped against the hardwood floor as he walked to his office door. A bead of sweat dropped from Napo's forehead and onto the floor. He stepped on it and kept his head down. No telling what the white man would do if he knew his floor had just been tainted with water from a black man's body. The steps got closer. Louder. Then they stopped.

"Napo, come in. I'd like to talk to you about something."

Napo looked up at his master's face. There it was. A long, young, unavoidable red scar. Indentions on each side of it where catgut stitches had been. Jack Johnson would bear it the rest of his earthly life. No doubt, when he asked about it, he'd be quick to say a slave was the cause.

Jack Johnson offered no smile. No scowl. Nothing. Napo stepped inside and stopped, his eyes fixed on the floor. His heart jumped and his shoulders flinched as the door banged shut behind him. Jack Johnson walked past him and headed for his desk. Before he sat down, he raised his hand toward a chair. "Sit down."

"Yassa."

Napo hastened to the chair and eased himself down. Now, more than ever before, it was time to talk and act like an ignorant, naïve, obedient slave. Napo sat on the chair's edge, his shoulders forward. He kept his eyes down to avoid be tempted to stare at the imperfection on Jack Johnson's face.

"The horse stable be finished before the end of next week . . . yassa. Show will. I knows you wantin' to go to that big horse sale down in Montgomery first of next month." Napo adjusted in the chair and rolled the brim of his hat in his hands. "Don't you worry none. That stall be all ready for some more new horses. Show will."

The slave owner pressed his lips and leaned forward, his elbows on his desk, his fingers intertwined. "That's not what I want to talk to you about."

CHAPTER ONE

1995

The red Alabama dust powdered Mickey's bare feet and ankles as he walked on one side of the road. He could walk down the middle. Would be just fine. There was no traffic. Probably never was any. But his mama told him before he left the house, "Make sure you walk on the side of the road. People drive crazy." If she'd told him once, she'd told him a thousand times. Mickey always assured her he would. The road was more like two trails side by side separated by a knee-high growth of goldenrods, coffee weeds and bahiagrass. A log truck road perhaps. Or maybe a deer camp road. Mickey didn't know. He hoped it led to a pond or a creek. Hoped, if it did, they'd be fish and they'd be biting. Mickey had been run off from every pond within walking distance of where he and his mother lived. He'd never ventured down this road before. And for good reason. It had a bridge on it . . . and not just a regular bridge. A haunted bridge. Folks called it *Cry Baby Bridge*. The story was that one stormy night, years ago, a woman was walking on the road carrying her infant child. When she came to the bridge, a sudden gust of wind blew her against the railing. The impact knocked the baby out of her arms. It fell over the side and was gone . . . just like that. The event drove the lady mad. And every night, until she died, she returned to the bridge. Said she could hear her baby crying. And people say that, on windy nights, the ghost of the woman can be seen on the bridge. Leaning over the railing. Looking down into the water below. And that the sound of a baby crying can be heard. Whether or not the legend was true, Mickey was uncertain. Kids at school swore it was. True or not though, Mickey had to take his chances. He had to find a new fishing hole. *Cry Baby Bridge* notwithstanding.

Holding the fat end in one hand, Mickey leaned his cane pole against his shoulder as he walked. He'd wound the line loosely on the pole and stuck the hook in a knotty joint. The cork and sinker bounced from side to side as he stepped. He held a coffee can in the other hand. Dirt filled the can halfway. Inside were more than two dozen red worms. Bass, bream and catfish alike would hit red worms. No need to take chances with night crawlers. Sure, catfish would hit them. And maybe some bream. But any fish in any pond or any creek anywhere would go after reds.

The dirt was cool to the soles of Mickey's feet, thanks to the shade cast by the mature oaks, sweet gums and poplars that grew on each side of the road. A welcomed change from the sunbaked gravel shoulder of the blacktop he'd been walking. A breeze blew through the trees. Mickey stopped, faced it and shut his eyes. The warm moisture at his temples and hairline cooled and dried pleasantly as the gentle wind rustled through his hair and caressed his scalp. When it subsided, he opened his eyes and resumed his walking. He passed a rolling pasture to his right. A whippoorwill called in the distance. A long, crooked tree limb or something lay in the middle of the road up ahead. As Mickey drew closer, it moved. Chicken snake. It slithered away. To his left, about two hundred yards away, a willow tree draped its limp branches to the ground. A stone's throw away from it, a patch of cattail plants swayed in the breeze near a big water oak. Two good indications.

The sign on one of the fence posts read, "No Trespassing." So what? That was for grown-ups. Not kids. Mickey tossed his pole through the fence and climbed between two of the strands of barbed wire, careful not to snag his britches or dump any of the reds. He repositioned his pole on his shoulder and trounced through the waist-high grass. Mickey's heart jumped at the sudden sound of a nearby flapping. He halted and cut a glance. A quail ascended from the tall grass, then disappeared into the nearby woods. A quail lifting off never fails to startle a passerby, regardless of how young or old the passerby may be. Mickey shook his head and smiled and resumed his pace.

Wait. There. There it was. The sight of it caused his blood to pound through his veins. A little bigger than half of a football field. A pond. A slough at one end. An overflow dam at the other. What a find! Who could possibly know about THIS pond? No telling how many fish were in it.

He chose the dam side near the willow. Catfish and bream, the best eating fish, would be in the deepest water. He unrolled the line of the pole. Set his cork at four feet. Adjusted his sinker. Loaded up his hook with the reds and plopped it in. The cork hit the water at the edge of the willow tree's shadow. In less than a minute, the cork bobbed once. Three more times and down it went. Mickey lifted the pole to set the hook, then raised his line clear of the water. A bream twice the size of his hand. Yes! Mickey craned it to the bank and let it flop while he pulled his stringer from a front pocket. He strung the fish, eased it into the water and stuck the stringer's metal spike in the ground. He reloaded his hook with reds and plopped it in again at the same spot. This time, the cork bobbed almost as soon as it landed in the water. Another two times and down it went. Success again. Another bream. A little larger than the first. Mickey repeated his process. When his cork hit the water the third time, it sat still for thirty seconds, then went down hard. "Now, we're talking," Mickey said. He figured it to be a catfish. He gripped the pole with both hands and battled the fish for a few seconds. A catfish it was. Eighteen inches long. Head as wide as a bar of soap. Mickey landed it on the bank and bent down to get the stringer.

"The sign says, 'No Trespassing'," came a voice.

What the heck! Mickey froze, his hand only inches from the stringer spike. He pressed his lips together and lowered his chin to his chest. Lie or just tell the truth? Apologize or play dumb? Mickey stood up and turned around. A man stood ten yards away. At his side, he held a carbine rifle, then end of the barrel pointed at the ground.

Mickey swallowed hard. "You ain't gonna shoot me, are you?"

The man relaxed his shoulders and shook his head. "This world. This world," he said. With his free hand, he removed his straw hat and wiped the moisture from his dark brown forehead with the back of his forearm.

Staring toward the horizon, he pushed the hat back on. He locked his eyes on to Mickey's. "Now, why would you ask me a question like that?"

"Well, you gotta gun," Mickey said, one side of his faced wrenched, his brow wrinkled.

The man looked down at the gun, then back up at Mickey. "Yes, I do have a gun. But what if I had an axe or a bush hook or a sledgehammer or a garden hoe? Would you ask me the same kind of question?"

"Of course not. Them's tools."

"Well, in the hands of a wicked person, any one of them can do evil just like a gun. But in the hands of a respectable person, they can be used to do good. Same with a gun. Didn't your daddy teach you that?"

"No sir. I don't have no daddy no more. Just a mama. Our check don't come till the first of the month. We need some meat. That's why I'm fishing."

Mickey's words seem to melt the man's expression. "How many have you caught so far?" he asked, his eyes suddenly kind and accompanied with a subtle smile.

"I got two bream on the stringer. The cat makes three."

"Sounds like you're a REAL fisherman. How many more do you plan on catching?"

"I'd like to get another three or four more cats."

The man stroked his graying beard. "I tell you what. I've got to get home. You catch me a couple of cats and you can keep fishing. I live further down the road, just past the bridge. You bring me my two before you head back home. Deal?" the man said and winked.

What! Mickey could keep fishing. The man wasn't running him off.

Mickey beamed and nodded. "Deal!"

"Well, then, I'll plan on seeing you a little later." The man tipped his hat and started toward the road, his rifle at his side, its barrel pointed downward. Mickey bent down and pulled the stringer stake from the ground. He strung up the catfish, loaded up his hook with reds and plopped his line back in the water. In a few seconds, the cork bobbed again.

. . .

Mickey walked the cobblestone path to the front steps of the house, his eyes rounded as if he were watching the fireworks at the county fair. Was the place out of a book? Or a movie? It had to be the most beautiful house he'd ever seen. Not a wooden house. Not a brick house. But a rock house. Large stones the color of an evening sunset held together by wide joints of gray concrete. Its high, sharp sloping roof swooped up a bit on one side like the big sliding board at Mims' Swimming Lake. Numerous white-framed windows. Two white columns held up the triangle shaped awning that covered a small porch. Mickey held the loaded fish stringer at his side as he climbed the steps. He looked down at his dirty feet. They'd be the reason he wouldn't be able to see the inside of the magnificent house. Should he knock or turn the strange looking knob in the middle of the door? What was the knob for? Best to play it safe. Mickey extended a fist, but his curiosity wouldn't be denied. He hesitated. If it was a doorbell, reckon what it sounded like? He released the fist and gave the knob a turn. It sounded like the bell at school, only not as loud. Footsteps thumped inside the house, their sound getting closer. He wished he was tall enough to look through the window near the top of the door. Being a kid had many setbacks. Not being able to see things high up was one of them. The doorknob turned. What? The man didn't even have his door locked? What was he thinking? Mickey and his mother KEPT the door of their trailer locked. Always! Drug addicts steal stuff. And they don't care if it's daylight or dark. The door opened. The man wasn't wearing his hat, but he did have the same smile. A big white one like a movie star's. His hair had some gray in it, but not as much as his beard had.

"Well, looks like you had success," the man said. "Come on in."

"But Mister, my feet are dirty."

The man made a downward motion with his hand. "Not a problem."

Wow! The man actually invited him in. Dirty feet and all. The neighbors who lived close to Mickey would've made him wash at their water spigots. They'd never let him in with dirty feet even though they lived in crappy old trailers like Mickey and his mama. Mickey stepped through the doorway. The smell of something freshly baked greeted his nostrils. He inhaled. Oh, how he wanted a piece of whatever it was.

"Let's get those fish to the kitchen," the man said.

Mickey followed the man through the front room, through another room filled with books and into the kitchen. In the middle of it, pots and pans hung from a suspended grid over a buffet island.

"Just put them here in the sink," the man said and pointed an index finger. Mickey dropped the stringer of fish in one side of the double sink.

The man began inspecting the catch. "Let's see what you've got. Eight bream and four cats. Yeah, I thought the cats might stop biting for you. It was getting close to the heat of the day. That's when they move to the middle of the pond and lay on the bottom till the sun starts setting."

"Mister, your house is beautiful," Mickey said. "I believe it's the most beautiful house I've ever been in. Are you rich?"

The man laughed then looked down at Mickey. "The Lord's been good to me." He raised his brow and looked Mickey dead in the eyes. "He'll be good to you too, if you use the brain He gave you." He patted Mickey on the head then turned his attention back to the fish.

Mickey wrenched his face. "But what about someone like me who don't have much of a brain?"

The man started pulling the fish off the stringer. "And just why do you think that?"

"Because I don't make good grades."

The man continued unstringing the catch, his back to Mickey. "So, not making good grades means you don't have much of a brain? Is that what you think?"

Mickey noticed a picture on the wall of the kitchen and walked over to inspect it. "Well, that's what my teacher says. Told me I was just trailer trash with not much of a brain. Said it in front of the whole class too. Who are these people in the picture?"

"And, just who is your teacher?"

"Mrs. Fletcher."

"I'm sure your mother paid Mrs. Fletcher a visit after that." The man drew down his brow and cocked his head. "What a terrible thing to say to a child."

Mickey turned his attention to an item on the counter. A wooden block filled with antler-handle knives. He pulled one out of its slot. "No. Mama can't go nowhere. She's sick. These're cool," he said and touched the cutting side of the blade with his thumb. "Sharp too."

"What's your name?" the man said in a commanding tone.

Mickey returned the knife to its slot and pulled out another one. "Mickey Tucker," he said, checking the sharpness of the second knife's blade as well.

A garbage can with no lid sat on the floor at the end of the counter. What kind of garbage do people with nice houses have? Mickey looked down. Three empty bottles lay in the bottom of the can. The label on one of the bottles was turned upward. It read *Jack Daniel's Old No. 7 Brand Sour Mash Whiskey*. Best not to ask about them. Mickey put the knife back. A sign about the size of a dollar bill was affixed to the refrigerator door. Mickey walked over to inspect it. The sign read READY TO LEAD, READY TO FOLLOW, NEVER QUIT. Mickey pulled it off and let it snap back in place. A magnet. Cool.

The man washed his hands under the kitchen faucet and dried them on a small hand towel. "Well, Mickey Tucker, look at me," he said.

Mickey turned and looked at the man. The man pointed at Mickey with an index finger, "You may live in a trailer, but you're not trash. Don't you ever let anyone convince you that you are. You hear me, Son?"

Mickey nodded.

"Now, come over here and let's talk about these fish."

Mickey walked over to the sink. The man had all the fish off the stringer.

"Let's see now," the man said. "You have four catfish and eight bream. Two of the catfish are mine already. If you're willing to sell two of your bream, I'll give you two dollars for them. What do you say?"

Mickey gazed at the fish. Going home with enough fish for him and his mother for the next few days plus two dollars in his pocket—now, that was too good to pass up. But maybe, just maybe, the man would pay fifty cents more? Mickey looked up at the man and shot him his best dickering expression.

"How about two fifty?"

The man laughed. "Boy, your brain works just fine. Okay. Two fifty then." He re-strung Mickey's fish, leaving the two smallest catfish for himself. He washed his hands and dried them on a dish towel. He lifted the lid off one of the canisters on the countertop and pulled out two one-dollar bills and two quarters. Mickey reached out an open hand, grinning like he was receiving a birthday gift. The man paused and fixed his eyes on Mickey's. "Mickey, let me ask you a question. Would you rather have two fifty now or five a little later . . . say in two or three days?"

Mickey wrinkled his brow. "You mean you'll give me five dollars for the catfish in two or three days?"

The man shook his head. "No. That's not what I'm saying." He peered into Mickey's eyes again. "But what I am saying is the money you have can be doubled if you use that good brain the Lord gave you."

"Hmm. Just two or three days, huh?"

The man shrugged his shoulders. "Maybe just one."

"Alright. Tell me how."

"It's called investing." The man put the money in Mickey's hand. "Here, you hold this." He walked across the kitchen to a pantry and opened the door. He stepped inside. Mickey watched as the man sorted through some of the items. The man turned and walked back to Mickey. He held up five candy bars. "You see these?"

"Uh huh."

"These were on sale at the grocery store yesterday. I paid fifty cents apiece for them. I'll sell them to you for what I paid for them. Then, you sell them to some of your friends or neighbors for a dollar each. And, just like that." The man snapped his fingers. "You will have turned two dollars and fifty cents into five. Got it?"

"Yup," Mickey said and nodded, his lips pressed together.

"Good," the man said and winked. "Now, when you get the five candy bars sold, don't run out and spend the money. You hang on to it. Then, come back and visit me. And bring the money with you. Will you do that?"

"Yeah."

The man pulled the stringer of fish out of the sink. "Here's your fish." Mickey took them. "And here's your candy," the man said.

The man shoved them into a plastic bag and handed the bag to Mickey. He held out his hand and Mickey gave him his money back.

The man put the money back into the canister and raised an index finger. "Just a minute. I've got something else for you, too.

Mickey hoped it was some of whatever smelled so good. The man opened the oven door and pulled a frying pan of cornbread from the top rack. With one of the knives from the wooden block he cut the bread in several triangled pieces. He left two pieces in the pan. He wrapped the others in foil and placed them in a brown paper bag. He rolled down the top of the bag and gave it to Mickey.

"You can leave your fishing pole and worm can here if you need to. I'll put them in the shed. You can get them when you come back. You don't have enough hands to carry everything."

"Thank you, Sir."

Mickey followed the man back through the house, the bag of cornbread in one hand. The stringer of fish in the other. The man opened the front door and held it for him.

Mickey stopped and looked up at the man just before stepping out on the porch. "I told you my name," he said. "But you never told me yours?"

The man's brown cheeks arched as he grinned. "Abraham. Abe for short."

"Okay, Mr. Abe. I'll come back when I have the five dollars."

"I'll be looking forward to it."

Mickey walked out onto the porch and down the steps. He looked around. The sun was almost gone for the day.

"One more thing, Mickey," the man said.

Mickey turned back to the man. "Yessir?"

"All that talk about the bridge is just that—a bunch of talk. Don't give it any thought. You're too smart to believe any nonsense about a ghost or a crying baby. You hear me, now?"

"Yessir."

The man shut the door.

CHAPTER TWO

Mickey climbed the steps, five George Washingtons in one pocket of his cut-off blue jean shorts. Why did Abe want him to bring the money? Mickey had gone to bed the night before wondering. He wondered all day at school. Whatever the reason might be, Mickey was certain it was a good one. He turned the doorbell knob then put an ear to the door. A wide grin stretched across his face as he heard Abe's footsteps get closer and louder. Mickey stood up straight and swelled his chest, excited to inform Abe that he'd turned two dollars and fifty cents into five. The door opened.

"Well, look who's here," Abe said, a welcoming grin on his face. He held the doorknob in one hand and motioned with the other. "Come right on in. Come right on in."

Mickey stepped inside and Abe shut the door.

"You came at just the right time. I was about to make myself a chicken salad sandwich. Do you like chicken salad?"

Mickey nodded, his eyebrows peaked. "I sure do."

Abe winked as he lowered his chin. "Well, alright then. Let's head to the kitchen."

Mickey followed Abe as they made their way through the house.

"I got the five dollars," Mickey said.

Abe stopped and turned back to Mickey, his head cocked to one side, his brow pulled down. "Sure enough?"

"No kidding. I sold the candy bars at school today. Could've sold more."

A big smile stretched out on Abe's face. He bent down. "You know, I'm not a bit surprised. A smart boy like you," he said and rubbed the top of Mickey's head with an opened hand.

Abe's words were medicinal to Mickey. As different as daylight and dark compared to the regular comments of many other grown-ups. "Get off my property," several men had yelled when they caught him fishing in their ponds. "I'm watching you, Mickey Tucker. You put anything in your pocket, and I'll call the law," the man behind the counter at T-Bone's Quick Stop said every time Mickey went there. Even though Mickey had never taken so much as a straw from the store's fountain drink station. Once, while standing outside the principal's office, Mickey overheard him talking to Mrs. Fletcher. "Just do the best you can, Carol. By the time he gets to high school, Mickey Tucker'll be hooked on drugs just like his mother anyway." Why weren't there more people in the world like Abe? Mickey wondered.

"Have a seat," Abe said when they reached the kitchen. Mickey slid one of the two chairs from under the small breakfast table against the wall and sat down. He heard Abe pull open the refrigerator door.

"I'm having me a grape soda pop with my sandwich. You want one too?"

"Yessir. I love grape," Mickey said, his attention fixed once again on the picture that hung just above the table. Perhaps Abe didn't hear his question about it the day before.

"Boy, these two fellas are sure dressed up fancy. Who are they?"

"The one with the harmonica is my great grandfather. You want some chips?"

"Yessir. I'd love some. Who's the man with the guitar?"

Abe hummed a tune as he continued preparing their meal, his vocals seasoning the room with the pleasantness of baritone in perfect pitch. As he walked to the table, he mumbled some phrases. Something about coming into a kitchen and about it raining outdoors. Mickey couldn't make out the other words.

Abe set a loaded plate in front of Mickey. A generous amount of potato chips surrounding a thick chicken salad and lettuce sandwich. And a glass bottle of grape soda.

"You know soda in a glass bottle taste better than soda in a can or plastic bottle, don't you? The reason is cane sugar," Abe said.

"And, who's the other man. The one with the guitar?" Mickey said, his attention fixed on the antique photograph.

Abe made a shewing motion with one hand. "Oh, I'll tell you about him some other time." He turned back toward the kitchen counter. "What I want to hear about is how you turned your two fifty into five. Let me get my plate and get sat down and you tell me all about it." Abe retrieved his meal from the counter and sat down at the table opposite Mickey.

"I took them five candy bars to school and sold'em for a dollar a piece. Just like you recommended."

"Was it hard to do?" Abe said.

"Heck naw. It was easy. Could've sold ten of'em. Hardest part was not eatin' one or two of'em myself," Mickey said and took a big bite out of the sandwich.

Abe laughed. "I know what you mean. Chocolate is awful powerful. Especially at night when it's time to go to bed. Just seems like it tastes better then. Say you could've sold ten, huh?"

"Yessir. Ain't no vending machines at school. Word started getting around. 'Mickey Tucker's got candy bars for a dollar.' Kids were coming up to me wanting to buy'em way after I'd sold the five I had."

Abe took a drink of his soda pop and set the bottle back down on the table. "I think I've got about ten more in the pantry. I'll make you the same deal. Sell them to you for five. You can do the same thing tomorrow. Then you'll have ten dollars. What do you say?"

"I'd like that a lot."

Abe pushed his chair back, stood up and walked to the pantry. He returned with ten candy bars in a plastic shopping bag in one hand, a single candy bar in the other.

"Here you go, Businessman."

Mickey pulled the five singles from one of his pockets and counted them out to Abe. "What're you gonna do with that eleventh one?" Mickey said.

"This one's special," Abe said, holding up the bar of candy, "It's for celebrating."

"For celebrating what?"

Abe looked at Mickey, a grin on his face. "For celebrating Mickey Tucker. A young businessman who used his brain to make five dollars."

Mickey felt his cheeks warm as he relished in the affirmation. "Heck, I ain't no businessman. I'm just a kid who sold some candy bars."

Abe clicked his tongue and shook his head. "Now, Son, what does a businessman do?"

"Uh . . . I don't know. Make money and stuff I guess."

"Well, that's what you did yesterday. So, yesterday, you were a businessman. And a darn good one at that. You doubled your money in less than twenty-four hours. That's something very, very few businessmen anywhere have ever done in their lives. But you, Mickey Tucker, you did it. Now, what you do from here on is up to you and the Lord. Not your teachers or other kids at school." Abe lowered his chin and looked Mickey dead in the eyes, his brow raised. "You and the Lord. Do you hear what I'm saying, Son?"

Mickey nodded attentively. Like he was being let in on a secret.

"And don't you let anyone tell you that you have a bad brain. You may have to go about learning things in ways different than other people, but that's okay. It's like going to town. If a man's driving a car, he'll probably take the highway—it's quicker. If another man's walking, he'll probably take the back roads—it's safer. Either way, both get to town. Just depends on the way they're traveling."

"You sound like my mama. She's always telling me to walk on the back roads. She's always worrying I'll get run over on the big roads. She worries about me A LOT," Mickey shook his head and rolled his eyes. "Besides, I ain't got no car. Ain't got no driving license neither. You gotta be 16 in Alabama. I ain't but 11."

Abe pumped his opened hands just above the table. "I know, Mickey. I know. But 16's not that far away. Trust me. It'll be here before you know it. Now, listen. When someone tells you you're not smart or you can't do something, you do two things. First, you ignore them. Because you'll never climb the mountain of your dreams if you let your ankles get stuck in the mud of what people say. Got it?"

"Got it."

"And, second. When someone tells you that you can't do something, let it motivate you to prove them wrong."

Mickey wrinkled his brow. "What?"

"You know who Popeye is, don't you?" Abe said.

"Of course. Everybody knows who Popeye is. I watch him most Saturday mornings. He comes on right after Tom and Jerry."

"What happens when Popeye eats a can of spinach?"

"He gets strong and tough! Does amazing stuff."

Abe slapped the top of the table with a palm. "That's right. That's right. He becomes like a superhero. His muscles explode in his arms like volcanoes. The courage of a lion rises up in him. Nothing can stop him when he eats spinach. He shows whoever or whatever that you never can afford to count Popeye the Sailor Man out. Now, when someone tells you that you can't do something, let it be to you what a can of spinach is to Popeye. When they say you can't, you prove them wrong by showing them you can."

Mickey pondered Abe's words for a moment. "It's that easy, huh?"

Abe cocked his head to one side. "I didn't say anything about easy. Sometimes it'll be hard. So hard you'll feel like you have a sack of bricks on your back and a chain around your neck. It's during those times that you have to keep going and not quit."

Mickey pressed his lips together and nodded. He'd start putting Abe's advice into practice.

Abe lowered his chin and peered into Mickey's eyes. "You know why your mother worries about you, don't you?"

"Because she loves me."

Abe relaxed his expression and smiled. "That's right. Because she loves you."

Mickey turned up the pop bottle and swallowed down the last of the grape soda. "When you gonna eat that celebration candy bar?" he said and set the empty bottle down on the table with a clack.

"Well, Mickey, you know I've just been thinking about that. I'm so full of chicken salad I probably could only eat, say___" Abe looked up at the ceiling and rubbed his beard. "I don't know. Maybe about half of it right now. But if I wait till later . . . say right before bed, I could eat the whole thing which probably would make it harder to go to sleep. So, I'm thinking." He cut his eyes to Mickey's and grinned. "I'll eat half now if you'll eat the other half."

Mickey pulled down a victory fist pump. "Yes!"

Abe rose from the table and walked to the counter. He pulled a knife from the collection in the block. With his back to Mickey, he cut the candy bar into two uneven pieces. He gave Mickey the longest piece and kept the shorter piece for himself. Mickey went to work on his piece like he was in a competition.

"Alright, Mickey. It'll be getting dark soon and I bet you have some homework to do. Before you go, tell me the two things we talked about today," Abe said and bit off a small bite of his portion of the candy.

Mickey raised an index finger as he chewed. He moved the candy in his mouth to one side between his teeth and jaw. "Okay. First, when Mrs. Fletcher and everybody tells me I'm not smart, I ignore them." He chewed a few more times, raised his chin and swallowed hard.

"How about another bottle of pop?" Abe said.

"That'd be great, Mr. Abe."

"Hold your thoughts for a second. I got you."

Abe pulled open the refrigerator. Took out another bottle. Pried the top off with an opener and handed the fresh soda pop to Mickey. The boy chugged down about a third of the soft drink and picked up where he'd left off.

"Second, I prove them wrong because when they tell me I can't do something, it's gonna be like Popeye eating spinach," Mickey said and shoved the rest of the candy into his mouth.

Abe slapped his knee. "That's what I'm talking about, Mickey. Come on and I'll walk you to the door. You can drink the rest of the pop on the way home."

When they reached the front door, Abe opened it and held it as Mickey stepped out onto the porch.

"You come back and see me when you get that ten dollars," Abe said.

Mickey looked back and grinned, his teeth decorated with the ingredients of the candy bar. "I will. Probably tomorrow."

"It wouldn't surprise me one bit."

Mickey descended the steps and headed for home, ten candy bars in the plastic bag he held.

CHAPTER THREE

Mickey looked at the clock on the wall. 9:38 AM. The bell would ring in twelve minutes and his least favorite class . . . no, the class he loathed, the class he'd dreaded every day of his sixth-grade year would be over. At least until Monday. As soon as he was freed from the temporary prison he was in, he'd hurry over to the library. And, standing out front, he'd be a businessman. Just like Abe said. Word had gotten around that he had ten candy bars to sell. Two kids had already told him they had their money. Mickey was sure others would be waiting with theirs as well.

Mickey's desk was the last one in the third row. The place assigned to him by none other than Carol Fletcher. She'd assigned the first two desks on each row of her five-row classroom to her favorite students. Her pets. Kids whose parents were the "somebodies" in Claxton. Sons and daughters of business owners, local politicians, other teachers, medical people, and the like. The kids who wore nice clothes. Had the latest and best sneakers. Got cool stuff for Christmas. Acted and sang in the school's drama presentations. The kids who weren't on welfare. Who talked about eating at the best restaurants. Kids who went on vacation to cool places like Panama City Beach and the Smoky Mountains. The kids who had braces on their teeth so their smiles would be perfect by the time they entered high school. Kids who played little league baseball and peewee football. The ones whose parents helped raise money for the school and went to PTO meetings and stuff. Key players in groups like the Chamber of Commerce, the historical society, and a host of civic clubs that Mickey knew nothing about. Mrs. Fletcher's class was a public-school exhibit of socio-economic distinction. A "Who's Who" of southern, county-seat-town pecking order. And Mickey and his kind didn't meet the standard. The kids in the back desks of Mrs. Fletcher's class were the nameless, the powerless, the unpopular, and the insignificant. Their clothes weren't name brand. Often times no brand at all. And they didn't always fit perfectly either because they were handed down from their older siblings. They didn't get invited to birthday parties. After Christmas break, they didn't come back to school talking about all the awesome gifts they got. The school supplies they used were basic and minimal. Their lunches were free in the cafeteria. Their parents didn't own stores, drive nice cars, run for alderman, dress for fashion, or get their hair done at salons. They ran cash registers at grocery stores or one of the numerous convenience stores around town. They drove wreckers, log trucks, tractors that cut the grass along the interstate, and worked in labor unions. They stacked winter firewood next to their not-so-nice houses. Had wrecked cars in their yards and dogs that slept outside. They clipped food coupons out of the local newspaper, paid for groceries with food stamps, and shopped at the Methodist donation store. They were like modern-day low characters from a Charles Dickens novel.

Mickey's head bobbed forward. He shifted in his desk to shake off the slumber. If Carol Fletcher caught him dozing, she'd take a point off his final grade. It was the classroom Fuhrer's cardinal rule. She didn't enforce it with blind justice, however. She'd been known to pass by her pets and bump their desks or ask them a question to snap them back to alertness. She never extended such mercy to those in the back desks. She'd give them the death penalty if it were in her power. At least Mickey and his fellow nobodies believed so.

For Mickey, losing a final point could prove hazardous, potentially. He expected to take home a "D." And a low one at that. If he failed Mrs. Fletcher's English class, he'd be held back a year. The principal had already sent a letter home to Mickey's mother stating the threat. The absolute last thing Mickey wanted was to have to sit in Carol Fletcher's class for another full school year. She disliked Mickey. He knew it. So did everyone in the class . . . everyone in the rest of the sixth grade . . . probably everyone in the entire school.

The wheels squeaked as Mrs. Fletcher pushed back her chair and rose to her feet. As she stepped, the heels of her shoes tapped against the tile floor. She stood at the front of the room like a head of state, repositioned her designer frames and raised an index finger.

"As you know next week is the last week of the school year which means final exams. I've given much thought to the kind of exam we will have. In the past I have given multiple-choice questions on the literature portion of the test and a paragraph in need of correction for the grammar portion."

A sigh rose from the class. Mrs. Fletcher smiled and moved her finger back and forth like a car's windshield wiper. "No. We'll have none of that."

The students quieted. Mrs. Fletcher put her hand on her hips and began touring her classroom.

"Next year is seventh grade for all of you."

She gazed at Mickey. "Perhaps," she said and cut her eyes to the students at the front of the room. "Seventh grade is very significant in your development as students. Next year you'll begin forging the habits that will prepare you for high school. It is my intention to help you toward your future matriculation."

What did matriculation mean? Dang. You'd think she'd pause and define it. After all, she WAS an English teacher. Oh, well. What did the old bat have up her sleeve?

"To do so, your final exam will require you to draw upon all we've studied this year. You are to demonstrate what you've learned both in literature and in grammar by making a presentation before the class."

A boy in one of the front desks raised his hand. Dillan Masterson. Son of Mayor Aaron Masterson.

"Yes, Dillan," said Carol Fletcher, her attention piqued, smiling as if she were talking to the mayor himself.

"What does matriculation mean?"

Mrs. Fletcher smiled. "What a great question. I used the word in hopes of arousing the curiosity of one of you brighter, more promising students. So, good for you, Dillan. You represent your family well." She nodded once then focused again on the class. "Matriculation means college acceptance. I want you to start honing those skills that will help you in your college career. So, you have all weekend to review what we've covered this year and come up with your own creative presentation. You will be graded on both accuracy and creativity." She spread her hands. "Stretch your thinking. Give us something that really impresses us. Feel free to use notes, props or whatever you feel will make your presentation the most effective and the most memorable. Starting Monday and going through Thursday, we'll review the key things from the year. Then, we'll have presentations on Friday. You'll each have three minutes. This final exam will count for one half of your final grade. We'll take a class vote. Whoever gets the most votes will automatically receive a perfect score plus ten bonus points. I'll grade all other presentations myself."

What the heck? Mickey didn't feel he'd learned a single thing all year. And now he was going to have to stand up before the entire class and say something. He was toast. It'd be an "F" for him, no doubt about it. He'd have to spend all next year in Mrs. Fletcher's class again. And, if that wasn't bad enough, he'd have to watch everyone else move up to the seventh grade while he stayed back in the sixth. A major setback. He'd all but lose the few friends he'd made over the past six years and have to make new ones. He'd have to watch his current classmates graduate high school a year before him because he'd be a junior when they'd be seniors. Mrs. Fletcher had set this whole thing in motion just so he'd fail.

The bell rang. The familiar sounds of voices, shuffling back packs, and sliding desks rose in the room. With his head down and the dread of the next Friday torturing him, Mickey slid out of his desk and shrugged on his pack. He'd been looking forward to selling the candy bars. Mrs. Fletcher's conspiracy, however, had all but extinguished the entrepreneurial fire that had been blazing ever since he'd gotten out of bed. He'd just go stand in front of the library. Sell the bars to those who asked for them, then go to his next class.

Mickey turned the corner and looked up the hallway. Seven kids gathered around Billy Joe Speed. How was that for a name? Billy Joe Speed. It was as if he were destined to be a famous race car driver, football player or Olympic gold medalist. But not only did the kid have the coolest name in the school, he had money. His father, Albert Speed, owned the county's only Chevrolet dealership. From Birmingham to Montgomery ads plastered on billboards, ads announced on radio stations and ads printed in newspapers etched Speed's slogan in people's minds. *When It Comes to Cars and Trucks Nothing Beats Speed.* People forever gossiped and speculated about just how much money Albert Speed had. A truly juicy mystery. One matter, however, was clear and out in the open. The Speed family lived in the most opulent home in town. Only a few kids in school had ever seen the inside of it. Those that did told a consistent story: the house had an indoor swimming pool, a two-lane bowling alley, a movie theater, and an elevator. Everyone wanted to be Billy Joe Speed's friend. Especially the girls. The boy was an eighth-grade celebrity. Good looking and the tallest kid on campus.

As Mickey drew closer to the fanfare, Billy Joe held up a candy bar. "One dollar. "One dollar. Line up if you want one." The most popular kid in school had gotten wind of Mickey's gig.

Like frantic shoppers on Black Friday, boys and girls lined up, money in hand. Two of the kids in line were the very ones who'd committed to buy from Mickey. What could Mickey do? He was no match for Billy Joe Speed. Then, Mickey had an idea. Something Abe hadn't mentioned. Mickey hoped his new friend would approve. He unzipped his backpack, pulled out one of the candy bars and held it up.

"Seventy-five cents. I'll take seventy-five cents for mine," he said.

Everyone in the line turned and looked back at Mickey.

"Seventy-five cents, huh?" said the girl at the back of the line.

Mickey glanced up at Billy Joe. One side of the rich kid's lip was raised, his jaw tight and eyelids narrowed. Mickey's heart pounded against the wall of his chest. Oh crap.

Mickey cut his attention to the girl. "Ah . . . yeah. That's right. Not a dollar. Just seventy-five cents."

The boy standing closest to Billy Joe turned to him. "So, Billy Joe. You matching Mickey's deal?

"No. I'm not matching that trailer trash's deal. My candy's better any way," Billy Joe said.

"It's the same candy," the girl said.

"Yeah. It's the same candy," said the heftiest boy in the line.

"Money's money," said the first boy. "I'm buying from Mickey."

The boy stepped away from Billy Joe and walked up to Mickey. "Here's three quarters," he said and peeled off three of the four he held. He dropped them in Mickey's opened hand. Mickey handed him the candy bar.

"I'll take one too," said the girl and handed Mickey a dollar bill.

Mickey gave her one of the quarters. Pulled another bar from his backpack and handed it to her.

"Here's my money," said the pudgy boy and handed Mickey a buck.

Mickey gave him his change and a candy bar.

Six more students handed over their money and, just like that, Mickey had turned the ten bars into seven dollars and fifty cents. The businessman had struck again. Two kids remained, ready to fork over their money. But Mickey was out of inventory.

"That's all I've got," Mickey said to the kids. "I'll try to have more on Monday."

They turned back to Billy Joe. "We'll give you seventy-five a piece. Right, Tommy?" one said and looked to the other.

"Right," Tommy said. "Seventy-five and not a penny more."

Billy Joe looked Mickey up and down and then glared at the two dickerers. "You heard me. I'm not matching that trailer trash's price."

The two looked at each other and smirked. "Okay, fine," the first one said and gave his partner and elbow nudge. "Let's go, Tommy."

"You were ready to pay a buck till he showed up," Billy Joe said, motioning toward Mickey.

"Yeah," Tommy said. "But not now. You're just wanting to gouge us."

The two walked away and the bell rang. Billy Joe Speed stepped up to Mickey. He put an opened palm on Mickey's throat and pinned him against the wall. With his other hand he made a fist and held it two inches from Mickey's face. "You basically stole money from me, Welfare Boy. Nobody takes money from a Speed—nobody. And, on top of it, you made me look bad. You're gonna regret this. Trust me."

Billy Joe squeezed Mickey's throat and then let go. He reached down, picked up his pack and pulled it on his shoulder. "You got it coming. I'll get you. Wait and see."

Mickey rubbed his throat as he watched Billy Joe walk away. Why would a rich kid get SO bent out of shape over ten bucks? He probably got that much as an allowance every day. And would he really do something to Mickey?

Mickey sat down in his usual seat in Mr. Thornton's US History class. Second desk from the front. First row closest to the door. Mr. Thornton didn't assign seats. The kind historian pastored a rural Baptist church east of town close to the Coosa River. Few churches in the county, relatively speaking, could afford to provide a full-time salary for their pastors and thus most clergy had full-time secular jobs. Mr. Thornton was one of them. He had a good sense of humor, wore a necktie every day and treated all his students the same. He was Mickey's favorite teacher.

Each day Mr. Thornton stood at the door and welcomed his students. When the class time bell sounded, anyone not inside his classroom was counted tardy. No exceptions. The bell rang, Mr. Thornton shut the door and proceeded with his ritualistic roll call. After noting all who were present by each student's response of "here," he placed the class roll book in the top middle drawer of his desk and proceeded. His communication skills as a preacher flowed over into his classroom lectures. He fluctuated his tone of voice for emphasis. Used dramatic body language when appropriate. Gave interesting details not mentioned in the textbook. Asked thought-provoking questions. Sometimes, he rewarded student participation with individually wrapped hard candy. At other times, he awarded bonus points. His classroom was a real experience for his students. Not at all the drudgery that most of his fellow faculty members were. Kids enjoyed conversing with him during lunch in the cafeteria, brought him gifts at Christmas time and showed him great respect in the classroom. Mickey often wondered why there weren't more teachers in the school like Mr. Thornton.

"Well, class, today we're going to learn about one of the truly great leaders in our country's history. Many of you, I'm sure, will become leaders in the future. And the man we'll focus on today is someone you can all learn from. He had a cool nickname—TR. Anyone want to take a shot at what his name was?" he asked.

Two hands shot up. Phillip Askew and Lolita DeRosa. Lolita lived three trailers down from Mickey. And, like Mickey, lived with only one parent—her mother. Mr. Thornton, looked at Phillip. "Phillip, you answered yesterday. So, we'll give someone else an opportunity today." He turned to Lolita. "Okay, Ms. DeRosa, who do you think our person of interest is today?"

"Theodore Roosevelt," she said, her uncertainty evident in her pronunciation of the famous man's name.

Mr. Thornton clicked his tongue and nodded. "You got it." He tossed her the piece of peppermint he had concealed in his hand.

"Can I eat it now, Mr. Thornton?"

"You certainly can."

For the forty minutes that followed Mr. Thornton dramatized before his students Roosevelt and his Rough Riders' courage and valor during the Spanish-American War. For Mickey, the minutes flew by like seconds. The bell rang.

"Well, our time is up for today. I'll have a study guide ready for you to help you prepare for your final. I look forward to seeing you Monday." He then proceeded with his end-of-class routine. "And remember," he said and put a cupped hand behind one ear.

"There's no history like US history," the class responded in unison.

"That's right, men and women. Have a great rest of the day."

Mickey shouldered on his backpack and walked out of the classroom and into the already densely populated hallway. His next class was gym which meant flag football. After that, lunch. Then math. Followed by science and then it would be the twenty-minute bus ride home. He'd check on his mama, take out the garbage and then walk to Abe's. Mickey wasn't sure how Abe would feel about him having to reduce the price of the candy bars. He hoped his new wise friend would say he'd once again been a good businessman.

When Mickey reached the end of the hall, he took the flight of steps down to the ground level and exited the main building. The quickest way to the gymnasium was to walk across the ball field. As he walked, he thought about Teddy Roosevelt. What a soldier. Mickey never saw the hand. It shoved him hard against the side of the brick building. Mickey turned and looked up into the hate-filled face of Billy Joe Speed.

"I told you, Welfare Boy. Nobody takes money from me."

Billy Joe's first punch knocked the wind out of Mickey. Mickey grabbed his stomach and bent over. Billy Joe's second punch caught Mickey's above his right eye. The impact of it thrust him back against the wall once again. Billy Joe shoved his forearm hard against Mickey's throat.

"Next time, I'll put you in the hospital. You hear me."

Mickey gagged under the force of Billy Joe's arm. He tried to speak but the words wouldn't come. Billy Joe backed off enough for Mickey to breathe.

"Ah . . . yeah, I got it," Mickey said.

"You better, Trailer Trash." Billy Joe slapped Mickey on the side of the face and walked away.

Mickey nursed the soreness in his midsection and did his best to be competitive in his gym period. Mickey's eyelid and the skin under his eye looked like they'd been inflated with an air pump. Redness began turning to purple. Everyone asked about it and all seemed concerned . . . that is until the name Billy Joe Speed came out of Mickey's mouth. Then, it was like flipping a light switch from "on" to "off." Comments like "Dude, it looks bad." And "You need to go to the first aid station" quickly downgraded to compassionless remarks such as "I'm sure it'll be fine," and "Toughen up Mickey, it ain't nothing but a black eye." Within two hours of the episode every kid from the fifth grade to the eighth grade was talking about it. Embellishments made the story grow like a rolling snowball. By the time it reached the principal's office, word was that Mickey had pulled a knife on Billy Joe Speed. Did it in an effort to steal the rich boy's stash of candy bars. Billy Joe had no choice but to defend himself by beating Mickey to a semi-pulp.

Mickey's math teacher was in the middle of roll call when the principal interrupted via the intercom.

"Mrs. Ellison, do you have Mickey Tucker in your classroom?"

"Yes," she replied.

"Please send him to my office at once."

Mickey picked up his backpack and left the classroom. He was all too familiar with the principal's office. Mrs. Fletcher had ushered him there no less than three times for unpleasant conferences about Mickey's poor grades and what she considered his "inability to pay attention."

Principal Floyd Howell sat at his desk. Four chairs were stationed in his office. Two along one wall. Two along the other. School counselor, Heidi Smith, sat in one of the chairs. Next to her was a vacant chair.

Principal Howell motioned toward it with an open hand. "Have a seat, Mickey."

Mickey dropped his backpack next to the empty chair and sat down. On the other side of the room sat Billy Joe Speed and Billy Joe's best friend, Michael Baxter. Son of William Baxter, owner and founder of Baxter and Sons Construction Company. Mickey gripped the arms of the chair with clammy hands. This was going to be a one-sided affair.

Principal Howell leaned forward, his elbows on the top of his desk, his fingers interlocked. "Alright, boys. You both know why we're here. So, let's get down to it." "First of all." He looked Mickey in the eyes, "Mickey, did you pull a knife on Billy Joe?"

"No sir."

Howell turned his attention to Billy Joe. "Is this the truth?"

Billy Joe cut a glance at Mickey then focused on Principal Howell. "Not exactly. He didn't actually pull a knife on me, but he did say he had one and that he would use it if I didn't give him my candy."

Mickey jumped to his feet, his emboldened eyes fixed on Billy Joe's. "That's a lie and you know it is!" He turned to Principal Howell. "I've never even brought a knife to school."

The principal raised an index finger toward Mickey. "You'll control yourself, Young Man, or you'll find yourself in even more trouble than you're in already! Now, sit down!"

Mickey sat back down. How could Mickey be already in trouble? Mr. Howell hadn't even heard Mickey's side of the story—the real story. This was a railroad job if there ever was one.

Howell turned to Michael Baxter. "Michael, I understand you witnessed the whole thing. Did Mickey threaten to use a knife if Billy Joe refused to give him the candy?"

Mickey protested. "Mr. Howell, Michael wasn't there. Nobody else was. It was just me and Billy Joe. He planned it that way."

Howell slammed an opened palm down on the top of the desk. He looked at Mickey with fiery eyes. "That's enough, Mickey Tucker! I told you to control yourself. I think I've heard enough. It's a wonder Billy Joe didn't do more than just black your eye. Who knows what some other student might have done? Billy Joe's older than you and bigger than you. He's been brought up to be honorable and respectful. I know because I attend church with his family. His father's in my Sunday School class. He's as fine of a man as I've ever known. I've no doubt that he's raised Billy Joe to turn the other cheek when at all possible. It's apparent that Billy Joe felt he was in harm's way and had to do what he did. I'm sure he held back. Probably just punched you and ran to get away. Mickey, you're suspended for three days for threatening another student with a knife. You're not to return to school until Thursday. I'll talk with all your teachers and have them provide any final exam study guides they plan on passing out. Your mother can pick them up at the front desk at 3 PM on Monday. When you return on Thursday, the two of you stay clear of each other. Do you understand?"

Billy Joe nodded, his face resembling that of a lying politician. "Yessir."

Mickey looked down at the floor. Was there no justice for a poor boy like him? "Yessir," he said, a defeated tone in his voice.

Principal Howell turned to Heidi Smith. "Mrs. Smith would you take Mickey to the library? Tell Mrs. Wiggins to monitor him the rest of the day until school is over. I don't want him going to his other classes. I don't want to risk him retaliating against Billy Joe during class changes. Tell Mrs. Wiggins to see to it that he gets on his bus without causing any further conflict with anyone else today."

"Yessir," Smith said.

"Also, will you make out a report of this session and place it on my desk?"

"Of course, Sir."

"That'll be all then. You're all dismissed."

The four of them stood from their seats and walked into the hallway.

"Oh, Mrs. Smith, would you come back in here for just a moment?" Principal Howell called out.

"Mickey, you wait here. Don't you move. I'll be right back," she said and walked back into Howell's office, closing the door behind her.

Mickey leaned against the wall and stared at the floor, his backpack in one hand. Billy Joe drew in close to Mickey and leaned down, his mouth inches from the crown of Mickey's head. "What do you say now, Trailer Trash? You get suspended and I get off free and clear. Did you hear all those nice things he said about me? I can do anything I want. I'm Billy Joe Speed. I'll be in high school next year. In two years, you'll be in high school too. And I'll be waiting for you."

Chapter Four

The doors squeaked behind Mickey as they twisted and slapped shut. The airbrakes swished as they disengaged and bus number fifty-seven pulled away, leaving Mickey standing at the end of the driveway. He looked at the low-cost metal dwelling. Four wooden steps led up to a small square porch. Both the steps and the porch bore witness to the eroding effectiveness of wind and rain, heat and cold over the years. Duct tape dangled from one side of the air conditioner. The small cooling unit stuck out of the window closest to the entry door. As it ran, water dripped from it and formed a small puddle on the ground next to a dented metal garbage can. The place wasn't attractive. Not even close. Mickey could still hear Billy Joe standing over him. Trailer trash.

Mickey climbed the steps. His mother wasn't waiting to greet him with the door held open. She never was. He pulled the key from under the mat and unlocked the door. As he entered, the cool air dabbed his face and arms. The window unit was doing its job.

"Mickey, is that you, Honey?" came an affectionate female voice.

"Yeah, Mama."

"Well, come on back here and tell me about your day."

Was she ever in for it? And the eye. It was going to send her through the ceiling. Mickey dropped his backpack on the recliner, took a deep breath and started towards the back room of the trailer. The door of her room was open just like always. He stopped short of the threshold and leaned against the wall.

"Mama, is it okay if I go out. I've got some things I'd like to do."

"Mickey, I haven't seen you all day. Come sit and talk with me. At least for a little while."

How could he say no? He was all she had. She seldom kissed him without shedding tears. Every day she told him how much she loved him. How proud she was of him. And every day she apologized. For not playing ball with him. Or going fishing with him. For not washing his clothes or helping him with his homework. For not meeting his teachers or having lunch with him in the cafeteria. For not giving him money or buying him new clothes. For not making him birthday cakes or buying him Christmas presents. And the one that pained Mickey the most—for not being a good mother.

Mickey walked through the doorway to a familiar sight. His mother sitting up in her bed, pillows stacked between her back and the headboard. A plastic tube from a portable metal tank fitting snug around her head and under her nose. A port in each of her nostrils providing a continual flow of oxygen. The absence of muscle in her arms and legs causing her skin to cling to her bones like thin plastic.

His mother's eyes shot open wide. "What happened?"

"Billy Joe Speed."

The ailing lady strained to adjust herself in her bed. "Oh, baby. Come sit beside me and tell me all about it."

Mickey sat on the edge of the bed and told his mother about selling the candy, how Billy Joe had punched him and the ordeal he'd experienced in Principal Howell's office.

"I'm so sorry, Mickey. Does it hurt?" she said and touched his eye with boney fingers.

"It hurt when he hit me but not now. It just feels heavy."

"I'd go up there and meet with that principal if I could. I'd tell him a thing or two." She stroked his hair. "I know you're telling the truth, Baby. Don't think I don't. I'd pay Billy Joe's parents a visit too." She made a feeble fist and made a downward motion with it. "I'd walk right up to that mansion they live in. Knock on the door and give them a piece of my mind."

"I know you would."

"So, you can't go back to school till Thursday?" she said.

"Nope. I can't even go to the school and get stuff for my final exams. Mr. Howell says you'll have to go by the school office Monday at 3 PM and pick it up."

"I'll call the school on Monday and talk to someone in the office. I'll tell them about my situation. Surely, they can give it to your bus driver and he can hand it to you when he comes by here that afternoon."

Mickey perked up and snapped his fingers. "I bet Abe would go pick the stuff up for me. That's the kind of man he is."

Mickey's mother gazed into his eyes. She pressed her lips together and lowered her chin. "You've been going on and on about this Abe fellow ever since you met him the other day. Maybe I'll get to meet him sometime."

"I'm telling you, Mama, you'd really like him. I bet he'd come over if I ask him. Please let me ask him. Please."

She shook her head. "I don't know, Mickey. I can't get the house cleaned up and ready. I can't cook a meal for him. I can't—"

Mickey interrupted her, his hand on top of one of hers. "Mama, I can do all that. I've got some money now from selling the candy bars. I can pick up a bag of chips and some stuff for sandwiches at the store. And, you know I know how to make Kool-Aid. It'll be great. Let me ask him, Mama. Please!"

She exhaled, gripped his hand and smiled. "Okay, Mickey. If you want to have him over, go ahead and ask him."

Mickey leaned down and hugged her. "Thanks, Mama. You're the best." He raised back up and looked into her wet eyes. "You're gonna really like him. I just know it."

"Make sure he knows that we don't live in a fancy house."

"Can I go see him right now?"

She patted him on the hand. "I guess so. But make sure you're back home before dark. I don't want you out walking after dark."

• • •

Abe had his back to Mickey as he worked. Mickey watched as the water spewed from the nozzle of the hose, washing the suds off the beautiful black truck and onto the driveway. Mickey walked up to him.

"Hello, Mr. Abe."

Abe looked down at him and jutted his head back. "Boy, what happened to you?"

"A boy at school beat me up."

Abe raised an index finger. "One second. Let me rinse the rest of this soap off and then I want to hear ALL about it."

Judging by the look on Abe's face, Mickey couldn't tell if he was mad or disappointed. But he knew that Abe was curious to hear the story.

With the gumption of a machine plugged into an outlet, Abe finished spraying the truck. He dropped the nozzle and motioned with one hand. "Let's sit on the back patio."

Mickey followed him past the truck and around the corner of the house. The color of the stone patio complemented the stones on the house. To one side stood a metal fire pit. Four heavy iron chairs with multi-colored cushions were positioned around the front of it in a semicircle. A glass top table with a green metal frame sat in the middle of the patio. Six matching chairs were pushed under the table and spaced perfectly around it. On the side opposite the fire pit, sat a large stainless steel barbeque grill. Ten yards from the back of the outdoor dining scene water gushed up in the shape of a cone from the center of a shallow rock-trimmed pond. It reminded Mickey of the one he'd seen while on a field trip at the Birmingham Zoo when he was in fourth grade. His mama had a job as a waitress at Earl Driver's Steakhouse back then. And they had extra money to do things like play mini-golf and go to the movie theater. She took off work the day of the field trip and went along with Mickey's class as a chaperone. Those were good days.

Abe pulled one of the chairs from the patio table. "Here. You sit here."

Mickey sat down. Abe pulled out another one and sat across from Mickey.

"Alright. What's the story?" he said.

Mickey told Abe all the details. Just like he'd told his mother. Everything from discounting the candy seventy-five cents per bar to being suspended for three days.

Abe pushed his chair back from the table, crossed his ankles and folded his arms over his stomach. "Alright. So let me get this straight. Billy Joe will be in high school next school year which means you won't be crossing paths with him for another two years. Correct?"

"Correct," said Mickey.

"And the last thing he told you was that he'd be waiting for you."

"That's what he said."

"Uh huh," said Abe as he rubbed his beard. "That'll give us time," he mumbled.

"What'd you say?"

Abe gave a tight smile. "Oh, nothing. I was just kinda thinking out loud. You say you lowered the price of your candy bars from a dollar to seventy-five cents?"

Mickey shrugged his shoulders and raised his opened hands. "I had to, Mr. Abe, or the kids would've bought Billy Joe's. I figured getting seven dollars and fifty cents was better than not getting nuthin'."

Abe grinned. "That was smart, Mickey. I would have done the same thing. Give me five."

Abe raised a palm to Mickey and Mickey slapped him five, a big smile on his face.

"Let's go in the house and we'll see if we can't start doing something about that eye."

They rose from the table and went inside. Mickey followed Abe to the kitchen and sat down. He studied the picture again of the two dapper men while Abe was in the pantry. Abe came back with a can of pineapple. He jammed the top of the can into the electric opener on the countertop and pressed down the blade. It whined as it circled the top of the can cutting through the tin lid. Abe took the top slice of pineapple out of the can and broke it into two pieces. He walked over to Mickey.

"Here," he said.

"I'm not hungry. Thanks though."

"It's not for you to eat. Hold it under your eye. It'll help the swelling go down."

Mickey took the piece of pineapple and held it under his bruised eye. "I never heard of this before. By the way, you never told me who the man with the guitar is."

Abe placed the other half of the pineapple on Mickey's puffy eyebrow and held it there. "We can talk about him some other time. What did your mother say about all this?"

"Oh, she wasn't happy. Said she'd like to give Billy Joe Speed's parents a piece of her mind. By the way, me and mama were wondering if you could come over to our house tomorrow for lunch. She really wants to meet you."

"I'd be honored. I've been wanting to meet your mother too. What are we eating?"

"I thought I'd use the money from the candy to buy some chips and sandwich stuff. And I'll make us some Kool-Aid to drink."

"Can you hold both pieces?" Abe said.

Mickey repositioned his hand so he could hold one piece below his eye and the other piece above it.

"I think I've got something else around here somewhere. Let me look."

Abe stepped back into the pantry and returned with a container of a white pasty substance. "This is coconut oil. When you go to sleep tonight rub some of it on. When you wake up in the morning, you'll see a difference." He placed the container on the table. "What time is lunch tomorrow?"

"How's straight up noon?" Mickey said.

"Alright. Straight up noon it is. Let me ask you a question. Would you rather have chips and a sandwich or burgers and fries from the Dari Delite?"

"What kind of question is that? Burgers and fries from the Dari Delite any day."

"What do you say, then, if I pick up some and bring them over for lunch and you keep your money?"

With one hand holding the pineapple pieces in place, Mickey raised his head and looked up, a grin on his face. "Deal."

Abe winked and smiled. "And what kind of milk shake does your mother like?"

"Butterscotch."

"And what about you?"

"Chocolate."

"Gotcha. Where do you live?"

"Smitherman's Trailer Park. Lot 61."

"Got it. I'll see you tomorrow. Noon. Straight up. I made some fried apple pies earlier today. You want to take a few home?"

"Sure," Mickey said. "Who doesn't like fried apple pies?"

Abe walked to the oven and pulled down the door. Mickey breathed in the delectable aroma of freshly baked apples and warm cinnamon.

Abe pulled out the tray of pastries and set it on the stovetop. Using a spatula, he began transferring some of the pies to a plastic bowl. "Mickey," he said, "You SURE your mother is okay having—" he stopped mid-sentence.

"Having what?" Mickey said.

Abe clamped a lid down on the bowl and turned and handed it to Mickey. "Oh, never mind. I'll see you tomorrow."

CHAPTER FIVE

The alarm clock chirped. 6 AM. Mickey never got up at 6. Not even on school days. And certainly not on Saturdays. But this was not a typical Saturday. Far from it. A man was coming for a visit. And not just a regular man like Mickey's bus driver or the man who read the electric meter or the man who picked up the garbage. Today, a rich man was coming. Abe had to be rich. A beautiful house that smelled nice. Good food—lots of good food. A room full of books. Land. A fishing pond. Didn't work a job. Yup, Abe had to be rich.

Mickey silenced the clock and stretched. The mattress and covers put up a good fight, but Mickey prevailed at freeing himself from their enticements. No rolling over and going back to sleep for him. He arose and made his way to the bathroom. After taking care of his needed morning business, he washed his hands in the sink and splashed some water in his face. Wait. They were working—the pineapple and the coconut oil were working. Hmm. How the heck did Abe know such things?

Mickey was determined that everything in the house would be perfect. Well, total perfection was impossible. The kitchen faucet dripped. The chairs around the dining table didn't match. The sofa had a rip on one cushion. The den carpet was stained in several places where Mickey had spilled things or tracked mud in. And one of the lamps had a blown bulb. However, the homely place could be perfect in other ways. The dishes in the sink could be washed and put in the cabinets. The console television could be dusted. The laundry piled in the bathroom floor could be washed, dried, folded, and put away. The carpet could be vacuumed. The linoleum floors could be swept and mopped. The garbage could be taken out. The mouse traps could be free of dead mice. And the debris in the yard could be picked up. The first thing Mickey did was make breakfast. He boiled two eggs. Toasted two pieces of bread. He would have fried two pieces of bologna, but he and his mama ate the last of it earlier in the week. When the meager food was prepared, he fixed two plates. He pulled the plastic pitcher from the fridge. Filled two glasses two-thirds full of orange Kool-Aid and put a drinking straw in one.

"Are you awake yet, Mama," he said as he walked down the hallway.

"Yes," she replied.

Mickey walked into her bedroom. She was ready for the meal, sitting up in the bed, pillows stacked behind her back. Mickey handed the plate to her and held the glass so she drank from the straw. After a few swallows, she stopped drinking and Mickey set the glass on the nightstand next to her bed.

"Mama, I know I usually sit and talk with you when we eat breakfast on Saturdays and Sundays, but would it be okay if I get started on the house? Mr. Abe'll be here at noon and I have a lot to do."

"Sure," she said, smiling. "Today is a big day to you, I know. But before you get started, would you put my hairbrush, cosmetic bag and hairspray on the bed next to me?"

Mickey did as she'd asked, then left the room. He scarfed down his breakfast and got busy. He washed and put away the dishes. Cleaned the countertop. Wiped off the table and dusted the few pieces of furniture he and his mother owned. He pulled the vacuum cleaner from the hall closet, plugged it in and flipped the switch. Nothing. He tried another outlet. Nothing. What was the deal? It ran fine the last time he used it. Couldn't have been more than a month ago. He inspected the cord, checked the filter and the belt. All seemed in order. He checked the clock on the wall. 9:53 AM.

Mickey darted out the door and ran to Lot 58. He shot up the steps and knocked on the door. Come on. Come on. Hurry, please. Mickey knocked again. This time louder.

"I'm coming. I'm coming," came a familiar voice from inside.

The door opened. A barefoot Lolita DeRosa wore Looney Tunes pajamas and had an unmistakable bed head.

"What's the problem, Mickey? It's Saturday and ain't even ten o'clock," she said just before a yawn overtook her.

"I need a vacuum cleaner and fast. You got one?"

"You mean to tell me you woke me up for a vacuum cleaner? Come on, Mickey. Couldn't it have waited?"

"I'm sorry, Lolita, but it's really important."

Lolita rubbed her hair and succumbed to another yawn. "Alright, give me a minute," she said and shut the door.

Mickey waited on the porch. He scanned the neighborhood. Randall Jones walked down his steps, shirtless and barefoot. His round belly jiggling as he made his descent. In one hand he held a clear plastic garbage bag that bulged with empty beer cans. Randall's driveway was packed with cars the night before and his home stereo system blasted half the trailer park with everything from *A Country Boy Can Survive* to *Back in Black*. He lifted the lid from his metal trash can and dropped the bag inside. The can was nearly full already. Randall packed the bag with an open palm. The sound of the bending, crunching cans stole the quietness from the air. After numerous plunges, the fat man had to settle for half the bag sticking above the can. Settling for defeat, he set the lid on top of the bag and turned to head back up his doorsteps. He cut a glance to Mickey, raised his chin as if to say, "Hey, man," and went back into his trailer.

Lolita opened the door, holding the handle of a Hoover upright vacuum cleaner. "Here you go," she said and handed it to him.

"Thanks, Lolita. I really appreciate it."

"I'm going back to bed so wait till after lunch to bring it back. If you need to keep it for a day or two, that's fine."

"Okay," Mickey said and turned and headed down the steps. He heard Lolita shut and lock the door behind him. He trotted back to his trailer, hurried up the steps and through the door. He checked the clock on the wall. 10:03 AM. Several chores were still on his list. Laundry. Sweeping. Mopping, Cleaning the bathroom. And finally, the yard. He'd have to hurry. He plugged in the vacuum and flipped the switch. It fired right up, and Mickey went to work. When it came to the bathroom, he turned on the bathtub faucet and sloshed the water over the tub's surface. And like he'd seen his mother do numerous times back when she was healthy, he sprinkled powdered cleanser over the wet interior and rubbed it into a pasty coating. He'd let it sit awhile so it could do its work. Mickey turned his attention to the sink. Washed it with the cleanser, scrubbed the toilet and washed the mirror. The bathroom was beginning to sparkle and smell better, thanks to the liquid pine cleaner he'd used to clean the toilet. He dropped to his knees and began the arduous ritual of scrubbing the tub, Mickey's least favorite household chore. He had an uncommon motivation this day, however, muttering the words to a *Black Crows* song as he labored. When the tub was clean, he rinsed out the sponge and returned it to its place under the sink. He pulled the bunched-up towel from the rack, dried his hands with it and tossed it in the empty hamper next to the washing machine. One piece of dirty laundry would be okay. Surely. He checked the clock again. 11:50 AM. He grabbed a plastic bag from a drawer in the kitchen and shot out the door. Like a little kid going after Easter eggs in a group hunt, he jetted around the small yard snatching up pages of newspapers, pop cans, an old shoe, and various other trash items that littered the lot. As he dropped the bag of trash into the garbage can, a shinning black Chevrolet Blazer pulled up in the driveway. Mickey looked up to see Abe sitting behind the wheel, a smile on his face. He raised an open hand and pointed at Mickey with an index finger. Mickey felt like the most important kid in town.

Mickey walked over as Abe was getting out of the truck.

"Hey, that eye's better already. Here, can you carry this?" Abe said and handed Mickey a pasteboard carrier that held three large milkshakes. He reached back into the front seat and picked up another carrier with three soft drinks in it as well as a large bag with a grease spot on it.

"You hungry?" Abe said.

"Boy, am I ever."

"Okay, lead the way and let's wage some war on that hunger."

Mickey led Abe into the house and set the milkshakes on the kitchen table. He pulled open a cabinet door. "We'll need to put mama's food on a plate. It's hard for her to sit at the table. She has to eat in her bed."

Abe returned a somber nod. "Sure thing." He perked up. "Why don't we put ours on a plate too," he said.

"Okay."

Mickey pulled three plates from the cabinet. Abe set the bag of food and the soft drinks on the table. He began pulling the burgers and fries out of the bag and placing them on the plates that Mickey put on the table.

"Mama will love this. We haven't had anything from the Dari Delite in a long time. Her room is in the back. We'll need to take two of these chairs for me and you to sit on."

Mickey pulled one of the chairs from under the table, Abe the other.

"Mama, Abe's here. You hungry?"

"I'm starving. Ya'll come on back here."

Mickey carried one chair down the hallway. Abe followed with the second one. When they walked into her bedroom, Mickey saw something he hadn't seen in quite some time—his mother with her hair styled and her make-up on. Mickey paused and gazed at her. "Mama, you look beautiful."

"Well, thank you, Baby. We do have a guest."

Mickey regathered his thoughts. "Oh yes." He turned to Abe. "Mama, this is Mr. Abe I've been telling you about." He lifted a hand to his mother. "Mr. Abe, this is my mama."

Abe put the chair down and stepped close to the bed. He reached out his hand for a shake. "Nice to meet you, Mrs. Tucker," Abe said and gave a tender smile.

She put her frail hand in his. "Call me Leslie. Is it okay if I call you Abe?"

"Of course."

"Mickey didn't tell me. I didn't expect a—" she caught herself before saying "black man."

Abe peered into her eyes and smiled again. "I hear you like butterscotch milkshakes."

Leslie Tucker's face lit up like a child's at a county fair. "You're kidding! You brought me a butterscotch milkshake?"

"I sure did. And a cheeseburger, some fries and a soda to go with it. From the Dari Delite."

"I haven't had anything from the Dari Delite in—" Her voice quaked. She paused, lowered her head. A tear dripped on her gown. She wiped her eyes and gathered her composure. "Well, since my health started failing."

Abe put his hand on her elbow. "Well, let's enjoy ourselves today. What do you say?"

"Yes. Let's," Leslie said.

Abe turned to Mickey. "Alright, Mickey, let's eat."

The two of them stepped out of the room and returned with the fast-food feast. Mickey handed his mother her plate and sat her milkshake and soft drink on the nightstand. He and Abe sat in the chairs, their plates on their laps, their drinks on the floor beside them.

"Leslie, would you mind if I said a blessing?" Abe said.

With her lips pressed tightly, she shook her head gently, her eyes revealing her heart had been touched. "Well, I've never been very religious, but that would be nice.."

Abe began. "Heavenly Father, thank you that we can enjoy this meal and bless our time together. I'm honored to be in this home. I thank you for letting me meet Mickey and now his mother. Bless our time today and bless this house. In Jesus' name. Amen."

"Amen," said Leslie.

Leslie took a bite of the cheeseburger. She closed her eyes and chewed slowly. "Mm. As good as I ever remember." She pushed a fry into her mouth and took a drink of the soda. "I used to love to go to the Dari Delite when I was a teenager. I can still see the concrete tables and benches behind it that overlook the railroad track below. We'd sit there for what seemed like hours. We'd eat and hope a train would pass by. If one did, then it was good luck. If the train had a yellow caboose, it meant double good luck. I remember one time a train came by that had TWO yellow cabooses. I'd never seen that before. Thought it was a sign I'd be the first in my family to graduate college or become successful or something." She took another drink of the soda. "Fell in love when I was a senior in high school. We got married right after graduation. Moved into this trailer." She took another bite of the cheeseburger and looked around the room. "Never even made it to the community college extension here in town," she said and took a long drink of the milkshake. She peered at Abe. "So much for yellow cabooses, huh?"

"There's nothing wrong with dreaming. Especially when you're young," Abe said.

Leslie nodded. "I suppose you're right."

Abe looked at Mickey. "So, Mickey, what are some of your dreams?"

Mickey's milkshake made a gurgling sound as he sucked air and the last of the creamy beverage through the straw. The top of the cup squeaked as he plunged the straw up and down through the plastic lid trying to find more shake in the bottom. "Well," he said, still laboring at the empty cup. "I guess my first dream would be to pass English. Principal Howell told me if I don't, he'll hold me back and I'll have to do sixth grade all over again. That means another year of Mrs. Fletcher. It'll be terrible. She hates me and I don't really care for her either."

"Are you not passing now?" Abe said and drank down some of his milkshake and shoved in the last portion off his burger.

"Just barely. I think I got a sixty-two average which is a low D. We got final exams next Thursday and Friday." Mickey stuck three fries in his mouth. "I dread the English one the most," he said, chewing and talking at the same time. "Mrs. Fletcher says we have to stand up and give a speech or something, using stuff we've studied. Counts for half your grade for the whole year. She said we'd take a class vote and whoever gets the most votes gets an automatic hundred plus ten bonus points. I don't know nothing about talking in front of people. I'll fail for sure."

"You suspended till Thursday. Right?" Abe said.

"Yup. And all because of Billy Joe Speed."

Abe turned his attention on Leslie. "Since Mickey is out of school for the next five days, why don't you let him come to my house. I'll pick him up in the mornings and bring him home in the evenings. I'll help him study and we'll see if we can't show this Principal Howell a thing or two and save Mickey from another year of Mrs. Fletcher."

"Abe, you probably have things to do with your job or something. I wouldn't want to put you out," she said.

"No, I don't have anything to do. I have a lot of flexibility. I'm basically retired. What about you? Will you be okay with Mickey not around as much next week?"

"I'll manage. A nurse comes on Mondays, Wednesdays and Fridays to check my oxygen, help me take a bath and what not. I'll be fine. Mickey can just leave some Kool-Aid here on the nightstand and maybe some loaf bread and crackers. It'll hold me over till he gets home."

"Mickey, get me a pen and paper," Abe said.

Mickey rose from his chair and went to the den. He returned with his backpack, set it on the foot of his mother's bed and unzipped it.

"Here's a pen," he said and handed it to Abe. He pulled out a spiral notebook. "And, here's some paper."

Abe flipped open the notebook. "Here's my phone number," he said as he wrote. "Call anytime. I'll put my address on here too. That way if we are outside or something and I don't hear the phone ring, you can send someone over if you need to." He tore the sheet of paper out of the notebook and placed it next to the phone beside Leslie's bed. He turned to Mickey. "Mickey, how much food is in the house?"

"Not much but we got a little."

"Our check will be here on Monday," Leslie said. "We'll be fine till then."

Abe shook his head. "No, I'll feel a whole lot better knowing you have everything you need while Mickey's with me. He and I are probably going to have a lot of work to do which means he may be late getting home some nights. You know, you can't be taking chances when you're working from a sixty-two average and a final worth fifty percent. Mickey and I'll run up to Walmart and be back in a bit."

Leslie adjusted herself in the bed. "Abe, you really don't have to go to all this trouble. I'll help him as best as I can to get ready for his tests. It'll be fine."

Abe squatted down beside her bed. He placed a hand on top of Leslie's. "Right now, Mickey needs a train with a yellow caboose to come down the track."

Leslie's chin began to quiver.

"Now, the Lord has sent more than one past me in my lifetime. I believe He wants me to be His engineer for Mickey. Do you understand?"

Leslie nodded, her eyes wet. "There's no way I'll EVER be able to repay you."

"Seeing this boy have some of his dreams come true will be more pay to me than you can imagine."

• • •

Though Claxton was the county seat of Baker County, the town had little more than a handful of places that could be characterized as venues for recreation. The local country club had a cinderblock clubhouse, no restaurant and only a nine-hole golf course. At one time the Claxton Drive-in boasted as being the "Show Place of Central Alabama" but a two-screen cinema opened and exterminated the nostalgic pastime. Within ten years of its conquest, the cinema shut its doors as well. A flooring chain based out of Mobile bought the building and turned it into a carpet outlet. This left locals with the options of a roller skating rink, a video arcade, a pool hall, a half-dozen dine-in restaurants, and a Walmart. Having no shopping mall, Walmart was the natural place to loiter. While shoppers combed the inside of the store, teenagers thronged the backside of the parking lot. They stood in groups and sat in cars and on the tailgates of pickup trucks. They took clandestine measures to drink beer and wine coolers. They played loud music and occasionally engaged in fistfights. The aspiration of the vast majority of middle school students was to move up to high school. Once this achievement was made the right to "hangout" in the Walmart parking lot was granted. The only Friday nights when the retail giant's real estate was not the most popular destination in town was during football season when the Claxton Tigers played at home. When this was the case, the multitude moved to the football stadium. Thanks to the Claxton Police Department, the loud music and beer remained outside the stadium. The occasional fistfight, however, didn't, especially when the visiting team was the in-county rival Jamison Panthers.

Abe and Mickey rolled into the Walmart parking lot and embarked on the quest of finding a parking place. A feat that often took two or three songs on the radio to succeed at. Mickey kept his eyes fixated on the high schoolers at the end of the lot. "You gotta be in high school to hang out there. I can't wait."

"I wouldn't be in such a rush. There's a lot of nonsense that goes on out there. More than a few have made some life-altering decisions in that pool of foolishness," Abe said, his eyes patrolling for a slot to park the Blazer.

"What do you mean, Mr. Abe, that's where all the big kids go on the weekends."

"I bet there's a few with enough common sense to occupy their time in other ways."

Mickey looked at Abe, a questioning look on his. "It's just kids talking and stuff."

"Uh huh. Well, talking is fine. Most of the time. But it's that STUFF you mentioned that causes problems."

"What problems?"

"We'll talk about that when you're a little older. But just know this. A wise man has wise friends. He doesn't run around with idiots. You know why?"

"Why?"

"Because he knows that the people he runs with affects the direction he goes in. Some people figure this out the hard way. After they've made a lot of screw ups. But you don't have to do that. You can start even at your age choosing friends that will help you go in the direction you want to go."

"How do you know who the ones are who can help you?"

"Hey, there's a car backing out," Abe said and whipped the Blazer around and pulled into the spot. It was close to the front of the store. A minor miracle. He shifted the Blazer into park and turned to Mickey. "Simple. They want to go in the direction you want to go. Got it?"

Mickey rolled it over in his mind for a few seconds. "Got it," he said and gestured with a quick, affirming nod.

"This has been an important conversation. Think about it. Don't forget it," Abe said.

"I won't."

Abe winked. "You ready to do some shopping?"

"Yup."

As they entered the store, Abe pulled a shopping cart from one of the rows near the front of the door. "You grab one too," he said to Mickey.

They went up and down the aisles, Mickey telling Abe the things he and his mama liked and needed. Without protest, anything Mickey mentioned, Abe put in the basket he was pushing. He put some extras too. Like paper goods, cleaners, condiments, tin foil, trash bags, and toiletries. When Mickey was out of suggestions, Abe pushed his cart towards the back of the store.

"Why are we going to the back? Ain't no groceries back here."

Abe didn't reply. He just kept moving. They reached the appliance area. Abe lifted a portable refrigerator from a stack and placed it in Mickey's empty cart.

"Do you need a small refrigerator?" Mickey said.

"Yeah. Just decided today. Let's go back to the sporting goods department."

Abe led the way. Mickey's cart had a loose front wheel that made the cart prone to swerve to one side. He wrestled with it as he pushed to keep it from crashing into the racks of merchandise. They passed the automotive department. Then the hunting and fishing section. When they came to the shelves with fitness equipment Abe stopped. "Let's leave our carts here for a minute," he said.

Mickey followed Abe over to the other side of the aisle. Bicycles of various sizes, styles and colors filled a two-tier rack display.

"Pick you one out, Mickey. Any one you want," Abe said.

Mickey's jaw dropped, his eyebrows raised. "What? You're kidding. Right?"

"No, I'm not kidding. It's a long walk from your house to mine. You need a bicycle. It's faster than walking and the reflectors make it safer. So, pick one."

After walking back and forth pass the inventory of bikes several times, Mickey focused on a green and silver one. It had the words "Lightning Bolt" on it.

"This one's cool," he said.

"Is that the one you want?" Abe said.

Mickey looked at the price tag.

"Now, don't you go worrying about the price. That's not your concern. Is that the one you like?"

"Yessir."

Abe pulled it from the rack. "Alright, try it out."

Mickey threw a leg over the bike and placed his foot on the pedal. He rode up the aisle and back again. "It's great."

"Okay. Let's take it to the front."

They walked back to the shopping carts. Abe pushed the cart filled with groceries with one hand and pulled the cart loaded with the compact refrigerator with the other. Mickey walked behind him, pushing the bicycle. He'd had a bicycle once before. He got it from Ricky Pledger. The Pledgers lived in the trailer park until Ricky's dad got a big job in Atlanta. He told Ricky he'd buy him a new bike when they got there so Ricky gave his old one to Mickey. The bike worked fine until he let Joey Perkins ride it. Joey said he was just going to ride it through the trailer park. That was a lie. He tried to cross Highway 31 to go to Snowy Milton's store and was hit by a car. Joey was banged up a little, but was fine. The bike, on the other hand, was smashed. Joey's parents said they'd buy Mickey a new one, but they never did. Every time Mickey asked about it, Joey's mama gave the same answer. "Next week when Joey's daddy gets paid." Mickey finally gave up but every time he saw Joey or his parents he thought, "You owe me a new bicycle." Now, those days would be over. He was about to get the coolest bike he'd ever seen. Store bought. With the tags still on it. Perhaps Abe already considered Mickey to be his best friend.

As they passed the electronics area, a tall boy stepped out into the main aisle. Mickey froze. The boy strolled up to Mickey like he'd pounce on him. He ran his hand along the middle bar of the bike, bumped the seat with his fist a few times and peered at Mickey.

"Nice eye," he said, his upper lip curled up one side.

"Young man, is there a problem here?" Abe said, his tone commanding.

The boy stepped back, caught off guard by Abe's intervention. "Who are you?" he said.

Abe shot him a cool gaze. "I'm Mickey's friend. And just who are you?"

Mickey said nothing, a look of terror on his face.

"Billy. . . Billy Joe Speed," the boy said.

A man walked up. "Son, did they have the headphones you're wanting?"

The man's presence stilled Billy Joe's nerves and his cockiness welled back up. He pointed an index finger toward Mickey. "Dad, this is the trailer park kid that threatened me with a knife."

The man's temperament turned fiery. "Listen, you little punk," he said to Mickey. "You ever threaten my son with a knife again and I'll see to it that you're sent away to a reform school."

Abe stepped in front of the man. "Now, you watch yourself, Mister. You're a grown man and he's twelve. Besides, your son is two years older and six inches taller."

"My name's Albert Speed," the man said. "And you'd do well to keep your nose in your own business."

Abe returned a tight smile. "Oh, I know who you are. And I never put my nose in business that's not mine. Make no mistake about it. This IS my business. Let me ask you a question. Have you ever caught your son in a lie?"

"Are you calling my son a liar?" Albert Speed said, his fists at his sides.

Abe glanced down then looked the man dead in the eyes. "I didn't call your son anything? Not a liar and certainly not a punk. After all, he's just a kid. I asked you a question. You're a grown man. Just like me." Abe lowered his head slightly and wrenched one of his eyelids. "And it'd be wise to keep your fists right where they are. Now, are you man enough and honest enough to answer my question?"

Albert Speed released his fists. His face softened like wax near a flame. "I don't believe this is the place to have this discussion."

"That's strange. You believed it was the place to threaten a twelve-year-old boy just a second ago. Now, all of the sudden, you don't believe it's the place to answer a simple question."

Albert Speed looked at his watch and turned to his son. "Billy Joe, we're supposed to meet the Howells at the Mexican Restaurant in fifteen minutes. Let's get going." He motioned with his head and started walking.

"Mister Howell is the middle school principal. Is he not?" Abe said, loud enough for people in the aisles nearby to hear.

Albert Speed didn't reply. He just kept walking, his son walking alongside him. Mickey stared at them. Stunned at what had just occurred.

"Mickey, you okay?" Abe said.

Mickey looked up at Abe and nodded. "Yeah. Thanks to you."

"Good. Let's pay for this stuff and get back to your mother."

CHAPTER SIX

Abe unboxed the refrigerator and carried it down the hall and into Leslie Tucker's bedroom. Mickey followed, a plastic bag full of food in each hand.

"What are you doing?" she said as Abe eased it to the floor.

"This will keep your drinks and perishables cool. It has a small freezer in the top," he said. He opened the door so she could see inside it. "It'll be handy here in your bedroom." He pointed to the outlet closest to her bed. "If I plug it in here, you can get to it without having to get up. Would that be okay?"

Leslie put her hand over her mouth. "You really don't have to do this."

"Wait till you see what I got, Mama," Mickey said and walked out of the room. He rolled the bicycle down the hall, maneuvered the handlebars through the small door then pushed it the rest of the way into his mother's bedroom. "Ain't she a beauty?"

Tears welled in Leslie's eyes. She wiped them with her fingers then lowered her chin to her chest. "Abe, why are you doing all this for us?" she said, her eyes closed.

"Because I want to," he said.

"See, I told you, Mama. Abe's the best man in Claxton," Mickey said.

"I believe it," Leslie said and sniffled.

Abe and Mickey filled the refrigerator with soft drinks, a gallon of milk, a package of sliced cheese, small containers of yogurt, apples, oranges, and apple juice. They put popsicles in the freezer section. Items such as crackers, bread, chips, peanut butter, and cereal they sat on top of the refrigerator and on the nightstand next to Leslie's bed.

"If there's anything you want that's not here, just let me know," Abe said, standing at the foot of the bed. "Do you like to read?"

"I used to read a lot, back when I could check out books from the library. But since I've been sick, I haven't been able to get out. So, it's been a while."

"Who do you like? Tolkien? Dickens? Jane Austen? Victor Hugo? Shakespeare? Or do you like more modern authors? Say James Michener or maybe Patricia Cornwell?"

Leslie looked up at Abe. "Are you an angel?"

"Sorry to disappoint you, but last time I checked, angels are not born on Navy bases."

"Which one were you born on?"

"Sauda Bay on the island of Crete. My father was a seaman during the Korean War. Now back to your reading preferences."

Leslie looked down, her lips pressed tightly. "Mm. Let me think." She looked back up at him. "Surprise me," she said and smiled.

"Alright. I think I know just the book." He looked at Mickey. "I have something to do in the morning. But I should be through by noon. So, I'll pick you up after lunch. Say 12:30."

Mickey nodded. "Okay. That means I get to ride my new bike before you get here."

Abe winked with one eye and made a pistol gesture to Mickey with one hand. "Now, don't you go breaking the speed limit, you hear," he said and grinned. And, with that, he turned and walked out of Leslie's bedroom.

Leslie gazed at Mickey. When she heard the front door shut she said, "Well, Mickey, he does seem to be a nice person. I can't believe the groceries. Not to mention the bicycle. Wow!."

"Yup. You shoulda seen him take up for me at Walmart. He made Billy Joe Speed's dad back down like a crawfish," Mickey said.

Leslie's eyes shot open. "You mean he stood up to Albert Speed?"

"Sure did. And Mr. Speed had his fists balled up and everything."

They heard the door of the Blazer slam shut and the engine start.

"You have got to tell me all about it," Leslie said.

· · ·

Mickey began looking through the kitchen window at 12:20. He'd parked the bike in the den after a more than two-hour ride. He must have ridden down all eight streets of the trailer park at least thirty times. Maybe more. He'd stopped counting at twenty-two. Several neighbors saw his new bike as he cruised through his low-income neighborhood. On one of his trips, he rolled by Randall Jones' place just as Randall was carrying another trash bag to his already packed garbage can. The bag was filled with empty beer cans just like the day before. And Randall was shirtless. Just like the day before. He drew down his brow and gave a thumbs up. "That's a sweet ride," he said.

Mickey saw the black Blazer when it rounded the curve and headed his way. He glanced at the clock. 12:29.

"Mama, Abe's here," he called out.

"Okay. You study hard," she said.

"I will." Mickey grabbed his backpack and jetted out the door.

He pulled open the Blazer's passenger door. "Hey, Mr. Abe."

"Did you put some miles on that bike this morning?" Abe said.

"I sure did," Mickey said and tossed his backpack onto the front seat. "You shoulda seen how people checked it out when I rode by them."

Abe smiled and handed Mickey a book. "Here. Run this back in the house and give it to your mother before we go."

Mickey looked at the title. "The Count of Monte Cristo," he said. "What's a count?"

"Someone who owns a lot of land and has a whole bunch of money," Abe said.

"Abe, are you a count?"

Abe laughed. "No, I'm just a regular ole country boy. Now hurry up. We've got a lot to do."

Mickey ran up the steps and grabbed the doorknob. Locked. He'd forgotten about that. He retrieved the key from under the mat, unlocked the door and flung it open. In less than a minute he was climbing back into Abe's beastly truck.

"You need to come up with another place to hide that key," Abe said. "Under the mat is the oldest hiding place in the book."

"Alright. I'll start thinking of one."

"Tie it on a string and carry it around your neck. Do you have all your school books?"

"Yup. Got'em all in my backpack."

"Good. Let's get going."

Abe backed out of Mickey's driveway and eased down the narrow street. An elderly couple sat on their porch and stared as they passed by.

"That's Big Ed and Erma," Mickey said, returning their stare. "I don't know why he's called Big Ed. He ain't that big. They moved here last summer from Maryland. You ever been to Maryland?"

"I have. Spent a few years there back when I was in the Navy," Abe said, resting one hand bent at the wrist on top of the steering wheel.

"Are people in Maryland friendly?"

"Friendly as any other people, I guess. Why do you ask?"

Mickey turned his head and raised up in his seat as they rolled further down the street, keeping his gaze on Big Ed and Erma. "Because those two are definitely not friendly. They don't answer the door for trick or treaters. They don't even put up Christmas lights."

He repositioned himself in the seat and turned to Abe. "How old are you?"

"I'm fifty-four. Be fifty-five in November. Tell, me something, Mickey."

"Okay. What?"

Abe stopped at the entrance of the trailer park and looked north and south, then north again. He pulled out and headed south on Highway 31. "Why do you think you have a low D in English?"

"That's easy. Because my average right now is sixty-two."

Abe shook his head. "Naw. I don't mean that. I mean why do you think your average is sixty-two instead of higher?"

Mickey turned and looked out the passenger window, his cheeks getting warm. "Mrs. Fletcher says it's because I have a slow brain. Just like my mama has. Just like my dad had."

"Look at me, Mickey."

Mickey looked at Abe. "I told you that kinda talk is a bunch of nonsense. Mrs. Fletcher may be a teacher but that doesn't mean she's right about everything."

"Well, I can't keep up with what she says. I make B's and C's in history. Mr. Thornton's the teacher. When he teaches it's almost like watching a show on television. You feel like you're watching all the stuff happen even though it happened a long time ago. Like Friday, for instance. He taught us about Teddy Roosevelt and the Rough Riders. I felt like I was in Cuba riding a horse right alongside TR. They used to call him just TR. Did you know that?"

Abe rubbed his beard as he smiled. "Seems like I remember that."

"But Mrs. Fletcher just stands up and talks. Sometimes she sits at her desk, but most of the time she stands up. When she talks, she talks to the kids in the front desks, mostly. Kids who have nice clothes and braces on their teeth and who have both a mom and a dad. Kids like me and Lolita DeRosa and Charlie Thompson, we sit in the back desks. She only talks to us when we make a bad grade or get in trouble for something. When she's standing up talking to the kids in the front desks, I can hardly hear her. Sometimes I can't hear her at all. When it comes time to take one of her tests, it's like stuff I've never seen before. The multiple-choice questions I can get right pretty much all the time. But it's the ones where you have to explain stuff that I'm not good at. Most of the time, I just skip 'em because I don't know what to put down."

"What about the other kids who sit in the back? What kind of grades do they make?" Abe said.

"Lolita makes A's. She's smart. Especially for a trailer park kid. Some of the others make A's too, but not as many as Lolita. Most of them make some B's and maybe a few C's. I'm the only one who makes D's and F's. That's why Mrs. Fletcher says I have a bad—"

Abe raised an index finger. "Stop! I don't want to hear those kinds of words come out of your mouth. They're nonsense. Just like we talked about. When she says that you just chew it up like Popeye chews up spinach!" he said. Abe's tone of voice reminded Mickey of some of his teachers when students made them mad. Mickey knew that Abe was not mad at him. He just wanted Mickey to stop believing what Mrs. Fletcher had been saying.

Abe pulled the Blazer into his driveway. "It's a beautiful day today," he said. "What do you think about studying on the patio?"

"Sure," Mickey said.

"I'll grab a couple of bottles of pop out of the fridge and be right out."

Mickey climbed out of the truck and walked around the house, his backpack slung over one shoulder. A rainbow radiated from the edge of the water that sprayed up from the middle of the rock-trimmed pond. Mickey slid the backpack off his shoulder and onto the patio table. He walked over to check it out and also to see if Abe had any fish in the small pond. Mickey counted seven fish, each about a foot long. Some were orange and white. Some were orange, white and black. He'd never seen fish like them before. And he'd certainly never caught one with a cane pole and red worms. He watched them as they wiggled through the water and nipped at the surface. The peaceful scene of Abe's backyard caused his mind to wander. He thought of a record his mother used to play and began singing it, moving to the beat.

"Johnny's in the basement
Mixing up the medicine
I'm on the pavement
Thinkin' about the government
The man in the trench coat
Badge out, laid off
Says he's got a bad cough
Wants to get it paid off

Look out kid
It's somethin' you did
God knows when
But you're doin' it again
You better duck down the alley way
Lookin' for a new friend
The man in the coon-skin cap
In the pig pen
Wants eleven dollar bills
You only got ten."

"How did you come to know the words to that song?" Abe said.

Mickey turned on his heels to see Abe standing next to the patio table, a bottle of pop in each hand.

"I didn't know you were listening," Mickey said, like he'd been busted for something.

Abe set the bottles down on the table. "That was great. I mean," he raised an open hand in front of his chest and pumped it and nodded as he completed the sentence. "REALLY GREAT. You know the words and, let me tell you, son, you've got some moves to go with them."

"Aw, it ain't nothing really," Mickey said, shaking his head, feeling the heat in his cheeks. "Just a song my mama used to play on the record player."

Abe clicked his tongue and twitched his head. "Well, you nailed it. Bob Dylan. *Subterranean Homesick Blues.*" He raised his brow. "Do you know all of it?"

"Yeah. I know a lot of the songs Mama used to play."

"Oh yeah. Let me hear another one."

"Okay. Here goes. 'A child arrived just the other day. He came to the world in the usual way, but there were planes to catch and bills to pay. He learned to walk while I was away.'"

"Harry Chapin. *The Cats in the Cradle,*" Abe said. "Hit me with another one."

Mickey raised one hand about even with his shoulders and closed his eyes, "Well, you wake up in the mornin'. You hear the work bell ring. And they march you to the table to see the same old thing. Ain't no food upon the table. Ain't no fork up in the pan. But you better not complain, boy. You get in trouble with the man."

Mickey stopped, opened his eyes and looked at Abe.

"Don't stop now. Give me the chorus," he said.

"So let the midnight special shine a light on me," Mickey sang and started moving his hips, his fists clinched, elbows bent as he moved and swayed. "Let the midnight special shine a light on me. Let the midnight special." Mickey made an air guitar and mimicked the famous three-note guitar break then picked the words back up. "Shine a light on me. Let the midnight special shine an ever lovin' light on me."

"*Midnight Special*. Creedence Clearwater Revival," Abe said. "Mm. Mm. Mm. Mickey, you got a gift. I'm telling you. How many songs do you know?"

"I don't know." Mickey raised one eyebrow. "I'd say a hundred."

Abe's eyes shot open. "You know the words to a HUNDRED songs?"

"Maybe more. Back before Mama got sick, she played the record player all the time. I'd hear a song once or twice and then I could sing it."

Abe suddenly looked like he'd seen a magician perform a magic trick. "Mickey, what all did Mrs. Fletcher teach this year?"

"Well, we started out with grammar. Then diagraming sentences. After that we studied some literature."

Abe made a rolling motion with one hand. "Okay, tell me what kind of literature," he said with increasing excitement in his tone.

"Well, for authors, we studied Mark Twain and L. Frank Baum. For poets we studied Robert Frost, Emily Dickenson and Henry Wadsworth Longfellow."

Abe slapped his hands together. "Mickey, you are going to pass that English test and I mean pass it with style."

Mickey wasn't buying it. "How? English is my worst subject and Mrs. Fletcher don't like me."

"Those songs you just sang. You know what they are?"

Mickey searched for an answer. "Ah . . . music?"

"The words. The words. What are they?"

Mickey rolled his eyes toward the top of his brow. "Well, they're kinda like poems, I guess."

"That's exactly what they are, Mickey. And you can memorize and sing songs better than anyone else in your class, I bet. Heck, I bet better than anyone in your whole school. Mrs. Fletcher says you have to stand before the class and demonstrate something you've learned by giving a speech or something. Right?"

"Right." Mickey said with a nod.

"Well, why not write your own poem about something and turn it into a song. Then, stand up and sing it to your class."

"I never thought of songs as poetry," Mickey said. He was starting to catch where Abe was going. "The kids at school love music. Especially rap."

Abe bumped Mickey on the shoulder. "Well, there you go. Write a poem and rap it then."

"But what should I write a poem about?"

Abe pulled a chair back from the patio table and sat down. "Sit down and let's talk about that."

Mickey sat down in one of the chairs and took a long drink of soda.

"Alright, Mickey. What or who interests you?"

Mickey burped. "Sorry." He let out another smaller one. "Well, like I was telling you, Mr. Thornton really got me interested in Teddy Roosevelt."

Abe wrapped his knuckles on the table once. "Write a poem about Teddy Roosevelt then. Henry Wadsworth Longfellow wrote a poem about Paul Revere."

Mickey grinned. "He sure did. We studied it. And, I have a book about Teddy Roosevelt in my backpack. Principal Howell made me stay in the library for over two hours Friday, so I decided I'd check out a book. And I thought why not check out a book on TR?"

"I'm telling you, Mickey, you are about to show Mrs. Fletcher and everybody else at that school that your brain is just fine. You get started on that poem and I'm gonna start cooking us some supper. You like fried pork chops and mashed potatoes?"

"I sure do."

Abe picked up his bottle of pop and went inside. Mickey pulled the Teddy Roosevelt book out of his backpack. He opened the cover and read the table of contents. One chapter was entitled, "The War in Cuba." Mickey fanned to it and scanned the chapter. The dates, names and many of the terms highlighted themselves in Mickey's mind because they were already there. It was as if they'd been stamped on his brain by Mr. Thornton's Friday lesson. Mickey closed the book and set it aside. He gazed at the fountain in the middle of the fishpond, the mist shimmering with hues of violet, indigo, blue, green, yellow, orange, and red. Maybe he could write a poem about Teddy Roosevelt. He took his pen and spiral notebook and words started coming.

I'ma 'bout to tell ya the story of Cuba
So you better listen up or I'ma gonna sue ya.
Seventeen thousand American troops
Had landed near Cuba
And the Spanish said, "Oops."

Mickey continued writing, the lines flowing from his brain and through his pen. Quickly. Effortlessly, almost. A word wouldn't feel just right and he'd scratch through it and write another one. He could hear the cadence in his mind. He imagined himself standing before his English class . . . Rapping. Pausing. Gesturing. Rhyming. Amazing his classmates. Entertaining them. Knocking them out. Mrs. Fletcher was not his concern. She'd probably didn't even know who 2Pac, The Notorious B.I.G. or Ice Cube was. His classmates did, though. And Mickey was about to show them that, not only did he KNOW who they were, but he could DO what they DID. Within minutes he'd written to the bottom of the page. He flipped to the next and never broke his creative stride. By the time Abe opened the back door and called out "Supper's ready," the poem was done.

Mickey pushed the chair away from the patio table and held up the notebook. "Hey, Abe. Come check this out and tell me what you think."

Abe walked over and took it from Mickey's hand. As he read the words, a broad smile stretched on his face. He chuckled a few times. When he finished, he dropped the spiral notebook on the table and raised his hands to Mickey. "Gimme ten, my man! Gimme ten."

Mickey slapped Abe's palms. Abe hoisted Mickey up off the ground and set him on one of his shoulders. He paraded him around the backyard, singing Queen's *We Are the Champions*.

• • •

Abe pulled into Mickey's driveway. Mickey hustled down the doorsteps and bolted to Abe's truck.

"How's your mother doing this morning?" Abe said as soon as Mickey opened the door.

"She's fine," Mickey said as he climbed in and slid into the passenger seat. "I can't tell you the last time we had so much good food in our house. Mama ate an apple and a bowl of cereal for breakfast."

Abe smiled. "And what did you have?"

"Two bowls of cereal . . . two Pop Tarts and a root beer. I didn't bring my books since you told me not to. What are we studying today?"

Abe shifted into reverse and backed onto the asphalt. He pressed the brake with a booted foot and pulled the gear shift into "D." Before he took his lifted his foot off the brake he looked at Mickey. "We're going to see someone I know and then we're going to do some shopping. By the time we're finished it'll be close to three o'clock. That's when I can pick up the study guides for your final exams. Correct?"

"Yup. That's what Principal Howell said. Three o'clock."

"Your mother give you a note to give to me?"

Mickey straightened one leg so he could get his hand in the pocket of his jeans. He pulled out a folded piece of paper and handed it to Abe.

"Here you go. She signed it and everything."

Abe unfolded the paper and inspected it, then refolded it and shoved it into the pocket of his shirt.

"Did you read the poem to your mother?"

Mickey grinned. "She thinks it's awesome."

"That's because it is." Abe raised a palm to Mickey. "You're gonna knock 'em dead. I wish I could be there," he said. Mickey slapped him five.

They passed Big Ed and Erma's. The two northern transplants sat in rocking chairs on their front porch.

"They sit out on their porch like that every day?" Abe said.

"Every day," Mickey said.

"You ever tried talking to them?"

Mickey scowled. "Them old grumpy people? Of course not."

Abe kept his attention on the road. "Everyone has a story. People's stories explain a lot about why they are the way they are. Why not try to be their friend and learn their story? You never know, Mickey. They may be just waiting for someone to be their friend."

"Really?"

"Give it a shot sometime. See what happens."

"I'll think about it," Mickey said, unconvinced.

Abe drove through Claxton and pulled onto the northbound lanes of Interstate 65. He kicked the Blazer up to sixty.

"We ain't stayin' in Claxton?"

Abe looked at Mickey and shook his head. "Nope. We're going up to Birmingham."

Mickey nodded and gave a lopsided grin. "Cool!"

•   •   •

Abe took the exit for the University of Alabama at Birmingham. Mickey's attention was glued to the sites and activity of the thriving south end of the Magic City.

"There's the Vulcan," said Mickey, pointing. "I went up in it back when I was in the fourth grade. My class took a field trip. Ate lunch at Milo's. Their burgers are pretty good, but their sweet tea is the best!"

"We'll have to go up in it at night sometime," Abe said. "You can see lights for miles."

Abe pulled off 8th Avenue and into a parking lot. A white Mercedes-Benz S600 was parked near the front door of the lime-colored office building. Eight other cars sat in random spaces, filling the lot to half capacity. A young oak tree cast a morning shadow over three cars. Between two of the cars a space was empty. Abe pulled into it and shut off the engine.

"I love it when this happens," he said, unbuckling his seat belt.

"When what happens?" asked Mickey.

"When I get a parking place in the shade," he said and removed his metal-framed sunglasses. He pulled down the sun visor and closed the glasses against the visor and the roof. "Come on, there's somebody I want you to meet."

He opened the door and got out. Mickey followed suit. Walking toward the front door Mickey read the sign on the side of the building.

"Everett Smith. Oto . . . Otolar . . . Otolaryngo."

"Otolaryngologist," Abe said. "It's the medical term for an ear, nose and throat doctor."

Mickey stopped, his forehead furrowed. "Doctor? I don't want to see no doctor. He'll give me a shot."

Abe put his hand on Mickey's shoulder and looked him in the eyes. "Now, Mickey, this doctor is not going to hurt you. He's going to check your ears to see why you have trouble hearing in school."

"Promise?" Mickey said.

Abe winked one eye and lowered his chin. "Promise." He nudged Mickey's shoulder. "Now, come on. Let's go."

They walked through the door and Abe stepped up to the receptionist. She hammered away at her keypad, oblivious to Abe's presence. The office smelled clean. The temperature was cool, but not cold.

"Hey, Margaret," Abe said.

She looked up. Her face turned gleeful. "Hello, Abe. I've been expecting you. Dr. Smith told me you'd be dropping in this morning."

She looked at Mickey and gave a warm, teethy smile. "And you must be Mickey."

Mickey nodded.

"Do I need to fill out anything?" Abe said.

"I don't think so," she said. "You and Mickey can go back to Dr. Smith's office. I'll tell him you're here."

She stood from her chair, walked around the side of her desk and opened the door to the waiting room. Abe and Mickey walked through the door.

"You know where it is. Just make yourself at home. He's got a new one on the wall since the last time you were here. Wait'll you see it," she said.

Abe and Mickey walked down the hallway to the back of the clinic. They came to a stately mahogany door. A brass placard read, "Dr. Everett Smith." Abe opened the door, Mickey following close behind him.

Mickey's eyes shot open. "Wow, this place is almost as big as my house," he said. On one wall hung a variety of animal heads. Mickey counted fourteen antler points on one deer. Another had antlers that seemed to be fused together in places almost like wings. Some of the points turned downward. Some extended out to each side. Others stuck straight up and some curved around in front of the animal's eyes. Mickey moved on to the next one.

"What's this?" he said.

Abe turned from the wall of pictures he was staring at. "That's an Aoudad sheep. He killed that one a couple of years ago in west Texas."

"And what about this pig-looking thing?"

Abe walked over to Mickey and placed a hand on Mickey's shoulder. "That's a javelina." He pointed to the animal next to it. "And this is an Alaskan mountain goat."

"That looks kinda like a bobcat," Mickey said. He walked over to a table in a corner of the room. On it a stuffed cat with pointed ears and mouth opened wide extended a paw towards a stuffed bird on a tree branch.

"It is kinda like a bobcat, Mickey. It's called a lynx."

"Isn't it beautiful?" Mickey said, stroking the cat between its eyes. He ran an index finger over its impressive top canines.

"It really is. I was with him in Canada when he got it."

Abe's attention turned to the animal head hanging above an African shield. "This must be what Margaret was talking about."

"Wow," said Mickey. "Ain't that a leopard?"

"It sure is. No telling how much it—"

"Abe!" came a voice.

Abe and Mickey turned on their heels. A fit white man stood just inside the door, his arms outstretched, a radiant expression on his face. He wore khaki slacks, a light blue golf shirt and was noticeably tanned. His blonde hair parted to one side, his straight teeth perfectly white.

Abe and the man walked toward each other and shared a long embrace, each man clapping the other on the shoulders. They released one another and took a step back.

"Abe, how are you staying so young?" the man said.

Abe cocked his head and grinned. "Me? Look at you. Dressed like Greg Norman. A tan like you live in Miami." Abe raised his hands. "You're the one that's been drinking from the fountain of youth."

"It's Lacy. She keeps me young," the man said.

"Tell her I said hello," Abe said.

"I will. She'd be thrilled if you'd come over for dinner sometime. You know she's a great cook."

"She certainly is," Abe said.

Everett looked down at Mickey. "You must be Mickey."

"Yessir," Mickey said, a tone of apprehension in his voice.

The man extended a hand for a shake. Mickey obliged.

"My name's Everett and I'm glad to meet you. What do you say if we take a look in your ears and see if we can't help you to hear better?"

Mickey swallowed hard and looked at the man. "You're not gonna give me a shot, are you?"

The man shook his head. "Nope. Just look in your ears with something like a flashlight."

Mickey released his tense expression. "Okay."

Everett rested a hand on Mickey's shoulder and looked at Abe. "The two of you go to room four. Let me finish up with a patient and I'll see you in bit."

The three of them walked out of the office. Everett opened the door to room two and stepped inside. Mickey and Abe continued on to room four. The door was already open. Abe walked in and sat down on a chair. Mickey hopped up in a seated position on the edge of the padded exam table.

"Y'all are good friends, huh?" Mickey said.

Abe tightened his lips, then clicked his tongue. "The best."

"Were ya'll in the Navy together?"

"Yup."

"He's sure killed some amazing animals. Must be some kind of good shot."

"He really is."

Everett stepped into the exam room, an otoscope in one hand. He held it up to Mickey.

"See Mickey," he said. "Something kinda like a flash light. Won't hurt. I promise."

Mickey smiled. Everett gently placed the instrument in the ear canal of Mickey's ears. "Uh huh," he said. "Now, turn your head, Mickey."

Mickey turned so that Everett could examine his other ear.

"Do you ever get dizzy?" Everett asked as he looked through the otoscope.

"Sometimes when I first wake up. This year in school we started doing some gymnastic stuff and I had to stop a few times because things started spinning."

"I'm not surprised," Everett said.

He raised up and walked over to the countertop in the room. He laid the otoscope in a plastic tray and turned to back to Mickey.

"Has a doctor ever cleaned your ears?"

Mickey shook his head. "No sir."

Everett looked at Abe. "He's got acute wax build-up in both ears. I think his left ear is totally obstructed. No doubt, it's causing some significant hearing impairment."

"Can you clean them out today or do we need to make an appointment and come back?" Abe said.

"I can do it right now. I'll tell Margaret to re-arrange a few of my appointments for the day."

The look of apprehension returned to Mickey's face. "How do you clean them out?"

Everett looked at Mickey with a compassionate expression. "I just go inside your ear with a small suction tube and remove the wax. It'll tickle a little, but it won't hurt."

"You need to get this done, Mickey," Abe said, his eyes narrowed. "Besides, we're already here. So, why wait?"

Mickey nodded.

"Okay, Mickey," Everett said. "You go ahead and lay down. I'll be back in a few minutes and we'll get you fixed up."

Everett Smith stepped out of the room. When he returned, a nurse followed him pushing a device. She plugged in the machine, then opened one of the doors of the cabinet that hung on the wall above a countertop. Mickey watched her every move, ready to protest at the first sight of anything resembling a needle. The nurse pulled a towel from the cabinet and walked over to Mickey.

"Okay, Mickey. I need you to raise your head a little," she said.

How did she know his name was Mickey? Dr. Smith must have told her. Mickey raised his head, and she slid the towel under him. She smelled somewhat like his mama smelled back when she used to get dressed up and go places. As she adjusted the towel under Mickey's head, her brown hair brushed the side of Mickey's face. It felt nice. She wore a light blue smock. A name badge was pinned to it that read, "Heather."

She stepped back and Dr. Smith rolled over on a chair that had wheels on the bottom. He flipped a switch on the machine and the machine began making a humming sound.

"Okay, Mickey, here we go," he said. "Now, this will sound like wind blowing in your ear and it'll tickle, but it won't hurt. You ready?"

"Yessir, I guess."

Mickey felt a cold, windy sensation in his ear. Dr. Smith was right; it tickled but didn't hurt. Once he was finished with the first ear, Dr. Smith had Mickey rotate to the other end of the examination table so he could clean the second one. When Dr. Smith finished, he turned off the machine.

"Okay, Mickey, you can sit up now," he said.

The nurse opened the door and pushed the machine out of the room.

Mickey sat up. The inside of his ears felt bigger and cooler, like a tiny air conditioner had been blowing in them. Dr. Smith walked over to the door.

"What's your name?" he asked.

"Mickey Tucker," said Mickey.

"How old are you?" he asked in a lower tone of voice.

"Twelve."

Dr. Smith turned his back to Mickey. "What's your mother's name?" he said, this time even lower.

"Leslie," Mickey said.

"What's your favorite ice cream?" Dr. Smith whispered.

"Chocolate."

Dr. Smith opened the door. Leaving the door opened, he walked out of the room and down the hall a bit.

"What color is your new bicycle?" he said in a conversational tone.

Mickey jumped to his feet and bolted to the door. He looked down the hallway. "Green and silver!" Mickey said, his eyes opened wide, a broad smile on his face. "My bicycle is green and silver! I heard you!" He looked back at Abe who was grinning. Mickey brought his palms to the sides of his temples as if he were shocked or amazed, "I heard him!"

Abe stood up. Mickey rushed to him and threw his arms around him. "I can hear just fine now, Mr. Abe! Just fine!"

• • •

The sign read "*Cowboy Earl's. Quality Western Wear since 1979.*"

"What are we doing here?" Mickey said.

"Preparing for your final exam," Abe said and opened the door of the Blazer. Mickey bailed out on the other side and fell in line behind Abe. They stepped up on the wooden wrap-around porch and Abe flung open the door. Waylon Jennings and Willie Nelson's famous counsel that mothers not let their babies grow up to be cowboys bellowed from inside the barn-like structure. The clang of the cowbell on the front door alerted the salespeople that a customer was on the scene. A man dressed in Wrangler jeans, Justin boots and a red checkered western shirt straightened up from leaning on the checkout counter. He pushed the front of his cowboy hat up a bit and smiled.

"How are you folks doing today? Looking for anything in particular?" he said.

"As a matter fact we are," Abe said. "We're looking for a pair of jeans. Gray or camel in color. A dark blue long sleeve shirt. A red bandana. A brown felt hat with a leather band. A pair of boots. And we'll take a pair of suspenders if you have any."

"I like a customer who knows exactly what they want," the man said. "For you or the boy?"

"For him," Abe said and motioned toward Mickey with a tilt of his head.

"Alright, we'll start with the jeans. Right this way."

They walked to the back of the store. Cubby holes filled with stacks of jeans lined one third of the back wall of the store. The man looked Mickey up and down.

"I'd guess a size 12-14. Would that be about right, son?"

With a wrenched expression Mickey looked at the man. "Probably, I ain't exactly sure."

"Be best to measure him," Abe said.

"Sure," the man said and walked back to the checkout counter. He returned with a cloth measuring tape and wrapped it around Mickey's waist.

"Twenty-four and a half," he said.

He went to a stack of the jeans.

"We got gray and light brown. Which one you prefer?"

"We'll go with the light brown," Abe said.

Mickey looked up at Abe. "What in the world are we doin', Abe? I ain't no cowboy."

Abe smiled. "We're making you a Rough Rider."

"Ah, I see now," the man said, nodding. "The boy's gonna be in a play or something, huh?"

"Something like that," Abe said.

The man measured Mickey's neck and the length of his arms with the measuring tape.

"A boys' medium," he said.

He walked to a rack of western style shirts, fingered through the hangers and pulled a dark blue one off its hanger. He held it up to Mickey's back.

"Stretch out your arms," he said.

Mickey extended them and the man checked the length of the sleeves against Mickey's arms. He handed the shirt to Abe.

"Now, for a pair of boots. I believe I'd go with a square toe and a low heel if I were you. What do you think?"

Mickey looked up at Abe. Abe shrugged. "Up to you."

"Square toe, low heel is fine, if that's what you recommend," Mickey said.

"What size shoe you wear?"

"Six," Mickey said.

The man led them to the opposite side of the store where boots were displayed. He pulled a box from a stack and opened it up.

"Too light," said Abe. "Let's aim for something a little darker."

The man pulled another box from a stack and opened it. Abe nodded. The man pulled the boots out of the box.

"Okay, son. Have a seat over here." The man pointed to a bench.

Mickey sat down and removed his sneakers. The man handed him the boots and Mickey pulled them on. He looked down at them. New boots. Right out of the box. Wow!

"Try them out and see how they feel," he said.

Mickey stood up and walked back and forth a few times.

"Do they slip up and down?" the man asked.

"No sir. They're a little tight though."

"That's normal for a new boot," he said and knelt down on one knee. With a thumb he checked where Mickey's big toes came to. He gripped and squeezed the side of one of the boots and then did the same to the other one.

"After you wear them a little, they'll loosen up. You can always put some mink oil on them, too."

"We'll take a can," Abe said.

The man stood to his feet. Mickey sat back down, took off the boots and put his sneakers back on. The man put the boots back in the box and took them to the counter. Abe and Mickey followed. Abe put the shirt and jeans down next to the boots.

"Alright, now for a hat," the man said. He looked at Mickey. "Are you going to be wearing this hat on a regular basis or just every now and then?"

Mickey closed one eye, pressed his lips together and pondered for a second. "Mm, I'd say just every now and then."

The man turned to Abe. "A Stetson's gonna run you about sixty. But since he's not going to be wearing it a lot, I'd recommend just going with an off brand. Just as good in my opinion."

"As long as it's brown felt with a brown leather band," Abe said.

Abe and Mickey followed the man to a vast collection of hats. The man pulled a small one from the wall display. It was made of brown felt and had a thin brown leather band. The man checked the size then set it on Mickey's head. Too big. He swapped it with another one of the same style. Mickey tried it on. Perfect.

"How about a belt?" the man said, looking at Abe.

"Yeah. And don't forget the suspenders," Abe said.

Near the display of hats, belts hung from a metal fixture, organized by size. The man pulled a brown one from one of the rows.

"It's a twenty-six. No need to try it on unless you just want to," said the man. "Now, let's get this boy a red neckerchief and a pair of suspenders and he'll be a bona fide Rough Rider if there ever was one. They're up close to the cash register."

The man started walking back to the front of the store, Abe and Mickey following close behind. He stopped at a rack and thumbed through the suspenders that hung on it. He pulled one from the collection then walked behind the checkout counter and pulled three red bandanas from a wire carousel that sat next to a collection of leather wallets. He spread the three bandanas out in front of Mickey. One was plain. One had small white stars. The other had black figures on it that reminded Mickey of some pictures in his science book.

"Which one suits you the best?"

Mickey pointed to the plain one. The man returned the other to the rack and started punching numbers on the cash register.

"Total comes to two thirty-seven forty-five," the man said and whipped a paper bag open.

Abe pulled his wallet from his back pocket and handed the man three one-hundred- dollar bills.

Abe must be rich, Mickey thought. First groceries. Then a bicycle. And now almost three hundred dollars' worth of cowboy stuff.

• • •

Mickey sat in the truck waiting for Abe to return. The school yard teamed with students. Most of them hustled to school buses. Many got into cars driven by their parents. A smaller number pulled their bikes from the bicycle rack. And a few just walked away from the school grounds. Mickey assumed they lived close by. He watched Lolita DeRosa come down the front steps of the main building. She'd no doubt just gotten out of math class, the last period of the day. Mickey thought about honking the horn of the Blazer to get her attention then throwing her a friendly wave. But he decided against it. Lolita was a nice girl. She and Mickey sometimes sat together on the bus. Sometimes they didn't. When they didn't, it wasn't because they were mad at each other. They just didn't sit together all the time. When they did, they talked about all kinds of things. Lolita even liked NASCAR. Imagine that. A girl liking NASCAR. Mickey thought that was cool. Wait! There he was. Billy Joe Speed. He carried a couple of books at his side. Mickey spied on the rich kid as he made his way across the school's green lawn. He stopped and spoke to a few girls. Punched a few guys on the shoulder and laughed. Mickey scrunched down a little as Billy Joe walked right pass Abe's truck. He didn't notice Mickey. Thank God. Billy Joe crossed the street and got into a white BMW. The woman driving didn't speak to Billy Joe. She just waited for him to get in then pulled away from the curb and drove away. Must be Billy Joe's mama, Mickey thought. Why was she driving a BMW and not some kind of Chevrolet? After all, Billy Joe's dad owned the Chevrolet dealership in town. He didn't sell BMWs. Weird.

The buses began pulling onto the streets. Mickey watched as the schoolyard turned into a virtual ghost town. What was keeping Abe so long? He'd been in the office since before school let out. All he had to do was show one of the ladies in the office the note his mother had written. Then, she'd give the study guides to Abe. That was all there was to it. Right? What was happening?

Mickey couldn't play the radio; Abe had the car keys. There was no place he could go to pass the time. No stores close by. He couldn't go anywhere on the school property; he was suspended. He opened up the bags from the western store. New clothes. He could hardly believe it. He had BRAND NEW clothes. The hat was okay. He'd wear it some. But the boots . . . well they were just flat out cool. He raised the top of the box. Why not put them on again? Just for the heck of it.

The driver's door clicked. Mickey looked up. Abe slid in under the steering wheel.

"What took so long?" Mickey said.

Abe pressed his lips and cocked his head. He retrieved his sunglasses from the visor, unfolded them and put them on. He took a deep breath and exhaled.

"Alright, Mickey, you ready to head on back to my house?" he said.

"Sure," Mickey said and closed up the boots and put the box back in the bag.

Abe cranked the Blazer, shifted into drive and pulled away. Mickey looked straight ahead. He wondered why Abe didn't answer his question. Abe didn't say a word the rest of the way home.

CHAPTER SEVEN

Mickey walked into Mrs. Fletcher's English class dressed in his new jeans and shirt, wearing his new belt and suspenders. He carried the bandana, the hat and the boots in a brown paper Winn Dixie grocery bag. Mrs. Fletcher shot him a look as he walked past her desk. Mickey suspected as much. He'd not worn new clothes to school a single day all year. Not even after Christmas break because Mickey didn't get any new clothes for Christmas. He didn't get anything new for that matter. The coat he'd gotten, the football, the baseball cards, and the Super Soaker water gun all came from the thrift store. Mickey didn't know exactly how they'd been purchased and transported to his house. It wasn't his mama. He was sure of that. He just came home from school the one day in mid- December and there they were. Wrapped and under the tree. The secret Santa, whoever the person was, forgot to remove the tags. Or maybe he or she left them on intentionally. Whichever it was, the tags left no question. The presents came from the Methodist thrift store. And not one of them cost over seven dollars. So what if they belonged to other people first? On Christmas morning they were new to him.

Mickey took his seat. He set the brown paper Winn Dixie bag on the floor next to his feet. If Mrs. Fletcher called students up in alphabetical order, he'd be last to make a presentation. No one in the class had a last name that came after Tucker. There was no kid with the last name of Williams or Wilson. Not even a Turner.

The bell rang and Mrs. Fletcher called the role. Everyone was present. Of course. Who would be stupid enough to miss a final exam? Especially when it was going to count for half your grade for the whole year. Mickey wondered why she even bothered to call the role. Just goes to show that teachers aren't smart about everything, Mickey thought.

After calling the role Mrs. Fletcher wheeled her chair from behind her desk to one side of the room next to Katherine Fairchild's desk. Katherine sat in the first desk closest to the windows. Her mother owned a beauty salon and sat on the school board.

"Do you mind if I sit next to you?" she asked Katherine.

Katherine smiled. "Not at all, Mrs. Fletcher."

Mickey looked over at Lolita. She rolled her eyes and shook her head. Mickey nodded in reply, a smirk on his face. They both knew Mrs. Fletcher wouldn't dare come sit in the back next to their kind.

"Alright," Mrs. Fletcher said. "Do your best to stay under three minutes. If you go a little over, I won't say anything. But if you go past three and a half minutes, I'll have to stop you. Everyone must get a turn." She sat down and called the first student. "Christy Adams."

Christy Adams sat in the second desk on the third row. Her father was a police officer and her mother taught Algebra I at the high school. Christy walked to the front of the room, a piece of poster board in one hand. She stood in front of Mrs. Fletcher's desk and held up a collage of pictures she'd drawn depicting characters from L. Frank Baum's The Wonderful Wizard of Oz. For just over two minutes she recapped the story, pointing to the characters as she mentioned them. When she finished, she returned to her seat.

"Very good, Christy," Mrs. Fletcher said. "It is apparent that you put a great deal of effort into your collage."

One by one Mrs. Fletcher called up the rest of Mickey's classmates. Each one sought to win Mrs. Fletcher's affirmation and the classroom's approval. Some made speeches about authors. Some read dramatically. Some acted out scenes from books. Some recited poems from memory. Lolita performed with sock puppets she'd made of Dorothy, the witch, the lion, the tin man, and the scarecrow. Archie Tanner displayed a miniature raft he'd constructed out of twigs and talked about life on the Mississippi River during the mid 1800s.

"And, for our final presentation, Mickey Tucker," Mrs. Fletcher announced.

Mickey picked up the Winn Dixie bag and walked to the front of the room, his heart rate increasing with each step. He set the bag on Mrs. Tucker's desk, rubbed his palms on his shirt and turned to the class.

"For my presentation, I'll draw from the example of Henry Wadsworth Longfellow," he said.

He cut a glance toward Mrs. Fletcher's. Her glasses were down on her nose and she glared at Mickey over the top of them. Two girls seated near her looked at each other and rolled their eyes. He felt like Lolita DeRosa and the other kids of his kind in the back of the room were a mile away and that he was standing in his underwear in front of Mrs. Fletcher and her pets. Mickey was certain his breakfast would be on the floor if he'd eaten it before leaving the house. Thank God he'd skipped it. Had no appetite anyway.

"Mr. Longfellow wrote a poem entitled 'Paul Revere's Ride.' I've written a poem entitled 'Roosevelt's Rough Riders.'" Mickey cleared his throat. "I'd like to perform it for you." He looked down and slipped off his sneakers.

Mickey reached a trembling hand into the bag.

"What are you doing?" Kevin Chalmers said. Kevin's dad was the high school basketball coach.

Mickey paused but didn't look at Kevin. "I'm putting on stuff like a Rough Rider wore," he said.

"Did they ride barefoot?" blurted out Mike Rogers, son of Alabama State Representative Richard Rogers.

The kids in the front desks laughed. Mickey looked at Mrs. Fletcher again. She swallowed the smile off her face. "Now, be respectful," she said, as fake as counterfeit money.

Mickey took out the bandana and tied it around his neck. He pulled the boots from the bag and worked them on his feet, making sure the legs of his jeans stayed tucked inside the boots' leather uppers.

"Wow! Those are the bomb," Keith Cleckler said from the back of the room.

Mickey smiled, thankful for the positive comment. Finally, he lifted the hat from the bag and pushed it on. He could hear Abe's voice in his head. *You're gonna knock 'em dead.* He'd practiced for the past four days in Abe's backyard. This was not Abe's backyard. This was real. How would Mrs. Fletcher respond? Would she stop him in the middle of his presentation and send him to the principal's office? He gave Lolita the signal and she started beatboxing just like he'd ask her to earlier on the bus ride to school. Mickey began moving his body, shuffling his feet, gesturing, and making animated facial expressions. And, then he launched into the rap song he'd written.

I'ma 'bout to tell ya the story of Cuba
So you better listen up or I'ma gonna sue ya.
Seventeen thousand American troops
Had landed near Cuba
And the Spanish said, "Oops."
Of course, you know
The USA won
American got two
And the Spanish were done.
One at El Caney, the other at San Juan Hill
But, of course, you know those Spanish
They were a pill.
There was a courageous group that were fighters
Led by Roosevelt, the Rough Riders
There was a man named Richard Davis
He wrote a letter and I say, "Save it."
He said General Hawkins had white hair
If I was that Hawkins
I'd say that just ain't fair
With Roosevelt mounted high on that horseback
He made you feel like you wanta jump back

As he said the final word of the song, Mickey threw up his right thumb as if he were thumbing for a ride and jerked his fist to his right side to drive home the point. He lowered his chin and pushed the back of the hat up so that the front of the brim covered his eyes. Lolita and the kids in the back of the room clapped. Dillon Masterson stood up and made slow, intentional, loud claps with cupped hands. Kevin Chalmers and Mike Rogers looked at each other and followed Dillon Masterson's lead. Dillon looked at the other front-desk kids and motioned for them to stand up too. The standing ovation gained momentum and the clapping grew into a hearty applause. Mickey held the pose till Mrs. Fletcher quieted the class and had them sit back down. Mickey picked up his sneakers and the Winn Dixie bag and walked to his seat. As he did, students on both sides of the aisle affirmed him with words, thrilled expressions and high-fives.

Mickey sat down and looked to the front of the room. Mrs. Fletcher stood in front of her desk, her hands at her hips. "Well, that was totally unexpected, Mickey."

"Looks like we just voted, Mrs. Fletcher," Dillon Masterson said. "It's Mickey. Hands down."

Mickey couldn't believe what he was seeing and hearing—Dillon Masterson, the mayor's son, had just led the class to declare Mickey the winner. Perhaps Mickey had some wrong ideas. Maybe some of the popular kids were good kids after all. And what could Mrs. Fletcher say? Her power was now compromised. And, to further debilitate her, the rest of the class chimed in with celebratory remarks like, "Way to go, Mickey!" and "Mickey, that was totally fly!" and "Cowabunga, Dude!"

Mickey felt the victory. This was his moment. For the first time in his entire life, HE was the most popular, the highest regarded . . . at least in Mrs. Fletcher's English class. He looked around at his new, cheering fans. He paused and stared at Lolita DeRosa for a few seconds.

"You did it, Mickey! You did it!" she said, clapping and grinning.

Mickey knew what she meant. He'd done more than just written a poem and turned it into a song. He'd broken a barrier . . . scored a victory. And not just a personal victory, but a victory for all the other unpopular, undesirable kids in the class—the kids who didn't have trendy clothes, well-to-do parents or nice houses. He'd shown Mrs. Fletcher that they could be every bit as smart and have just as much potential as the kids who sat in the front desks. Mrs. Fletcher would have to give him a perfect hundred plus ten bonus points. The class had spoken; the peer pressure was more than even she could withstand. If her plan was to flunk Mickey and make him retake the sixth grade, she'd failed. Abe was right. There was nothing wrong with Mickey's brain.

CHAPTER EIGHT

Mickey locked down the rear brakes. The back tire skidded on the loose gravel as the bicycle came to a stop. He dismounted and, with one foot, he pushed down the kickstand then shot up the steps. He turned the door ringer. The sound he heard amped up his enthusiasm. Abe's footsteps. Abe opened the door.

"I knocked'em out today. Just like you said I would," Mickey said, looking up at Abe, eyes beaming, a broad smile on his face, breathing deep from the hurried bike ride.

"I want to hear all about it, so come right on in," Abe said.

"It was so awesome," Mickey said, walking in, accenting his enthusiasm with his opened hands. "You should have seen it."

Abe shut the door behind him. Mickey looked up at him. "I was so nervous. I thought I was gonna throw up. I'm sure I would have if I hadn't skipped breakfast."

"Well, you still might if you don't slow down." Abe motioned to a chair in the living room. "Let's have a seat."

"You shoulda seen it, Mr. Abe. The whole class," Mickey said, collapsing down on one of the forest green wingback chairs. He put his palms on the sides of his head. "It's like I was somebody. Like I mattered. Not just to the kids in the back desks, but to the kids in the front desks too." He dropped his hands to the tops of his legs. "Abe, it was one of the best times of my life . . . no, it was THE best." Mickey crossed his arms at his wrist and then spread them apart. "Without question."

Abe snapped his fingers. "This calls for a celebration. What do you say we go to that new Mexican restaurant that just opened? I hear it's really good."

Mickey sat up in the chair, his eyes opened wide. "No way! I've never been to a Mexican restaurant!"

Abe cocked his head, winked with one eye and clicked his tongue. "Well, now you're about to," he said and grinned. "Let me grab my keys."

• • •

Restaurants in Claxton thrived on weekends. From the franchise pizza parlor to the locally owned catfish café. But no restaurant served as many hungry customers as Casa Amigos. The restaurant was a hit from the day it opened less than six months ago.

Abe and Mickey walked in. The sound of authentic Mexican music filled their ears; the smell of authentic Mexican cuisine filled their nostrils.

A lady stood behind a welcome station. Her black hair was pulled back tightly from her face. A white and pink orchid blossom protruded on one side from the bun formed on the back of her head. "Welcome to Casa Amigos," she said, dimples on her cheeks. "How many will be dining today?"

"Two," Abe said.

She pulled two menus from a stack. "Follow me."

Abe and Mickey followed her to a booth next to a window in the back of the restaurant. "How's this?" she said.

"Perfect," Abe said and slid in on one side of the booth. Mickey slid in on the other.

She glanced at Mickey then at Abe and smiled. "Your server will be with you shortly." She turned and walked back toward the front of the restaurant.

Mickey breathed in deep. Oh, the smell. Unfamiliar, but good—really good. And the music. Wow! What were those instruments? Certainly not electric guitars or drums or synthesizers.

"Look at this place," Mickey said, scanning the room. "It makes you feel like you're really in Mexico." He focused on Abe. "You ever been to Mexico?"

"A couple of times."

"What kind of stuff did you see when you were there?"

"I didn't go there to check out the place. It wasn't a vacation. I didn't stay long. Just in and out," Abe said and opened his menu.

Why would anyone go to Mexico and not check out the place? What did in and out mean? And why would anyone go there and not be on a vacation?

"What are you having?" Abe said.

"Tacos, I never had tacos before. I've just seen them on TV. We have pizza for lunch at school on Fridays sometimes. But we never have tacos. I asked one of the lunchroom ladies if we would ever have them. She said, 'Probably not.'"

"My name is Dahlia and I'll be your server this evening," came a voice.

Mickey looked up to a smiling lady in her early twenties. She stood at the end of the table, her shiny black hair hanging midway of her back. The light blue tee shirt she wore had "*Casa Amigos*" imprinted on it just below her left shoulder. "Can I get you something to drink?" she asked.

"I'll have a Coke," Mickey said.

I'll have a glass of sweet tea," Abe said and glanced at Mickey. "And I think we're ready to order."

Mickey nodded. Dahlia pulled a small pad and a pen from the pocket of the small black apron she wore.

"Okay, let's start with you," she said and looked at Mickey.

"I'll have three tacos."

"Crunchy or soft?"

"Crunchy."

"Okay." She turned to Abe. "What can I get for you?"

"I'll have a tamale, a beef enchilada and rice and beans. And can we get a large bowl of cheese dip?"

"Certainly," Dahlia said. "I'll bring it right out with your chips and salsa."

She turned and walked away. In a few minutes she returned, palming a large round tray in one hand. From the tray she took a large glass of iced tea and set it on the table in front of Abe, a large glass of Coca-Cola in front of Mickey. She placed a basket of tortilla chips in the middle of the table along with a glass container of salsa, two small plastic empty bowls and a large bowl filled with warm cheese dip.

"Your orders will be out shortly," she said.

"Thank you," Abe said, smiling.

After Abe prayed a brief prayer, the two of them dug in.

"So, what are your plans for the summer?" Abe said, pouring the salsa into the two bowls.

"Nothing much. Just riding my new bike and taking care of Mama." Mickey stuffed a chip half-covered with cheese into his mouth. "What about you?"

"I have a few chores around the house that need to be done. I could use some help. I'll pay you five bucks an hour and let you fish in my pond."

Mickey shot his eyes open. "Heck yeah." He drank down some of the Coca-Cola and set the glass back down on the table. "When do you want to get started?"

Abe cut into the enchilada with his fork. "I was thinking about tomorrow morning."

"Tomorrow's good."

"Okay, I'll pick you up at nine."

"You don't have to. I can ride my bike," Mickey said and bit off a large part of one of the tacos.

"That's right. You have your own transportation now."

Mickey cut a look toward the front door. His blood cooled in his veins. He dropped his chin to his chest and exhaled.

"What's wrong?" Abe said.

"Billy Joe and his dad just walked in."

Abe turned in his seat and looked back then turned back to Mickey.

"Don't you go worrying about them. We're celebrating. Remember?"

Mickey looked up at Abe, a flushed look on his face.

"You just keep eating your tacos and enjoying yourself."

Mickey nodded, his face expressing his sudden decrease in enthusiasm.

Dahlia came back to Abe and Mickey's table. "How's it going here? Need anything?"

Mickey shook his head.

"You think your mother would like some tacos?" Abe said to Mickey.

"I think so."

"I think we're about ready for the check," Abe said to Dahlia. "And we'll have three tacos to go."

"Okay. I'll be back with your check and your to-go order."

The cordial waitress walked away.

"Tell me again about your English final exam."

Mickey livened up.

"Abe, it was great. I did it just like we practiced. And everybody loved it. When it was all over, the whole class voted me as the best which means I get a hundred and ten points."

"Let me see," said Abe and narrowed his eyelids. "You had a sixty-two-average going into the final. That means you have a hundred and seventy-two points. Divide that by two and you come out with an eighty-six. A solid B."

"Yeah. And I don't have to look at Mrs. Fletcher next year."

Abe held up his tea glass. "Let's drink to that."

Mickey raised his glass and dinged it against Abe's. The two took drinks and grinned at each other. Dahlia returned with the check and a foam container inside a plastic bag.

"Here you go," she said and set the bag on the table. She slid the check face-down on Abe's side. "It's been my pleasure to serve you tonight and we hope to see you again soon."

"Everything was great and we'll definitely be back," Abe said.

Dahlia smiled and walked away.

"Here, let's put the rest of the chips in here for your mother," said Abe.

Mickey began pouring the leftover chips into the bag. Abe turned over the check and looked at it.

"How was your food?" came a commanding, masculine voice.

Abe and Mickey looked up. A man stood at the table, his defined muscles making his collared shirt look a couple of sizes too small. He wore a gold watch on one of his thick wrists, a gold curb link bracelet on the other.

"The food was fine," Abe said. "We'll be back."

"It'd be best that you don't," the man said with the tone and cool expression of an irritated state trooper.

Abe cocked his head. "Excuse me. I don't quite follow you."

The man put his fists on the table and leered at Abe.

"Let's just say Mr. Speed prefers that you don't come back," he said.

Abe nodded, a notable sarcastic look on his face. "Oh, I see. You relay Mr. Speed's messages for him when he's not man enough to speak for himself." Abe raised an index finger. "You tell Mr. Speed that I realize his preferences mean something to a lot of people in this town but I'm not one of them."

The beefy man leaned in. "Buddy, you have no idea what you're getting yourself into."

"Buddy, huh? So that's the pet name you're giving me. Buddy. Okay. Okay. Why don't you tell me what I'm getting myself into?"

"Let's just say that if you don't do what Mr. Speed suggests things could get unpleasant, maybe even hazardous."

"Well, Butterfly," Abe said with raised eyebrows and a condescending tight smile. "It is okay if I call you Butterfly, isn't it?"

The man flared his nostrils and wrinkled his brow.

Abe grinned. "Don't care too much for that pet name, do you?" He gave the man a patronizing look. "Well, that's just too bad. I don't like Buddy and you don't like Butterfly so we're even." Abe lifted an index finger in Albert Speed's direction. "Now, Butterfly, you walk right back over to Mr. Speed. You know the man who tells you what to do and you do it. That Mr. Speed. You walk right back over to him and you tell him that I'll come here and eat every day of the week if I want to. Tell him I'd be glad for him to join me anytime."

The man gritted his teeth and gave Abe a smirk then turned to walk away.

"Oh, and by the way, Butterfly," Abe said.

The man turned on his heels and looked at Abe through fiery eyes.

"You're welcome to join us as well," Abe added.

The man curled one side of his mouth and turned and walked away.

Abe snickered and looked at Mickey. "Well, Mickey, you ready to go?"

Mickey looked as though he'd seen a ghost. "You know what that big man means, don't you? He's saying he's gonna kill you, Mr. Abe."

Abe made a backhanded wave in the air. "Guys like him are a dime a dozen."

•   •   •

Mickey parked his bike next to Abe's front porch and ascended the steps dressed like he was in gym class. When he dropped Mickey off at home after eating at the Mexican restaurant, Abe said, "Tomorrow, wear something like what you wear for your gym class." Mickey didn't know why because Abe didn't say. But he'd come dressed as Abe had instructed. He turned the door ringer. Abe opened the door wearing sweat pants and a white tee shirt that had a Jamaican flag across the front.

"Good morning," Abe said. "You ready to get started."

"I guess so. What're we gonna be doing?"

"We're going to start preparing for the future. I'll meet you in the backyard."

Mickey walked around the house to the back yard. The water was not spraying up in the pond. Mickey stood at the edge of it and watched the fish cruise around close to the surface. A woodpecker hammered away in a nearby tree. Two squirrels frolicked on the rail fence that separated the backyard from a pasture.

"Alright, Mickey."

Mickey turned on his heels. Abe stood at the edge of the patio. He motioned with one hand. "Come over here."

Mickey walked over.

"Spread your feet out about shoulder width apart."

Mickey spread his feet.

Abe bent his knees as if he were sitting in an imaginary chair.

"Now, bend your legs like this so that your knees are directly over your feet. When you do it correctly, you shouldn't be able to see your feet."

Mickey did as Abe instructed. Abe clinched his fists and held them firmly at his sides. Mickey did the same.

"This is called a horse stance. Over time it'll build strength in your legs. When you throw a punch, you punch with these two knuckles," said Abe and pointed to the knuckles of his index and middle fingers. "The punch goes straight out in front of you and your fist twists at the very end. The power comes from your hips. Like this," Abe said and thrusts his right fist forward, rotating his hips slightly. "Every time you throw a punch, I want you to imagine that you are punching someone who wants to hurt you."

CHAPTER NINE

With his hearing deficiency corrected, Mickey sailed through the seventh grade. He didn't make a D. He didn't make a C or even a B. Mickey made straight A's. He proved to Mrs. Fletcher and to everyone else she'd poisoned that there was nothing whatsoever wrong with his brain. On the contrary. His brain was amazing. Names. Dates. Terms. Definitions. Formulas. He could nail them all. As his metamorphosis progressed so did his popularity. By the end of the eighth grade, Mickey was the man! Boys who used to ignore him wanted to be his friend. Girls who once thought they were above him passed notes to him in class. Mickey, however, stayed true. He was friendly to everyone, but his closest friends remained the same—the kids whose parents did manual labor for a living—the kids who didn't wear designer clothes or get regular dental exams. Kids like Wally Burton, Bobby Dawson, Shelly Bohannan, and Lolita DeRosa.

And then there was all the things Mickey had learned from Abe. Mickey could take down a tree with a chainsaw. Handle a twelve-gauge shotgun. Plow with a tractor. Replace an electrical outlet. Field dress a deer. Hit a jar lid with a twenty-two rifle from a hundred yards. Not only could Mickey drive a car, but he could change the oil and replace the spark plugs. Mickey was making up for lost time, filling in the empty spaces a boy suffers when his father is not in the picture. Mickey was growing. Maturing. Getting stronger.

Leslie Tucker, however, was declining. By the summer leading up to Mickey's freshman year of high school, the hospice nurse was coming five days a week instead of three. Leslie's days were filled with sleeping and with books. Great books. Both fiction and non-fiction. Abe brought her three books from his library every week. Sometimes four or five. For her birthday he gave her a leather-bound Bible with her name engraved on it.

"It's the book of all books," he said. "You start reading it and it'll start reading you. When you have questions, let me know and we'll discuss them."

Leslie began reading and she did have questions—questions that often resulted in long conversations with Abe. On more than a few occasions Abe altered the plans he had for Mickey and spent entire days at Leslie's bedside. Sometimes Mickey would listen in. Other times he'd ride his bike or practice the fighting and self-defense techniques Abe had been teaching him. He'd spend time with Lolita or visit Big Ed and Erma. Come to find out, the Maryland couple weren't so grumpy after all. They didn't put up Christmas lights because they had no one to celebrate Christmas with. Erma wouldn't allow candy in the house because of Big Ed's diabetes. She had to watch him like a hawk when it came to sweets. Before they moved from Maryland, Big Ed almost died from eating candy one Halloween. Erma had given him strict orders to give it out ONLY to kids. Between trick-or- treaters he'd sneak and eat some when Erma's wasn't looking. Big Ed's rebellion caused him to have a reaction that put him in the hospital for three weeks. When the doctor finally let him go home, Erma threw down the gauntlet. "No more candy in the house ever again." She'd stuck to her guns ever since. On Halloween they kept their porch light off and didn't answer the door. Not because they didn't want to give kids candy, but because Erma wanted to make sure Big Ed didn't fall victim to temptation. Abe was right. Everyone has a story.

• • •

Two long lines of yellow buses almost bumper to bumper striped the paved lot in front of Claxton High School. Mickey and Lolita stepped off bus fifty-seven and joined into the flow of streaming students.

"Here we are. High school," Lolita said. "You nervous?"

"Maybe a little, I guess. But think about it. It's just a bigger building, bigger books and different teachers. That's all." Mickey pulled her in tight. "We'll be fine, Lolita. It's like the internet. Remember? It took a little time, but eventually we got the hang of it."

"I'm not talking about that." Lolita stopped and scanned the scene, one palm turned up. "Look around, Mickey. Most of these kids have it all. Some of them even drove their own cars."

Mickey put a hand on her shoulder. "Look at me."

Lolita looked up into his eyes. "What?"

"Have you ever watched Popeye the Sailorman?"

Lolita wrinkled her brow and raised one side of her upper lip. "What the heck kind of question is that?"

"Come on, Lolita. Just answer the question. Have you ever watched Popeye the Sailorman?"

She rolled her eyes. "Of course. Who hasn't?"

Mickey grinned. "And what is it that makes him strong and powerful?"

Lolita shook her head. "Mickey, I'm really not following you. I'm telling you how I feel right now and you're asking me about a classic cartoon character."

"Come on. Come on. I'm going somewhere with this."

Lolita sighed. "Spinach. Spinach makes him strong. So what?"

"You know how people look down on us because we live in the trailer park and how we're never the teachers' pets and don't have the nicest houses and coolest clothes?"

"Uh huh."

"From this day forward, let's look at stuff like that as cans of spinach that will only make us stronger and more powerful. When a teacher overlooks us. That's a can of spinach. When a kid makes fun of something we wear. That's a can of spinach. Someone calls us trailer trash. That's a can of spinach. We just take stuff like that and eat it up like Popeye does spinach. See it all as something that makes us stronger. Then, one day we'll look up and we'll be living in nice houses. We'll have nice clothes.

We'll drive nice cars." Mickey bumped her on the shoulder with one hand. "What do you say?"

A loud voice interrupted before Lolita could answer. "Everyone, make your way into the auditorium for a general assembly with Mr. Williams! When you get there, sit in the section assigned to your grade!"

Mickey and Lolita looked toward the main entrance doors. A man stood at the top of the steps speaking into a bullhorn. "After the assembly, freshmen will move to the lunchroom! Sophomores will move to the gymnasium! Juniors and seniors will remain in the auditorium!"

Lolita inhaled through her nose then exhaled through her lips, her cheeks bulging. "Freshman. Why not just tell it like it is? We're high school peons."

Mickey put an arm around Lolita's shoulders. "Come on. Let's go. It might actually be fun."

Colbert Williams stepped up to the podium. The student chatter in the large room evaporated as the speakers amplified the fuzzy *bump bump bump* sound he caused when he tapped the microphone three times with his index finger. He gripped each side of the podium and launched into his pre-planned address. "Good morning. My name is Mr. Williams and I'm the principal here at Claxton High. On behalf of the entire faculty, I welcome you. We purpose to provide an atmosphere where your opportunity for learning is maximized. I'm sure as I look out over this crowd this morning that I'm looking at future doctors, lawyers, educators, business professionals, entrepreneurs, and political leaders. Upon graduation, many of you will go on to college. Some of you will go straight into the marketplace. Whatever career path you choose, we want to help you succeed. Rest assured; we are here for you. Today, you will be given a student handbook. It will inform you of all our school policies. Let me encourage you to read it and abide by it. In doing so, you will help ensure a healthy, safe learning environment for yourself and your fellow students. I want you to know that my office is always open. Feel free to come see me should you ever have a need or concern."

Colbert Williams looked down to the front row of seats and lifted an opened hand to a man. "Mr. Capshaw, would you please stand so all our sophomores can see you?"

The man stood to his feet and re-tucked the back of his blue shirt into his pleated khaki pants. He pushed the rim of his glasses up on the brim of his nose. His thick mustache matched his sandy-blonde hair and raised up as he gave the student body a big, teethy smile.

Colbert Williams turned his attention back to the students. "Okay, if you are a sophomore, would you please form a line and follow Mr. Capshaw to the gymnasium."

The sound of spring-loaded chair seats folding back into place reverberated throughout the auditorium as more than one hundred students stood up. They filed into the main aisle, formed a line and followed Mr. Capshaw out the double-doors near the front of the large room.

Colbert Williams looked down at the front row again and motioned toward a lady. "Miss Ferguson, would you please stand so all our freshmen can see you?"

Judy Ferguson stood up, a leather padfolio cradled in one arm and held close to her chest. Her black hair hung below her shoulders. She gave a friendly wave with her free hand then walked to the side-double doors where Mr. Capshaw and the sophomores had just exited. She stopped at the doors and turned back to face the room.

Colbert Williams leaned in close to the microphone. "Alright. Freshmen, you'll be following Miss Ferguson to the lunchroom for an orientation and to receive your homeroom assignments."

Mickey and Lolita stood to their feet along with one hundred plus other new high school students. They joined in the flow of their fellow classmen and followed Judy Ferguson out of the auditorium and down the hallway leading to the lunchroom. Mickey paused at an opened door and stepped past the threshold. Lolita stayed close to him.

"Check it out, Lolita! Microscopes and all kinds of cool stuff." He pointed to the back corner of the room. "Look, there's even a full-sized skeleton."

Lolita tugged at the back of Mickey's shirt. "Mickey, come on. We're not supposed to be in here. We're supposed to go to the lunchroom."

Mickey made a few downward motions with one hand. "I know. I know." He continued surveying the room. "But the door was open. Can't hurt anything just to look."

Lolita tugged on his shirt again, this time harder. "Let's go. You're gonna get us in trouble."

"I'd listen to her if I were you," a boy said.

Mickey and Lolita turned back to the door.

Billy Joe Speed stood in the doorway. He wore a royal blue golf shirt, the letters *SGA* monogrammed in gold on the left side of his chest. He peered at Mickey, a condescending grin on his face.

"Well, Trailer Trash, I knew we'd eventually bump into each other, but I didn't think it'd be on your very first day."

Billy Joe raised his eyebrows. "We've got some catching up to do. But that can wait. For now, we best be making our way to the lunchroom."

Billy Joe motioned with his head and stepped out into the hallway. He raised a hand toward the mass of students who were filing through the lunchroom doors at the end of the hall. "After you."

Mickey and Lolita walked out of the room and headed down the hallway. Billy Joe followed close behind them singing the chorus of LL Cool J's "Mama Said Knock You Out" just loud enough for them to hear. Great. The very first day and Billy Joe Speed was already at it. They entered the cafeteria. The other students were already seated. Miss Ferguson was well into her opening remarks. She paused and smiled at Mickey and Lolita.

"Come right in and take a seat. Did you get turned around between here and the auditorium?"

"No, they stopped off at the biology lab and took a SELF-guided tour," Billy Joe said.

Mickey and Lolita sat down at the table in the back of the lunchroom.

Miss Ferguson fixed her attention on them, a congenial expression on her face. "Biology is offered as a sophomore elective. So that'll give you something to look forward to for next year, if biology interests you."

Billy Joe walked over and stood behind Mickey. He leaned in close to Mickey's ear. "Welcome to high school, Trailer Trash. You're in for a REAL education."

He straightened himself back up and shot Miss Ferguson a boy scout smile. The young educator raised an open palm toward Billy Joe. "Everyone, this is Billy Joe Speed."

In near perfect unison the students twisted in their seats and looked back.

"Billy Joe is the student government vice-president. He'll be assisting me with your orientation today. Please don't hesitate to ask either of us any questions you may have. We're here to help make your first day of high school a great memory. Isn't that correct, Billy Joe?"

Billy Joe took a few steps forward and launched into the playacting he'd learned by watching his father schmooze numerous indecisive car shoppers. "Absolutely. I know exactly how you feel. I still remember my first day as a freshman. Knots in my stomach. Mind filled with thoughts of insecurity and inferiority. Worried about having to compete against upper classmen in gym class. Not to mention the thought of having to take algebra and chemistry. I felt overwhelmed. It was then that I determined I'd help future incoming freshmen to have a better experience if ever given the opportunity. Today, as a member of the SGA, I'm in a position to do just that. So, let me know if there's anything I can help you with."

Billy Joe scanned the room as he continued. "And not just today, but tomorrow or next week or next month. Or next semester even."

He backstepped a few paces and resumed his position behind Mickey's chair and threw Miss Ferguson the same boy scout smile once again.

"You represent the best of this school, Billy Joe."

He returned a thankful nod and she picked back up with her orientation agenda. Billy Joe leaned down once again, his mouth inches from Mickey's ear. "None of that bull crap I just said applies to you, Trailer Trash. I've got some real surprises in store for you . . . FOR THE NEXT TWO YEARS."

Chapter Ten

Mickey stood on the pedals as he coasted into Abe's driveway. He stopped next to the front porch and propped the bike on its kickstand.

"I'm on the phone! It's gonna be a few minutes!" Abe said from his bedroom as Mickey entered through the front door. Mickey no longer knocked when he came to Abe's house. He just opened the door and let himself in. If the door was locked, no problem. Abe had shown him where the hidden key was. Hanging on a screw under the front porch.

Mickey fished in Abe's pond anytime he wanted. Had free rein to Abe's impressive library. Helped himself to anything in the refrigerator, the pantry or both. Mickey kept Abe's grass cut and his truck clean. He bush hogged and plowed parts of Abe's property with Abe's John Deere tractor. He and Abe hunted together. Jogged together. Ate together several times each week. Even went to church together.

Abe introduced Mickey to the Mount Pisgah Missionary Baptist Church on Easter Sunday of Mickey's seventh-grade year. The Reverend Jonah Washington ascended his pulpit donning a pink double-breasted suit, a white shirt with French cuffs, a silk red necktie with matching pocket cloth, and black and white wingtip shoes. He preached from Isaiah 53 and held Mickey and the rest of the congregation spellbound for an hour. From that day onward, Mickey never missed a Sunday service other than the rare times of personal sickness or the absence of the Hospice nurse at his mother's bedside.

Abe bought Mickey a wide-margin, calfskin-bound King James Version Ryrie Study Bible. It was identical to the one Reverend Washington preached from with but a handful of exceptions. The cover of the gifted preacher's was well worn. Handwritten notes and smudges from the traffic of faithful fingertips filled its pages in both the Old Testament books and the New Testament ones. Reverend Washington's Bible had "Preach the Word" stamped into the outside front cover. Abe had "Psalm 119:105" stamped on Mickey's. Mickey was the only white attender in the congregation. To a visitor he may have looked out of place. To the church members, however, Mickey was family. Not a Sunday went by that Mickey didn't take home a cake, a pie, a casserole, an entrée, or some combination compliments of the ladies of the church.

• • •

The sun beamed down with stinging intensity. It was the third Sunday of July. The summer prior to Mickey's eighth grade year. Reverend Washington stood below his congregants as they looked down in anticipation. The women battled the heat with the hand fans they'd brought from the church sanctuary. Most of the men fought it in like fashion with their fedoras. The men who didn't have a hat routinely wiped the sweat from their faces and necks with handkerchiefs. The young folks endured like only young folks can during the deep south's hottest, most humid time of the year. But no one complained. Quite the contrary. All were thrilled, eager to witness the long-held tradition of displaying faith. The waist-high brownish gray water of Yellow Leaf Creek tugged at Reverend Washington's purple robe as it flowed lazily on its southbound course. The white-robed candidate stood along the muddy shore, awaiting the good minister's invitation to come join him in the middle of the creek. History was about to be made . . . something never before experienced by any generation of believers in Mount Pisgah Missionary Baptist Church's ninety-eight years of existence. A church member would soon be added who would forever be remembered as the first of his kind. At the pastor's bidding, the candidate stepped forward and took his stand in the natural, streaming water. . In his baritone pulpit voice Reverend Washington asked the candidate the question he always asked on such occasions. "Is it your testimony that you have repented of your sins and trusted Jesus Christ as your Lord and Savior?" The candidate responded in the affirmative and folded his arms over his chest. The preacher put one hand on the candidate's shoulder and raised the other high over his head. "Then it is my joy to baptize you, Mickey Tucker, my brother, in the name of the Father and the Son and the Holy Spirit." The minister lowered Mickey under the water and raised him back up. And with that, Mount Pisgah Missionary Baptist Church received its first ever white member into its fellowship. The witnesses of the momentous event joined in an a cappella rendering of *Amazing Grace*.

•   •   •

Mickey opened the refrigerator and took out an orange Fanta. He checked under the plastic cake cover. A heap of chocolate chip cookies. He grabbed three and sat down at the small table against the wall. As he chewed he gazed at the picture he'd often examined. Abe's great grandfather and the other dapper musician. The one who held a weathered acoustic guitar and had a perfect smile. Who was the man? Mickey had long stopped asking. Abe always changed the subject or gave the same pat answer: "Just a guitar player my great grandfather used to play with from time to time."

The hardwood floor told Mickey that Abe was through with his phone call and headed toward the kitchen.

"Sorry about that. It was an important call."

Mickey turned in his chair and looked back at Abe. "No problem."

Abe clapped a hand against the top of Mickey's shoulder as he walked past him. "So, tell me about your first day of high school."

Abe reached for the handle of the refrigerator.

Mickey sighed and lowered his head. "He started in on me already."

Abe pulled open the door and took out a bottle of root beer. "Who?"

"Who do you think? Billy Joe Speed."

Abe took a bottle opener from a cabinet drawer. "I see," he said and popped the top off the bottle. He turned and leaned back against the kitchen counter, took a long drink and looked at the bottle. "Ain't nothing like a Frostie. Got a little something other root beers don't have. Been my favorite since I was a kid. My daddy and I used to sit on the back porch and solve the world's problems while we ate Cracker Jacks and drank Frosties." He turned his attention to Mickey and tilted the top of the bottle toward him. "Anything with a bearded old man on it is ALWAYS good."

Mickey cocked his head back. "Did you hear what I said?

"Of course, I heard you. Billy Joe Speed wasted no time. Set his affection on you the very first day."

Mickey raised his eyebrows and lowered his chin close to his chest. "YEAH! And you start talking about you and your daddy eating Cracker Jacks and drinking your favorite brand of root beer."

Abe smiled as he walked over and sat down in the chair opposite Mickey. "One of the problems my daddy and I solved was a problem I had."

"And what problem was that?"

Abe took another drink of the root beer and set the bottle down on the table. "Gerald Matthews."

"So what does some guy name Gerald Matthews have to do with anything?"

Abe fixed his attention on the bottle and began rotating it on the table. "I entered Claxton High School in 1969 as a freshman. It was different back then. The first year of integration in Alabama. Black kids and white kids going to the same school. A new day in the south. Gerald Matthews was a football player . . . quarterback to be exact and the son of Charles Matthews who just happened to be the high school football coach. Gerald was the back-up quarterback his freshman year. The starter his sophomore year. Ran for nine touchdowns and passed for eight hundred and twenty-three yards."

Abe paused turning the bottle and looked up at Mickey. "Not bad for a sophomore . . . not bad at all."

He returned his attention to the bottle and began rotating it again. "When I arrived he was a junior. It was a foregone conclusion that the starting job was his. He was all over the local papers. The local radio station too. Couple of scouts even came over from Alabama and met with him at his house."

"Wait a minute," Mickey said. "Alabama? THE Alabama? BEAR BRYANT Alabama?"

Abe looked at Mickey again and nodded. "Yessir. Bear Bryant Alabama."

He took another drink and continued. "It was in the cards for Gerald. A proven track record. Father was the coach. Then came the first day of practice. I was the only black kid on the team. We lined up on the forty-yard line. The coach said, 'Boys, the first man to the goal line can choose the position he wants to try out for.' He blew the whistle. And I beat everyone else by ten yards. Everybody thought I'd say running back or wide-receiver."

Mickey perked up. "But you said quarterback, didn't you?"

Abe laughed. "I definitely said quarterback."

"Then what happened?"

"We started competing for the job."

Mickey leaned forward, his attention locked in as if he were watching a suspenseful movie. "And?"

"I learned the plays quicker. Ran the offense better. Read the defense faster. Threw the ball more accurately."

"So, you won the starting position!" Mickey said, nodding.

"I was better, but I didn't become the starting quarterback."

"Well, why not? Did you quit or get hurt or something?"

Abe pressed his lips and shook his head, "No. I was named the third-string quarterback behind Melvin Derryberry."

Mickey slammed a fist down on the table. "Third-string? What a rip off!"

"That's what I thought too. And that brings us back to Frostie root beer."

Mickey wrenched his expression like he'd just smelled something foul. "I'm not following you."

Abe pushed back in his chair and interlocked his finger in front of his stomach. "I was mad and hurt. I wanted to quit the football team. And then my dad and I had Cracker Jacks and Frosties on the back porch. He told me that, if I quit, I'd miss out on one of the greatest experiences of my high school football career."

"And what was that?"

"The experience of being on a team where all the other players and all the coaches would know that I was the best. And, knowing that every time we lost, and we did lose, those players and those coaches would go home thinking, 'We might have won had Abe Loomis been our quarterback tonight.'"

Mickey smiled. "Especially Gerald Matthews."

Abe winked an eye. "ESPECIALLY Gerald Matthews."

Mickey bit off a chunk of a cookie. "Whatever happened? Did he go play for Bear Bryant?"

Abe shook an index finger in the air. "Funny you should ask. One day. Unannounced. Those same two scouts came to watch him practice. He was so focused on me he didn't complete a single pass and threw two—" Abe held up two fingers. "Not one but TWO interceptions."

Mickey pulled down a clinched fist. "Yes!"

Abe lowered his head and looked at Mickey from under his brow. "Now don't you go celebrating. It was sad . . . really sad."

Mickey washed the expression from his face. "Was it really?"

Abe began shaking his head slowly, a smile stretching on his face. "No, it was one of the greatest days of my life!"

Abe raised an open palm and Mickey slapped him five and the two laughed.

"Did they ever get to see you play?" Mickey said.

"Yes. I threw eleven straight completions. Three for touchdowns. And ran for another two."

"What did they say?"

Abe's expression turned somber. "They didn't say anything."

"They didn't say anything?"

"Nothing."

"You gotta be kidding me."

Abe stood from his chair and walked over to the trash can near the pantry. "They didn't say anything." He dropped the bottle into the can. "THAT day. But they did come back and say something when I was a senior."

He opened the pantry door and looked inside.

Mickey rolled a "come on, spit it out" open hand, "Which was?"

Abe closed the pantry door and turned back to Mickey. He stroked his beard. "Well, it seems like it went something like this. Mr. Loomis, we'd like to offer you a full scholarship to play football at the University of Alabama."

Mickey put his hands on the sides of his head. "You mean you played for Bear Bryant?"

"I did."

"Quarterback?"

"Wide-receiver. I was the third-string quarterback but the starting wide-receiver all four years of high school. And Bama needed a wide-receiver. So, when they came calling, I was ready."

"Good thing you didn't quit."

Abe nodded. "Good thing I didn't quit."

"And, what about Gerald Matthews? Did he play for Alabama too?"

"No. He wound up going to a small college in Florida. Flunked out his sophomore year. Came back home to Claxton and went to work driving one of those trucks that pumps out portable toilets. You know, the kind you see at construction sites."

"Dude, he went from being the starting quarterback to driving a honey wagon?"

"Is that what kids now days call those trucks?"

"Yeah. Among other things."

Abe leaned against the kitchen counter again, his expression serious. "Alright now, Mick. Listen to me."

Mickey locked in as Abe continued.

"Gerald Matthews knew I was a better quarterback than he was and it drove him crazy. He was always cutting me down and trying to get me in trouble. He'd lie and make stuff up that wasn't true. He and some of his buddies even beat me up a few times. But he knew and I knew that I was better than him. Now, Mick, you're a better man than Billy Joe Speed."

"You think so?"

"No, I don't think so. I know so. He may have money and he might be the pet of half the teachers at school. But he's got the same problem Gerald Matthews had."

"What's that?"

"Bad character. He knew I was a better quarterback than he was, and he couldn't accept it. So, he treated me the way he did. He flunked out of college because of bad character. A man's character defines everything about him. How he handles success. How he handles disappointment. How he treats other people. How he handles his money. Everything. Now, you sort of beat him in middle school when you sold those candy bars cheaper than his. Hurt his ego. It's bothered him ever since. Now, he's made it his mission to make you look bad. He's going to work overtime to get under your skin. Make you lose your cool. Don't let him do it. He might even put his hands on you again. But remember, things are different now. Got it?"

Mickey nodded. "Yessir."

Chapter Eleven

Mickey studied the campus map, planned his daily transition routine and stuck to it. All freshman classrooms were on the same hall. Junior classrooms were on another wing of the building. This meant Mickey didn't run the risk of crossing paths with Billy Joe Speed during class changes. Thank God for that! An awning connected Claxton High School's junior wing to the Kenneth Davis Gymnasium where Physical Education classes for all classmen were held. Down the junior hallway and under the awning was the shortest way to the gymnasium. Mickey, however, would exit the freshman wing through the glass door at the end of the hall and walk across the back parking lot. He'd enter the gymnasium through the single door next to the coaches' parking places. Mickey would stay alert when he walked from his first period Algebra class to his second period gym class. Students who drove to school parked in the back parking lot. Mickey would be ready to duck behind a car or pickup truck at the first sight of Billy Joe.

Lunch period. Well, that was more hazardous. All classmen had lunch together. Encountering Billy Joe was inevitable. Mickey would have to take things as they came at lunchtime. He'd stay close to other students. That way they'd be witnesses if, and when, anything went down. And he'd take note of where Billy Joe sat and sit as far away as possible with his back to a wall.

Mickey's route to and from the gymnasium was uneventful. He hoped it'd stay that way—always. He entered Room 10 and surveyed the near full classroom. English. Lolita sat halfway back in the middle row, an empty desk behind hers. Their eyes made contact. She motioned with her head. Mickey walked over, shrugged his backpack onto the floor and sat down.

"I've been saving it for you."

Mickey cracked a smile on one side. "Thanks."

Judy Ferguson stood at the front of the classroom behind a lectern, two stacks of new textbooks on her desk. She tapped an index finger in the air as she counted the students, mouthing the numbers silently. She gave Mickey a tight smile when she counted him as if to say, "I remember you from yesterday." The bell rang just as she counted the last student. She walked to the door and closed it, then returned to the lectern.

"When I call your name, please come forward and take a textbook from the stack."

She began calling the students' names in alphabetical order. Each textbook had a number written inside the front cover. Miss Ferguson noted the book number for each student during the process. Just as she was about to call Lolita's name someone knocked on the door.

Miss Ferguson looked up from the role book. She smiled and motioned with her hand when she saw the person on the outside through the door's glass pane. The door opened and Billy Joe Speed walked in. He handed her a sheet of paper. While she read it, Billy Joe scanned the classroom. He paused when he came to Mickey and shot him a contemptuous grin. Mickey held the stare, his jaw tight, his face expressionless. Abe's advice from the evening before fresh on his mind. Brad Logan sat in the desk behind Mickey. As the son of Willard Logan, the county probate judge, Brad was well connected to the power brokers of Claxton High School both student and faculty. He kicked one of the back legs of Mickey's desk. Mickey got the message. Brad was Billy Joe's stooge and would be informing him of Mickey's every move. Billy Joe raised his chin to Brad and winked as if to say, "I'm counting on you, Bro." Mickey shut his eyes and lowered his head. It was only a matter of time.

Miss Ferguson wrote some words on the sheet of paper and handed it back to Billy Joe. "Thanks, Billy Joe."

"Yes, ma'am," he said as courteous as an angel and exited the room.

Miss Ferguson resumed calling the students to her desk to get their assigned textbooks. When Robbie Zimmerman returned to his seat she took her position once again at the lectern.

"I want you to put your books away."

Unzipping and zipping accompanied by the moving and dropping of backpacks filled the room. The young teacher continued talking. "We won't be using them today. However, for your homework read chapter one. Be ready to discuss it tomorrow. I make notes of class participation for everyone. If you contribute to class discussion, it'll benefit you at report card time. You are students. Not statues. I am convinced that interaction and communication is a key part of the learning process. The difference in a C plus and a B can be your class participation. So don't shortchange yourselves. Today, we are going to start by getting to know one another. I'd like for each to come forward and tell us your name, your favorite dessert, the place of your dream vacation, and what you think you'd like to do as a career. We'll start with you, Mr. Zimmerman and move up the roll."

By the time Lori Abbott took her place at the front less than five minutes of class time remained. After the freckle-faced, strawberry blonde concluded her remarks about being a professional barrel racer on the national rodeo circuit, Miss Ferguson took up the rest of the time by giving an inspirational speech about the endless possibilities that a good education would secure. She was getting to the climax of her own story about how she worked her way through Ole Miss by waitressing when the bell rang. The metal dinging sound commanded the students to cease listening, grab their backpacks and move on to their next class. They obeyed as if they'd be arrested if they did otherwise.

Gary Martindale was the Baker County Tiger's linebackers' coach. The head coach was the school's only full-timer. Assistants had to teach subjects in addition to their coaching duties. Coach Martindale's classroom, a portable pod commonly referred to by students as "the trailer," was located outside the freshman wing. While regular classrooms had the benefit of the campus' HVAC system, the trailer had "Ole Elmer", a window unit that pulled double duty, cooling the makeshift educational facility during the warm months and heating it during the cold ones. Ole Elmer was a temperamental piece of equipment that was prone to letting Martindale and his students down at the MOST critical times. This meant that freshmen had to be mentally prepared to sweat a day or two in August and September and freeze a day or two in December and January. The school board members talked continually of expanding Claxton High in the near future and doing away with "the trailer" altogether. Therefore, in their minds, replacing Ole Elmer was a waste of money. Better to keep repairing the undependable noisy box.

Mickey and Lolita climbed the steps to Martindale's classroom, Ole Elmer battling the day's ninety-eight-degree temperature, howling like an injured hound dog. They walked in and took their seats along one of the paneled walls. Coach Martindale sat at his desk, a bookcase behind him. Two football helmets sat perfectly positioned on the top shelf close. One was white with an angry-looking black and yellow bee on the side of it. Mickey had no clue what school it represented. The other was bright red with a big black "G" inside a white oval. Mickey recognized it right away. Georgia Bulldogs.

Curiosity ate at Mickey. He just had to ask. He raised his hand. Martindale acknowledged him.

"Coach, did you play with Herschel Walker?" Mickey said.

Gary Martindale sighed and smiled. "I get asked that question all the time. No, I'm not that old. Do I look that old?"

Mickey didn't know how to respond so he said nothing.

"Herschel graduated in 82. I graduated in 93."

Students continued to come in. Coach Martindale looked toward the back of the small room. "Please keep that door closed. Ole Elmer's working as hard as he can."

The class erupted in a short-lived episode of laughter. An older student entered the classroom and made his way to the coach's desk. He leaned in close and whispered. Gary Martindale nodded and looked at his class role. He touched it with an index finger. "Yup. He's supposed to be in here."

The coach looked up at the class. "Mickey Tucker!"

Mickey raised his hand again.

"The principal needs to see you in the office."

Mickey turned to Lolita. She gave Mickey a "What's going on?" look. Mickey shrugged his shoulders and turned his palms upward. "I have no idea," he mouthed. He picked up his backpack and followed the older student out of the room and into the main building.

"Do you know why the principal wants to see me?"

The student looked back at him. "I don't have a clue. I was just told to come to Martindale's trailer and get you."

A girl sat on a stool behind the front counter of the office. She studied a catalogue with numerous pictures of cheerleading outfits. When Mickey approached the counter, she looked up at him. Her expression was feelingless. "You Mickey Tucker?"

"Yeah."

She turned and pointed to a door behind where she sat. "Through that door and all the way back. Mr. Williams is waiting for you."

Mickey's throat felt tight, his saliva warm in his mouth. He walked past the counter and to the door. To one side a woman fed paper into a shredder. As Mickey reached for the door handle, he glanced at her. Her eyes were already fixed on him. She quickly looked down as if Mickey had some deformity on his face. Mickey opened the door and headed down the hallway. The placard on the door had one word on it—*PRINCIPAL*. Mickey tapped on the door. He heard the sound of wheels rolling on the floor, then footsteps. The turn of the doorknob sounded like two pieces of metal scrapping together close to a microphone. Mickey felt his heart rate spike.

The door opened. A tall man with gelled salt and pepper hair stood before Mickey. His chest and arm muscles bulged under the black golf shirt he wore. Mickey didn't recall Colbert Williams looking so athletic during the orientation. Maybe Mickey wasn't paying close enough attention or maybe he was seated too far away to tell. Whatever the case was, there was no mistaking it now. Colbert Williams looked like an older version of Superman minus the cape and letter S on his chest. The top two buttons of the shirt were unfastened, allowing for a clear view of the gold herringbone necklace that lay snug against his tan skin. He smelled of cologne.

"You must be Mickey Tucker."

Mickey swallowed a hard lump. "Ah . . . yessir."

"Come on in, Son. We need to have a conversation."

Mickey walked in. The man shut the door and motioned to the empty chair in front of his large, wooden desk. "Have a seat."

Mickey sat down. The man walked around the side of the desk and sat down in his high-back leather executive chair. He rolled himself forward and put his elbows on top of the desk.

"I think you know why you're here. So, own up to it and things will go a lot easier."

"Mr. Williams, I don't know what you're talking about."

Colbert Williams pressed his lips together and shook his head. He interlocked his fingers and leaned toward Mickey. "Mickey, you just made things harder on yourself and they're only going to get worse the more you lie. So, stop it and just tell the truth. Now, I know you had a situation a couple of years ago where you lied about pulling a knife. I called Mr. Davis at the junior high school and talked to him before I had you brought to my office. He told me all about it. You're older now. And this is high school. You better start shooting straight with me or you're going be in a world of trouble. Do you hear me?"

"But Mr. Williams, I don't know what you're talking about. Honest."

Colbert Williams put a hand to his face. He pressed his temples with his thumb and index finger. He rubbed his eyes and pinched the bridge of his nose. He lowered his hand and looked at Mickey from under his brow.

"Alright. I gave you your chance."

He inhaled and exhaled through his nostrils. "When I dismissed the freshmen from assembly yesterday did you or did you not stop off at the biology lab?"

"Yessir."

"And what exactly did you see that got your attention in the biology lab?"

"Well, I thought the microscopes were cool. So are the pictures on the walls."

Colbert Williams nodded slowly. "Uh huh. Was there anything else?"

"Yessir. I thought the skeleton was really cool too."

"Well, Mickey, that's why we're here. Mrs. Blackman is the biology instructor. Has been for years. Has had that skeleton in her room for years. She paid for it herself and it cost a lot of money. When she got to her classroom this morning, the hand of the skeleton was missing."

"I didn't take it."

"Come on, Mickey. Isn't it true that Billy Joe Speed found you in the biology lab and had to escort you to the cafeteria?"

"Well, it is true that he came in while I was there, but he didn't have to ESCORT me to the cafeteria. I was going to go. The door to the biology lab was open and I just took a minute or two to check it out. That's all. I didn't even touch the skeleton. So how could I have taken its hand?"

Colbert Williams pushed his chair back from his desk and stood to his feet. He bumped his knuckles on the top of the back of the chair and starred Mickey in the eyes, shaking his head all the while. He sighed again then walked around to where Mickey sat. He leaned back against the top of the desk, folded his arms over his chest and crossed his feet at the ankles. "Mickey, listen to me, Son. At the rate you're going you're going to ruin your life. Probably wind up in prison or even worse—dead."

"Honest, Mr. Williams. I didn't take the skeleton's hand. I promise."

Colbert Williams raised an open palm to Mickey. "Stop it, Mickey. Just stop it."

Mickey's eyes welled.

"Unbelievable, Son. Just abso-lutely unbelievable. Open your backpack for me."

Mickey picked it up and unzipped it. Inside were textbooks, a calculator and the skeleton's hand.

Chapter Twelve

The skeleton's hand in his backpack might just as well been a gun to Mickey's head. His blood cooled in his veins.

"Mr. Williams, someone planted this. I—"

Colbert Williams raised both his palms to Mickey, fire in his eyes. "Stop it, Mickey. Just stop it. Hand it to me."

Mickey lifted the hand from the bag and gave it to him. The principal stood to his feet and walked to the door. He grabbed the knob and pulled it open as if he were opening a jail cell. "Go, call one of your parents to come pick you up. Stay in the waiting area till they get here. You're starting off your freshman year with a three-day suspension. In all my years in education, this is first time I've ever had to do this. When your parent gets here, we'll have a sit-down."

Mickey stood as if he were nauseated and tired. He walked past Colbert Williams and into the hallway.

"He needs to use the phone!" Williams said, his tone communicating to everyone in the office to the fact that Mickey Tucker was a bad seed.

Mickey heard the door clang shut behind him as he lumbered to the front desk.

The paper-shredding lady paused from feeding the machine. She pointed to a phone on a secretary desk. "You can use that phone over there."

Mickey walked over to the desk and picked up the phone. He dialed the only helpful number in his life, the noise of the shredder grinding paper in the background.

•   •   •

In less than fifteen minutes, Abe walked through the double glass doors of the school office. Mickey stood up. The two embraced.

"It's okay, Son. I'm gonna help you through this."

As Abe released him, Mickey caught a glimpse of the girl behind the counter rolling her eyes, a smirk on her face as she turned a page in the catalogue.

"Mr. Williams wants to meet with both of us before you take me home."

Abe put a hand on Mickey's shoulders and gave him an affectionate grip. "That's good because I have no intention of leaving until I talk to him."

A heavy-set lady sat at her desk writing on index cards, her glasses down close to the end of her nose. She'd been silent up to this point. She raised her head and looked over the rims. "The principal office is down at the end of the hall. Mickey knows the way."

Abe pulled Mickey close to him and they walked to the sit-down session Colbert Williams made mention of. When they reached his door, Abe knocked. The sound of wheels rolling on the floor again. Abe clapped Mickey's back a few times. Mickey looked up at him. Abe smiled and winked. Mickey's heart slowed down in his chest. His own personal superhero had his back.

Mr. Williams opened the door. He lowered his chin to Abe, but did not smile. "Please come in and have a seat."

The principal took his place in the chair behind his desk. Abe and Mickey sat in the chairs across from him.

"I assume you are Mickey's stepfather."

"Now, why would you make that assumption?"

Abe's question thickened the atmosphere like molasses in a refrigerator. Colbert Williams relaxed his expression and leaned forward, his palms flat on the top of his desk. "Look . . . I, ah . . . what's your name again?"

"Abe Loomis. And there's no need to end the question with the word 'again' because this is just the first time you asked me my name. Not the second."

"I'm sorry. I didn't mean to offend you."

"I'm not offended at all. But it is commendable when a man in authority like yourself is big enough to say, 'I'm sorry.'"

Colbert Williams pressed his lips together, the edges of his mouth extending. He wiped his forehead with a palm then sat back in his chair again. "We're here today because Mickey took one of the hands off the biology lab skeleton."

"No, he didn't. I asked him if he took it and he said he didn't." Abe raised his brow and peered into Williams' eyes. "Did you ask him if he took it?"

Williams tightened his jaw and rocked in his chair a few times.

"I did ask him."

"And what did he say?"

"He SAID he didn't take it."

"Well, then. There you have it. He told me he didn't take it and he told you he didn't take it. So, why would you start out by saying he TOOK one of the hands off the biology lab skeleton?"

"Look, Mr. Loomis—"

"No need to tell me to look. I assure you, Mr. Williams, I can see just fine."

The veins in Colbert Williams' neck rose underneath his skin. He lowered his chin to his chest and closed his eyes. He opened them and looked up at Abe once again. He pulled open a drawer, took out the skeleton hand and placed it on the desk in front of Abe. "It was in his backpack."

Abe looked down at the hand and smiled. He raised his eyes and locked into Williams' once again. "Do you eat the cafeteria food or bring your own?"

"I don't understand."

"Simple question. Do you eat the cafeteria food or bring your own?"

"Most times I eat what our cafeteria staff prepare for our students. But sometimes I bring my lunch."

"Do you bring your lunch in a lunchbox or a bag or small cooler or something?"

"I have a sports cooler I bring it in."

"And on those days when you bring your lunch, who puts it in your sports cooler? You or your wife?"

"Mr. Loomis, we're not talking about a wife packing her husband's lunch. We're talking about a theft of school property. The hand was IN Mickey's backpack. He took it. He LIED about it. And that's it."

"There you go. Saying he's lying again. Why have you come to that conclusion when it's entirely possible, I say certain, that someone else put it in his backpack. Then got word to you after they did it because they have it in for Mickey."

Colbert Williams stood to his feet and leaned over his desk. "I know the kid who told me wouldn't lie."

Abe stood up and leaned in close to William's face. "How do you know that kid wouldn't and Mickey would?"

The vexed principal plunged his fist down on his desk. "Because!"

Abe retaliated. "Because why, Mr. Williams? Because the kid who informed you lives in a nice subdivision? Wears nice clothes? Has parents who are members of the same country club as you and the other Who's Who of this town?"

Colbert Williams shot an index finger toward Mickey. "Just what is your relation to this kid anyway?"

Abe paused and held a dead stare at Colbert Williams. "Consider me his father."

"Then be informed that your son's suspended for three days."

Abe turned to Mickey. "Come on, Son. Let's go."

Mickey stood up and the two of them walked out of Colbert Williams' office. Abe was silent all the way to the truck. When they reached it, Abe unlocked the passenger door for Mickey and opened it. Mickey climbed into the front seat. Abe went around and slid in under the steering wheel.

Mickey looked at Abe. "I bet I know who did it."

"Who?"

"Brad Logan. He's friends with Billy Joe. His dad's a judge. He sat behind me today in English. He never sits close to kids like me. He knew I'd sit behind Lolita."

"That would make sense. Willard Logan's boy, huh?"

"Yup. Billy Joe came in and gave Miss Ferguson a piece of paper to sign. While she was reading it Billy Joe motioned to Brad kinda. Bet it was a signal."

"Get a pen and some paper out of your backpack. Let me know when you're ready to write."

Mickey obeyed. Abe pulled the gear shifter into drive and drove out of the parking lot.

"Okay. I'm ready."

"Name a kid who sat close to you in English class. Someone who may have seen Willard Logan's boy slip the hand into your backpack."

"Charlie Smuthers."

"Write his name down. Do you know where he lives?"

"No."

"Do you know where his parents work?"

"His dad works at the sawmill, I think."

"Okay. Write that down next to Charlie's name. Name someone else."

"Teresa Baldwin. I know where she lives. We ride the same bus."

Abe nodded. "Good. Write her name down and put a check mark by it. Who else?'

By the time they arrived at Mickey's house, there were six names on the list. Two with check marks. Three with nothing next to them. Charlie Smuthers' name had the word "Sawmill" written by it.

Abe reached out a hand. "Give me the list." Mickey tore the page from the notebook and gave it to him.

Abe looked at his watch. "I'll be back to pick you up at four."

"Okay."

Mickey opened the door and got out. He hesitated and looked back at Abe.

"You were great."

Abe drew down his brow, a look of uncertainty on his face. "What are you talking about?"

"Back at Mr. Williams' office. You were great. I never had anybody stand up for me before."

Abe smiled.

"The best part was when you told him to consider you my father."

"I meant it too."

"I know. You've acted like my father since the day you caught me fishing in your pond. Mama says God sent you to me."

Abe's eyes moistened. "I believe God sent you to me, Mick."

Mickey grinned and started closing the door.

"One more thing before I leave."

Mickey pulled the door back and looked up at Abe. "Yeah."

"I love you, Son."

There they were. Three words. They'd been spoken times without number by his mother. But Mickey had concluded he'd never hear them from anyone else. And yet, they'd come from the mouth of a man. A black man at that. Words that had already been vindicated by actions time and time again. A broad grin of a new inspiration stretched on Mickey's face, accented by warm cheeks and grateful eyes.

"I love you too, Mr. Abe."

Abe winked. "I'll see you at four."

"See you then."

Mickey closed the door and watched Abe drive away. The black Blazer was more than just a cool looking truck with big tires and chrome wheels. It was a chariot driven by a knight.

Mickey flung open the door and walked in. The cool air inside the mobile home pricked his cheeks. Pleasant. Refreshing. Approaching footsteps caused the lightweight domicile to creak as they drew closer.

Mickey gazed at the hallway as he lowered his backpack from his shoulder. A lady in her mid-forties dressed in beige scrubs stepped into the den. She had a plastic name badge pinned just below one shoulder. Evelyn.

"What are you doing home so soon? I didn't hear the bus go by."

"It's a long story. Abe brought me home."

"Your mama is having a great day today. She'll be so excited to see you. I just finished changing her oxygen tank. I need to run to the store. It'll give ya'll some time alone."

Evelyn walked to the counter, fisted a bulky ring of keys and shouldered on her purse.

"Will you be back by four?"

"Oh, heavens yes. Shouldn't be gone more than an hour or so. Can I bring you anything back?"

"No ma'am. I'm good."

She opened the door and held it open before exiting. "Alrighty then. Be back in a bit."

Leslie Tucker lit up when she saw Mickey. She adjusted herself in the bed and did the best she could to fluff her matted hair with one hand.

"Hey, Darling. Shouldn't you be at school?"

Mickey sat down in the chair next to her bed. "I got suspended for three days."

Leslie shot her eyes open. "What in the world for?"

"Somebody took a hand off of the skeleton in the biology lab and put it in my backpack. Then they told the principal that I stole it. He called me to the office and told me I was suspended."

"Did you tell him you didn't take it?"

"Yeah. But he didn't believe me. I didn't know the hand was in my backpack till Mr. Williams told me to unzip it. When I did, there it was."

"How'd you get home?"

"I called Abe. He came to the school and met with Mr. Williams in his office. It was EPIC, Mama. You should've seen it. He even told Mr. Williams to consider him to be my father."

Leslie put a hand on one of Mickey's and squeezed. "Abe's special to you, isn't he?"

"He told me he loved me, Mama. And I believe him."

Leslie reached up and caressed the side of Mickey's face. "I do too, Baby. I do too."

Mickey fell against her and the two shared a lengthy embrace. They released one another and Mickey sat back up in his chair. They each wiped the tears from their eyes.

Leslie cleared her throat. "Hand me the phone, Baby. I want to give Abe a call. I'd like to speak to him privately. Okay"

"Sure."

Mickey set the phone on the edge of the bed next to her and left the room.

CHAPTER THIRTEEN

Mickey stood at the edge of the one-lane street and watched for the black Blazer. It rounded the corner where his street met the main road of the trailer park. Mickey stepped to the other side of the tiny road and waited. Abe drove up and stopped the truck in front of him. Mickey climbed in and they drove off. The sheet of paper Mickey had given him looked much different than before. Addresses and phone numbers were by each of the six names he'd written down. Mickey picked up the paper and studied it as Abe navigated through the trailer park to the highway.

"How'd you find all this out?"

Abe checked both ways for traffic. "I made a few phone calls."

"So, what're we going to do? Go visit these kids and their parents?"

"Yup."

"If any of these kids know anything they may be too scared to say it. Folks like Billy Joe and Brad Logan can make things hard for regular kids."

Abe raised an index finger. "That's why we're going to their houses. They'll be with their parents and that'll help them have courage."

Abe turned into the entrance of Broadview Apartments. He drove cautiously through the parking lot of the section 8 complex as kids darted around on bicycles. Small, barefooted, dirty-faced children scurried around laughing and playing. He eased the truck into a parking place and he and Mickey got out. They climbed a corridor of steps to the second floor and walked to apartment twenty-four. Abe knocked on the door.

Someone yelled from inside. "Who is it?"

"Abe Loomis and Mickey Tucker. We'd like to talk to you about a school matter," Abe said.

A brief pause. Then, the sound of scratching metal as the person on the inside freed the door's security chain followed by the slide of the dead bolt. The knob turned and the door opened. Teresa Baldwin stood inside, her mouth open, her eyes rounded.

"Mickey, what're you doing here?"

A mid-thirties lady made the scene from an adjoining bedroom. Mickey recognized the logo on the blue and green fast-food smock she wore. *Super Burger.* A favorite, locally owned fast food.

The woman stepped up next to her daughter, her brow drawn down, her eyes narrowed. "Teresa, do you know these people?"

"I know one of them." Teresa raised a hand toward Mickey. "This is Mickey Tucker. We go to school together."

Abe smiled. "I'm Abe Loomis."

"He's like my dad," Mickey said.

"I'm Pamela. What can we do for you?"

Abe put his hand on Mickey's shoulder. "There's a school matter we'd like to talk to you about."

Pamela relaxed her expression and shrugged. "Well, okay. Come in, I guess, and have a seat. Pardon the mess. I just got home from work."

Abe and Mickey walked in and seated themselves on the sofa. Steam rose from the pot on top of the stove. The aroma of the skillet of cornbread baking in the oven gave the apartment a pleasant smell. Pamela sat down on the recliner and Teresa pulled a wheeled chair from under the small dining table and rolled in into the living room.

Abe began. "Ms. Baldwin—"

"It's Pamela, please."

Abe nodded and smiled. "Today, there was an episode at school. Mickey got a three-day suspension. It seems someone took one of the hands off the skeleton in the biology lab. The principal's convinced that Mickey's the one who did it. Which is not the case."

Pamela grimaced. "So, why does he believe Mickey's responsible?"

"Someone put the hand in Mickey's backpack without Mickey knowing it. Someone got word to the principal that Mickey stole it. He called Mickey to the office. Had him open the backpack and there it was."

Mickey read the look of suspicion on Pamela's face. "I had no idea it was in my backpack till I got to Mr. Williams' office. Honest."

Pamela looked at Mickey, her eyelids narrow, her lips pressed together. "Uh huh. And, who do you think would do that?"

"Someone who's friends with Billy Joe Speed."

"Albert Speed's kid?"

"Yeah. He hates me. Beat me up when he was in eighth grade and I was in sixth. And all because I sold some candy bars cheaper than him. Told the principal I pulled a knife on him. It was a lie. I got suspended back then too, because of him."

Pamela looked at Abe and shrugged her shoulders, her open palms just over her knees. "So why are you here telling us about all this?"

"Since Teresa and Mickey have classes together, we thought she might know how the hand got into Mickey's pack."

Pamela raised her palms to Abe. "Now, wait a minute. I'm sorry that you're having to deal with this. But I really don't want my daughter drug into it. Albert Speed pulls a lot of weight in Claxton. The last thing we need is for Teresa to get crossways with his son."

Abe leaned forward. "I understand your concern for Teresa, and I hope you understand mine for Mickey. Now, Albert Speed may have a lot of money and pull a lot of strings in this town. But at the end of the day, he puts his pants on one leg at a time like everybody else. His kid might wear the nicest clothes and be the pet of most of the teachers, but that doesn't give him the right to lie and bully other kids. And I, for one, am NOT going to sit back and do nothing when it's in my power to do something. If Teresa has seen or heard anything that might help me to help Mickey I sure would appreciate it if she'd tell us."

"Brad Logan did it in English class," Teresa said.

Pamela looked at Teresa. "And just who is Brad Logan?"

"Judge Logan's boy," Abe said.

Pamela shook her head. "Teresa, are you sure you want to get involved in this?"

"Mom, kids like Billy Joe Speed can get away with anything at school. Do anything. And teachers just let them. It's true. Billy Joe has it in for Mickey. Everybody in the school knows it. He's not going to stop either. He'll keep going after Mickey. His friends will help him too."

"What did you see Brad Logan do?" Abe asked.

Pamela raised an index finger to her daughter. "Don't say anything. I don't want you to get in the middle of this."

Teresa stood to her feet. "But Mom, I WANT to help Mickey. Kids like Billy Joe and Brad look down on the rest of us," she said with a hand motion toward Mickey. "They hardly even speak to us. We're nobodies to them. It's like we don't even exist."

"Okay, Teresa. But just know that you're probably going to experience some repercussions if you get involved."

"If there are, then I'll deal with them."

Pamela folded her arms. "Well, if things start getting difficult for you, don't say I didn't warn you."

"Fine." Teresa turned her attention to Abe and Mickey. "Today, Miss Ferguson had each us stand at the front of the class and say what our plans for the future are. When Mickey was walking to the front, I saw Brad slip the skeleton hand in Mickey's backpack."

"Would you be willing to write it down on paper and sign your name to it?" Abe said.

"Yes."

• • •

"There it is. Twenty-six thirty-nine," Mickey said, and raised an index finger toward the leaning mailbox up ahead on the right side of the road.

Abe eased on the brake and turned the Blazer onto the long dirt driveway. Before they reached the shanty home, the front door opened and a man wearing a blue work uniform stepped from inside the house and onto the uneven front porch, pulling the door closed behind him. He kept his eyes fixed on Abe and Mickey as the Blazer rolled up to the house.

William Fleming had a potential net worth of more than a quarter of a million dollars. His house and the three acres it sat on, however, had a market value of a mere twenty-five thousand. He'd bought the place on the front steps of the county courthouse. The auctioneer yelled, "Sold," at the high bid of seventeen thousand five hundred dollars, and William and the missus took possession of the foreclosed property. They moved in and for eighteen winters and summers the extreme weather of the deep south had etched its gruesome autograph on the abode. Several missing shingles in sporadic places gave the roof a patchy balding look. Two Bluetick Coonhounds lay under the low end of the porch. A crooked, loose shutter hung on one of the two front windows All in all, the house looked like a prop building in a western movie. William Fleming's untapped wealth could be seen strewn throughout the yard. Inoperable, classic cars. The man loved them and had a knack for acquiring them. He could locate and pick up barn finds, backyard rollers and abandoned projects with the ease of a squirrel gathering acorns. And he was forever on the lookout to add to his collection. The man had the gift of gab and dealt in cash. The combination of the two had secured graveyard automobiles for a fraction of their true values. He capitalized on people's naivety, apathy and/or need for quick money. Over time, William Fleming had accumulated more than two dozen highly desirable non-running automobiles. A 1971 Road Runner Super Bird. A 1970 GTO Judge. A 1967 Shelby Mustang GT500. And a 1955 Chevrolet Bel Air. Just to name a few. He envisioned restoring the automobiles and selling them for hefty profits. A feasible plan should he ever come up with the funds necessary to do the restorations. And therein lay the problem. The classic car enthusiast drew an hourly wage as an employee of Durant Paving Company. After covering his family's monthly necessities, he had just under four hundred dollars left over. Each month he saved the excess money with every intention of using it to begin the restoration process. His intentions never became reality, however. Without fail, money that could have been used to restore one of the rollers ended up being used to buy another one.

Abe and Mickey got out of the truck.

"How ya doin'?" Abe said and shot Fleming a big smile.

"Alright, I guess. What can I do for you?"

Abe and Mickey came together at the front of the truck. Abe put his hand on Mickey's shoulder.

"My name's Abe Loomis. This here is Mickey. He and your son, Bobby, go to school together. In the same grade as a matter of fact."

The two of them stopped just short of the front steps.

Abe looked up at Fleming, the smile no longer on Abe's face. "Mr. Fleming, we've got a situation and I was wondering if we could talk to you and Bobby about it."

Fleming cocked his head and narrowed one eye. "What kind of problem? Bobby ain't one to cause problems. He's been raised right. Besides, he don't keep secrets from me and his mama. He ain't said nothing about no problem between him and . . . ah."

"Mickey. Mickey Tucker," Mickey said.

Abe smiled again. "Oh, the problem's not between the boys. They get along just fine. The problem's with another boy. I thought maybe Bobby might know something that could help us solve it."

Fleming relaxed his expression and nodded. "I see." He motioned back and forth with a raised index finger, a look of perplexity on his face. "Just how do you two know each other?"

Abe pulled Mickey close to his side and looked down at him. "Mickey and me." He winked one eye and grinned. "Well, we're pretty much the best of friends."

Mickey returned a wink and smiled, his cheeks warm, his heart grateful. He gazed up at William Fleming. "We're pretty much family."

Fleming turned back to the front door. He opened it halfway and leaned his head inside. "Bobby! Come outside, Son!"

"Yessir!" came a young male voice from inside the house.

Fleming left the door open and stepped to the front of the porch. "Abe, you say."

"Yes. Abe Loomis."

"What do you do for a living?"

"Retired Navy man."

Bobby Fleming walked onto the porch, his rounded eyes and half-opened mouth revealing his amazement. "Hey Mickey. What's going on?"

"This is my friend, Abe. We'd like to talk to you about me getting suspended from school today."

The tinge of apprehension washed from William Fleming's face. "Let's go round back to my shop. Got some chairs we can sit in."

He descended the steps, Bobby following. Abe and Mickey followed Fleming and his son to the tin structure behind the house. Fleming flung open one of the large double doors. "Y'all come on in."

Near the front of the shop an engine sat in the middle of a puddle of oil. Two folded lawn chairs leaned against a wall of the shop. William Fleming unfolded one and slid it across the concrete floor to Abe. He raised an index finger toward the classic muscle car inside the shop. "Bobby, there's a couple more behind that—"

"67 Super Sport," Abe cut in before Fleming could say, "Car."

Fleming shot Abe a look. "You a car man?"

Abe squatted down and began studying the engine. "I know a little about them. Did this 396 big block come out of it?"

Fleming unfolded the second chair and sat down. "Yup. It needs a camshaft. Having a tough time finding one. Been to every junkyard between Birmingham and Montgomery. It's like trying to find a gold brick."

"A friend of mine has a shop in New Orleans. I'll give him a call and see if he knows where one might be."

Fleming warmed up to Abe like a puppy to a kid. "That'd be great. I'm glad to pay you for your trouble."

Abe shook his head. "No trouble at all."

The clang of metal against concrete interrupted the men's gearhead conversation as Bobby unfolded the two chairs he'd retrieved from the back of the shop. He sat down in one. Mickey the other.

Abe took his seat. "Someone took one of the hands off the biology lab skeleton and planted it in Mickey's backpack to make it look like Mickey tried to steal it. Whoever framed Mickey tipped off the principal. The principal called Mickey to the office and had him open his backpack. The hand was in it, so the principal suspended Mickey. A student saw another kid slip the hand in Mickey's pack during Miss Ferguson's English class. Since Bobby's in the same class we're wondering if he saw it too. And, if he did, would he be willing to put what he saw down on paper?"

Fleming nodded, his lips pressed together. He inhaled and exhaled through his nostrils, then turned his attention to Bobby. "So, Son, did you?"

Bobby gazed down at the floor and adjusted himself in his chair.

"Son, if you know something you need to speak up. If Mickey's been set up and you can help him, you should."

Bobby shook his head. Paused for a few seconds then stood up. He walked over to the countertop along one wall of the shop, his back to Abe, Mickey and his dad.

"Come on, Bobby. Speak up," his dad said as Bobby handled and moved some of the tools around that lay strewn on the counter.

"Bobby, we'd really appreciate it if you could help Mickey out," Abe said.

Bobby turned to face them and leaned against the countertop. He wiped the sweat from his forehead with the back of one hand.

"Come on, Son. You know me and your mama's always taught you to tell the truth."

"Dad, you don't understand. Me and Mickey are friends and all, but if I write down what I saw it'll cause a whole lotta trouble at school. Kids like me and Mickey ain't the teachers' favorites. I think some of the teachers don't even like us. The kid that put the hand in Mickey's backpack. He's one of the popular kids. Teachers talk to him. Even joke with him. If I write down what I saw and word gets out it'll make things worse than they already are."

"Brad Logan did it. Didn't he?" Mickey said.

"Yup. And you know who he's friends with. Don't you?"

"Billy Joe Speed."

"Exactly. And you need to watch yourself, Mickey. It's all over school that he's got it out for you."

William Fleming stood from his chair and walked over to Bobby. He rested a hand on his son's shoulder and bent down to make eye contact with his son. "Listen, Bobby. You just do what's right and if anything starts happening at school because of it, I'll go see the principal myself . . . and any teacher for that matter. Ain't nobody gonna mistreat my boy and get away with it. Understand?"

Bobby looked up at his dad and nodded, trepidation displayed on his face.

Chapter Fourteen

Mickey felt as welcome as head lice. Not one of the five ladies on the other side of the counter even so much as glanced at him and Abe. Each one busied herself with her job duties, bull crap sloshing around in her head all the while, no doubt. Mickey Tucker is a loser. A liar. A thief. A problem. Your typical white trash destined for a pathetic future. A food stamp and government aid case. Will end up in prison . . . probably. And whatever else Billy Joe Speed and his kind had circulated throughout Claxton High over the past few days. The women didn't know Mickey and certainly didn't know the truth. They'd bought into a pack of lies. Billy Joe Speed came from money. And in Claxton, Alabama, as in any small southern town, money mattered. It swayed and persuaded. Gave credibility even when credibility was not earned.

Near the door that opened into the hall of staff offices a lady sat at a desk. At the speed of popcorn popping, she typed away on a large typewriter, pausing occasionally to proofread her work and slurp a sip from the cup near her typewriter. The telephone on her desk buzzed. She hammered several more strokes then stopped and picked up the receiver.

"Yes, Mr. Williams."

She listened for a few seconds, then replied. "Okay, I'll send them in."

The lady hung up the phone. She looked at Abe and Mickey. "Okay, the principal will see you now." Her words as feelingless as a Nazi's, her facial expression as stoic and prude as a head mother at a nunnery.

Abe stood to his feet, his right hand clutching a leather binder at his side. The swinging wooden doors in the middle of the counter squeaked in their hinges as he pushed them open and walked into the ladies' work area, Mickey following his lead. The efficient typist pointed to the door near her desk, her eyes fixed on Abe. "Through that door. I'm sure you remember which office."

"I do indeed. Thank you," Abe said.

The door to Colbert Williams' office stood open. Claxton High School's chief administrator sat behind his desk. He didn't stand as Mickey and Abe entered. With the confidence of a foreclosing banker Abe sat down in one of the two chairs opposite Williams. Mickey took the other.

The principal glanced at Mickey then looked Abe in the eyes. "So, Mr. Loomis, what can I do for you today?"

His demeanor reminded Mickey of the way the men used to talk to him when they told him he couldn't fish in their ponds and to get off their property or they'd call the law.

Abe crossed his knees and rested the leather binder on his lap. He interlocked his fingers and looked at Colbert Williams like a detective interrogating a suspect. "I know Mickey well. The boy is honest. The notion that he stole school property—in this case a hand from the biology lab skeleton—then lied about it." Abe grimaced and clicked his tongue. "Well, Mr. Williams, it just didn't make sense. So . . . he and I talked to some of his classmates. Two of them stated that, during Miss Ferguson's English class, they saw Brad Logan slip the hand into Mickey's bag when Mickey wasn't looking."

Colbert Williams shot Abe a look of disdain and exhaled through his nostrils. "Mr. Loomis, you're an adult. No doubt the two kids you talked to felt intimidated by you and said what they thought you wanted to hear."

Abe shook his head then clapped back like a courtroom attorney. "Their parents were with them when we talked to them."

Williams leaned forward and put his elbows on top of his desk and interlocked his fingers. "You have the word of two kids." He shrugged his shoulders. "So what?"

Abe opened the leather binder and slid two sheets of paper in front of Williams. "Here are copies of signed statements from those kids. Witnessed by the parents."

Colbert Williams picked them up. Mickey watched the principal's eyes move back and forth as he read the first one, then the second.

He looked up at Abe. "Do you mind if I keep these?"

"Not at all. That's why I made copies. I kept the originals in case my—" Abe paused for a moment and shot Williams a look. "'Well, let's just say in case someone ELSE needs to see them."

Colbert Williams relaxed his expression and nodded. He pulled open a top desk drawer and placed the pages inside. He shut the drawer and adjusted himself in his chair.

"Mr. Loomis, what's a number I can reach you at?"

The principal wrote the numbers on his desk pad as Abe recited them.

"Okay, Mr. Loomis. I'll have a conversation with Brad Logan and be in touch."

"I appreciate your time, Mr. Williams. Mickey and I will be looking forward to your call. Let's go, Mick."

Abe rose from his chair and walked out of Colbert Williams' office, Mickey tailing him. The ladies in the reception area didn't so much as look up when they walked past. When they reached the other side of the counter, Abe turned back to them. "You ladies have a nice rest of the day," he said. He fixed his attention on the typist. "Ma'am, you're pretty fast. How many words you type a minute?"

The lady paused, repositioned her eyeglasses and looked up at him. "Seventy-three," she said with a *what do you think about that* tone.

Abe blew a whistle. "Impressive. I type eighty-seven myself. I'd be glad to help you get your word count up if you're interested. Just let me know."

• • •

The next morning Mickey got on the school bus. He didn't know the details of Mr. William's conversation with Brad Logan. All he knew was that before he and his mama had dinner the night before Abe called and told him that he could go back to school. Said he'd talked to Mr. Williams and everything was fine. The suspension had been dropped and removed from Mickey's record. Once again, Abe had come through for Mickey. Took care of a situation. Mickey gazed out the window, the scenery sliding by like it was on a conveyor belt.

Brad Logan was different all the sudden. He no longer sat in the desk behind Mickey's in Miss Ferguson's class. He sat at the front of her class. And not in hers only, but in every other class he and Mickey had together. Brad seemed purposefully to avoid all contact with Mickey. When they passed each other in the hall, Brad looked away and never spoke. Mickey noticed that he no longer hung around with Billy Joe Speed either. It was as if a big switch had been flipped. Brad Logan went from being well-connected to the popular kids to being a loaner. What happened? Mickey wondered.

Football at Claxton High School was borderline cultic. Head coach Jimbo Saterwhite laid down his demands with the fervor of any David Koresh or Jim Jones. From August to January any member on Saterwhite's squad was expected to have a single, unrivaled priority—football. He referred to his players as "his boys." And "his boys" had to adhere to a rigid schedule of football discipline during the regular season. An hour each weekday in the weight room took the place of gym class. While other students were doing everything from volleyball to basketball, Saterwhite's boys pumped iron. When the school day ended, they were to be in pads and on the field. Inclement weather simply moved practice to the gymnasium. Saturdays and Sundays meant more practice. Off the record, of course. "If you wanna draw blood come Friday night, you gotta sweat blood the rest of the week," he preached. Saterwhite's philosophy paid off. "His boys" finished the season with eleven wins and one loss. While the team had several quality athletes, it had only ONE marquee player. Junior middle linebacker Billy Joe Speed. The local newspapers treated him like local royalty, giving him more ink than any other baller in the county. Talent scouts throughout the Southeastern Conference, including in-state powerhouses Alabama and Auburn had visited the Speed household. Each hoped to secure a letter of intent from the alpha-dog tackle monster. With each passing week new information surfaced concerning Billy Joe's promising potential as a Division 1 college football player. Billy Joe, for his part, made sure the student body stayed well-informed concerning his college recruitment. More days than not, his dress attire consisted of the caps and jerseys he'd received as gifts from the various universities courting him for his football skills.

The close of football season gave Billy Joe a break from Coach Saterwhite's gridiron expectations. The jock's relaxed schedule proved to be bad news for Mickey. Billy Joe strolled down the freshman hallway like a predator on the prowl. He seized every opportunity, whether in passing or by intentional confrontation, to insult and mock Mickey. Talk of Billy Joe's animosity toward the boy he contemptuously referred to as "Trailer Trash" resonated throughout Claxton High School like the Clinton and Lewinski sex scandal in the news media.

As if on a mission, Mickey snaked his way through the lunchroom crowd. When he reached his destination, he plopped his tray on the table and sat down next to Lolita. "Last day of school and they give us Alpo," he said. All the students on the campus sarcastically referred to the beef tips and rice served in the school cafeteria as the famous brand of canned dog food. "You'd think they'd give us burgers and fries or at least pizza. But no, they give us Alpo and green beans," Mickey said with his upper lip raised on one side accenting his discontent.

Lolita looked up at him. "It ain't half bad." She bit off a piece of her dinner roll. "Pretty good, actually."

Mickey pulled open the top of the cardboard carton and took a drink of his chocolate milk. "I guess it'll fill the hole. Hey, let's go to the movies tonight. The Matrix is showing. Everyone's talking about what a great movie it is."

"I don't know Mickey. This is rent week. I can't ask my mom for movie money."

"My treat. Abe paid me fifty bucks for putting new brake pads on his truck the other day."

"You sure?"

"Absolutely!"

"Okay. I'll ask Mom if I can go."

"Great! I'll get Abe to drive us. Pick you up at 5:30. We'll grab a pizza at the Pizza Hut then walk over to the theater. Movie starts at seven."

Lolita looked at him, her dark eyes filled with gratitude. She shoulder-bumped him and smiled. "Thanks, Mickey."

"Well, well, well. If it ain't "Trailer Trash" and his skank?"

Lolita turned her gaze to her food tray, the pleasant expression washed from her face. Mickey tightened his jaw and shook his head.

Billy Joe sat down at the table across from Mickey, his eyes filled with venom. "I don't know what you plan on doing this summer. But if you come into town on the weekends, I'd be careful if I were you." He leaned in closer. "Something could happen when you least expect it." He grinned with one side of his mouth.

Mickey fixed his eyes on Billy Joe's. "I got a question for you, Billy Joe."

"And, just what might that be?"

"How does it feel being a football?"

"What do you mean?"

"You know, to be the focus of the game. To have a big name on the outside and yet be hollow and filled with nothing but air on the inside?"

Billy Joe narrowed his eyelids. "I don't forget it when someone tries to make me look bad. Here at school, I refrain myself. Can't afford to let a maggot like you mess up my future. So, I just annoy and harass you around here cause I gotta keep my school record clean. But I'll catch you out somewhere. When I do, you'll remember it the rest of your life." He leered at Lolita. "Skank."

Billy Joe stood up, keeping his eyes locked on Mickey's. He grinned like a demon. "Besides, I know where you live."

Mickey shrugged his shoulders and raised his brow. "So what? I know where you live too. Everybody does."

Billy Joe huffed and walked away.

Lolita placed her fork in its slot on the tray and turned to Mickey, a look of disgust on her face. "You know he's gonna be crusin' around town tonight with his jerk friends. Let's just rent a video and stay home. If he sees us—"

"No, Lolita. We're not gonna stay home just because of him. He's not stupid. He's not gonna make a scene in public. He's too concerned about his image. We'll eat dinner. Go to the movie. Everything'll be fine."

"You sure?"

Mickey rested his hand on Lolita's knee. "I'm sure. Besides, Abe'll be waiting for us when the movie's over."

CHAPTER FIFTEEN

Claxton, Alabama's liveliest time of the week was Friday and Saturday nights. Though most businesses were closed during the evening hours, the town teamed with life. While adults nestled on their recliners and couches in front of their televisions at home, most of the town's teenagers engaged in their favorite pastime. Cruising "The Strip". "The Strip," as they referred to it, was the three miles of Highway 31 that ran from the Starlight Shopping Center on the north end of town to just past the Dixie Shopping Center on the south end. On weekend nights, headlights and taillights almost bumper to bumper illuminated the small-town as vehicles of various makes and models packed with the younger generation cruised up and down the popular route. One vital landmark was the Pizza Hut. The corporate chain restaurant's parking lot was the young people's preferred turnaround point at the south end of The Strip. Like a long train slowly easing its way down a railroad track, a continual caravan of cars rolled in the pizza joint's one-way entrance, circled behind the building, exited on the other side, and headed back north on the state highway.

Mickey and Lolita sat on opposite sides of a table in a booth next to a window. A large, thin crusted pizza with two missing slices between them. They'd occasionally pause their conversation and gaze through the glass at the cars that passed by. Sometimes they recognized the kids in each car. Having both just completed their freshman year, however, there were still several of their fellow high school students yet unknown to them.

Lolita shoved the last portion of a slice into her mouth and reached for another large triangle. "Abe sure is a great friend to you. Isn't he?"

"He's like my dad. I've learned more from him than I've learned in school. He teaches me how to do stuff all the time. Like right now, he's teaching me how to rebuild an engine."

Lolita's eyes shot open. She shook her head. "That is so cool! What does he do for a living?"

"I'm not sure. I know he used to be in the Navy. Must draw some kind of retirement or something." Mickey took a long drink of his soda and sat his glass back down on the table. "You should see him shoot, Lolita. I bet he can kill a deer from a mile away. He can do just about anything. And he's smart too. He's got more books in his house than anyone I've ever known."

"Does your mom like him?"

Mickey sat back hard against the back of the booth and displayed a stank face. "Oh yeah. He's like family to her too. They talk all the time." He raised his hands, his fingers spread apart emphasizing his point. "He's always bringing her over some of his books. She reads'em ALL the time."

Mickey loosened his expression and leaned forward a bit. He picked up a fresh slice and chomped on it.

"Can I get you some refills?" came a polite female voice.

Mickey and Lolita looked up at the waitress. "Sure," they said.

The waitress picked up their glasses and walked away.

Lolita turned her attention back to Mickey. "I wish I had someone like Abe in my life. It's rough being a girl and not having someone like a dad."

Mickey nodded then drew down his brow. "We've never discussed it, but what ever happened to your dad?

Lolita pressed her lips, a look of disappointment on her face. She turned to gaze out the window. As if hit by electricity, her mouth dropped opened, her eyes rounded. She shot a hand over the top of the table and grabbed one of Mickey's. "Oh, Mickey!"

"What?"

Mickey looked through the glass. A gleaming red, convertible Camaro idled outside the window. A boy and a girl sat in the backseat. Another couple sat in the front. The four of them leered at Mickey and Lolita. The driver pointed an index finger at Mickey, then made a fist, his thumb extended. He drew his thumb across the front of his neck. Billy Joe Speed. He maintained a demon-like stare at Mickey as he eased the car forward, keeping pace with the cars cruising in front of his.

Lolita cupped her free hand over her mouth and squeezed Mickey's with her other. The Camaro made the turn to circle behind the building. She lowered the hand from her mouth and looked at Mickey. "I told you we should have just stayed home. Call Abe and tell him to come get us."

Mickey tightened his jaw and shook his head. "No, Lolita. We're not gonna let him ruin our evening. The theater is just across the parking lot. I can pay the check and we can walk over there. He'll be cruising the rest of the night with his friends. We probably won't even see him again tonight."

• • •

The Claxton Twin Cinema featured two movies. *The Matrix* starring Keanu Reeves and *8MM* starring Nicolas Cage. Claxton buzzed with talk of *The Matrix*. *8MM* was little more than an afterthought. Reeves' stardom was rising at lightning speed. Most every girl in Claxton had bedroom walls adorned with posters of him. The ticket line for his latest blockbuster extended out of the theater and down the sidewalk. The dozen or so people in line to buy tickets for *8MM* had already seen *The Matrix*. For the past two weeks, everyone at school had been posing the same question: The red pill or the blue pill? So, for Mickey, it wasn't even a question. He and Lolita were going to see *The Matrix*.

The show was general admission. Mickey and Lolita chose the two seats closest to one aisle on the second row from the back. Taking Abe's counsel and planning ahead, Mickey purchased the tickets before he and Abe picked up Lolita. While other movie goers stood in line to get whatever seats fate dealt them, he and Lolita availed themselves to the seats of their own choosing. Thanks again, Abe.

"Want something to munch on and something to drink?" Mickey asked.

She put one hand on her stomach. "I'm stuffed. I had three pieces of pizza."

"I had four, but movies are better when snacks are involved."

Lolita returned a grateful smile. "Okay. I'll have some Milk Duds, I guess."

Mickey clicked his tongue. "Milk Duds it is. And, what to drink?"

"Can we just share a drink?" Lolita said. "You know? In order not to spend so much. The pizza was almost twenty bucks."

Share a drink? Mickey liked the way that came out. Maybe it meant something. Like he and Lolita were becoming more than friends? Did she consider herself to be Mickey's girl? Did she consider Mickey to be her man? Lolita was good looking. No doubt. Smooth skin. Dark eyes. Dark hair. Nice teeth. Not too skinny. But there was more than just her appearance. She was nice. Honest. Kind. Easy to talk to. Could be trusted. These things made her even better looking in Mickey's opinion. "When it comes to choosing a woman, choose one who has a heart that's prettier than her face," Abe had told Mickey on more than one occasion. He told him once while they were fishing. Another time when they were building a chicken coop. One time while they were changing the oil in Abe's Blazer. And several times when they were driving. In fact, Abe gave some of his most important advice when they were traveling.

Mickey smiled, a good feeling tickling his heart. "Sure, we can share a drink. I'll get an extra-large one."

In a few minutes Mickey returned with a box of Milk Duds, a medium bucket of popcorn, an extra-large soda, and just one straw. This was going to be a Friday night for the record books. Lolita looked up at him. Her facial expression made Mickey feel appreciated. Masculine. Confident. Mickey handed her the Milk Duds.

"Thanks," she said.

Mickey took his seat next to her. She took a long drink of the soda then passed him the bulky cup. He put his mouth on the straw. Her mouth had just been there. It was the best soda he'd ever tasted. He sang Van Morrison's iconic words in his mind. *You, my brown-eyed girl.* The lights inside the theater began to fade. Tonight, Keanu Reeves had nothing on Mickey Tucker.

Just as Morpheus was offering Neo the choice between the blue pill and the red pill, a theater employee shined a small flashlight toward Mickey and Lolita.

"Are you Lolita DeRosa?"

"Yeah," she said, her expression a mixture of irritation and confusion.

"Your mother just called. She asked that you call her back immediately."

"Okay."

Mickey rose from his seat and stood in the aisle. Lolita handed him what was left of the Milk Duds. "I'll be right back."

"I'll go with you."

"No. You continue watching the movie. This won't take but a minute or two. I'm sure she just wants to check on me."

Lolita followed the employee out of the auditorium and Mickey sat back down in his seat. Neo took the red pill, but Mickey didn't know what it meant. At the moment, he didn't really care. Why did Lolita's mom call? Mickey fidgeted in his seat. He checked his watch. Looked back at the door. Tossed a kernel of popcorn in his mouth. Took a drink of the soda. Fidgeted in his seat some more. Neo was reaching out to touch the liquid mirror and Lolita had still not returned. Mickey placed the soda in his chair's cup holder, put the box of Milk Duds in the bag of popcorn and set the bag on the floor. He got up. Walked to the door, flung it open and rushed to the concession area.

"Where's the payphone?" he said to the workers behind the food counter.

A female employee raised an index finger. "Outside between Hibbet's Sporting Goods and the hair salon."

"Thanks."

Mickey bolted out the door. He looked in the direction the lady had pointed to. The payphone was there just as she'd said. Lolita, however, was not. Mickey scanned the parking lot. She was nowhere to be seen. A blue Ford F-150 crew cab rolled up to the curb where Mickey stood. Dirk Ballard, the team's field goal kicker leaned out the passenger window.

"Tucker, you looking for Lolita?"

"Yeah."

"She caught a ride with some chicks. Said it was an emergency. Told me to tell you. "She was pretty upset." He motioned with his head. "Jump in the back seat and we'll run you to her house."

Mickey had never had a conversation with Dirk Ballard before. He was surprised the popular jock even knew who he was. Mickey climbed in and the driver, whoever he was, made the truck tires bark as they headed out of the Starlight Shopping Center parking lot.

"We'll take the side roads to Higgins Ferry. It'll be a lot faster than taking The Strip. The unfamiliar driver handled the truck like an ambulance driver racing to a wreck. Several dramatic turns, a few roll throughs at stop signs and they were southbound on Higgins Ferry. Instead of turning right on Kincheon Road toward the trailer park where Mickey and Lolita lived, the driver of the truck turned on Second Avenue and then made a left on Highway 31. Road was clear. The boy at the wheel kicked the F-150 up to seventy.

"This ain't the way to Lolita's house. Where're we going?"

Dirk Ballard looked back at Mickey. "First, we gotta pick up Mike's sister at the high school. She has to be home by eight. It won't take but a minute."

So, Mike was driving the truck. Mike who?

The high school was like a ghost town. Not a light on. Not a parked car anywhere. One thing was apparent to Mickey. Neither Mike's sister, nor anyone else for that matter, was on the school's property. The driver sped past it.

"Where are you taking me?"

Dirk Ballard turned on the dome light inside the truck. He looked back at Mickey again, all signs of courtesy now gone from his face.

"Tonight's a night you'll never forget, Trailer Trash. You just sit tight and get ready for a real life-changing experience." He turned to Mike. "Ain't that right, Mike."

Mike smirked. "Welcome to the jungle, baby."

Mike stopped the truck behind the club house of the Claxton Golf Course. Dirk Ballard got out and opened Mickey's door. "Alright, Trailer Trash. Let's go. The party's waiting."

Mickey stepped out into the darkness. Mike sounded the vehicle's horn. Like spotlights, five pairs of headlights from the edge of the paved lot pointed toward Mickey. Motors cranked and the headlights grew closer. They stopped about ten yards from Mickey. Doors opened and five members of the football team emerged from the vehicles, each player accompanied by a cheerleader. Billy Joe Speed stepped forward. He strolled over to Mickey and looked him up and down.

"Well, Trailer Trash, tonight is a good night."

Billy Joe looked back at his posse. "Good for me that is." They laughed and made snide comments. Billy Joe refocused his attention on Mickey. He tapped Mickey on the cheek a few times with an opened palm. "Not so good for you."

Mickey jerked his face away. Billy Joe began pacing back and forth in front of Mickey. "You see, this is our town. We do what we want. When we want." With his back to Mickey, he stopped and gazed up at the evening sky. "When someone useless and insignificant." He raised a hand in Mickey's direction. "Like you, Trailer Trash." The specimen of a dominate high school football player turned on his heels and sashayed over to Mickey. "When someone like you doesn't respect us, well, then they have to pay." Billy Joe shook his head. "Not with money." He shot Mickey a condescending look. "I know you like money. After all, you've been known to sell candy for it. Remember?"

Mickey kept silent, his eyes fixed on Billy Joe's, his upper lip curled up on one side.

Billy Joe backhanded Mickey across the face. "Don't you look at me like that."

Mickey, in slow, calculated fashion, turned his face back toward Billy Joe.

"You basically stole money from me three years ago. And now, I'm gonna teach you a lesson you'll never forget."

Billy Joe lowered his face close to Mickey's. "We're gonna settle it right here and now," he said through gritted teeth. "I'm gonna beat every dime out of you . . . with interest. You hear me, Trailer Trash?"

Mickey lowered his head. "I don't want to fight you, Billy Joe."

"It doesn't matter. We're going to fight anyway."

Mickey raised his head again. "So, is that going to make you look tough in the eyes of all these friends of yours?" He panned the faces of those who stood by. "What will all of you go back and tell everyone? That Billy Joe beat up a kid nearly three years younger than him. A kid who didn't want to fight him in the first place. Is that the story you plan to tell?" Mickey walked over to them. "Well, that'll make the team's star player look like a real winner, won't it? Just the kind of player Alabama or Auburn or Georgia is looking for. Right?"

The onlookers said nothing. They simply looked at Mickey, their faces displaying their second thoughts about the situation.

Mickey looked back at Billy Joe. "Well, there you have it, Billy Joe. They're not so sure about this little party of yours after all."

Billy Joe sighed. "We're going to fight. And you're going start it."

Mickey shot Billy Joe a look of disgust. "You're outta your mind. I'm going home." He looked at Dirk Ballard. "And don't worry. I can walk."

Billy Joe snapped his fingers. "Bring out his motivation," he said.

A boy stepped out from behind the headlights. He held Lolita by the back of her neck, her teeth clinched against the make-shift gag tied around her head, her cheeks moist. Billy Joe raised one hand toward her. "There she is, Trailer Trash. Just another welfare, food stamp, government-aid-dependent cockroach like you. She'll probably be pregnant before she's a junior. And who knows by whom or how many? Most likely by any dude that'll pay her."

Billy Joe stepped over to Lolita and peered into her face. "I bet you've already been making some spending money." He stoked her hair with one hand. She pulled away from him. "How much would you charge me?" He cocked his head to one side. "Ten bucks?" Lolita narrowed her eyelids. "Five? You would for five. Wouldn't you?"

Lolita kicked him on the shin. Billy Joe slapped her hard across the face.

Mickey rushed over. He put one hand on Billy Joe's shoulder and spun him around. He punched him in the face with the other. Billy Joe fell back against the hood of one of the cars. A drop of blood trickled from his nose. He wiped it away with the back of one hand, then looked at it. He grinned. "I told you that you'd start it. Now, it's a matter of self-defense."

The thick chested athlete stood to his feet. "I'm going to put you in the hospital."

He approached Mickey with his fists raised. Mickey began to bounce on the balls of his feet, his left fist raised, his right clutched tight at his hip. Billy Joe threw a right haymaker. Mickey blocked it with his left forearm and exploded a right punch into Billy Joe's solar plexus. The muscular boy fell back hard on his backside against the asphalt. Mickey continued to bounce and shift. Billy Joe's friends looked on in amazement.

"You come at me again and I'm going to hurt you bad, Billy Joe," Mickey said. "You better stay down. Apologize to Lolita and we'll go home. It'll be over."

The bully looked at his friends. Their surprised facial expressions enraged him. He jumped to his feet, let out a violent yell and charged Mickey. In a flash, Mickey stepped forward with his back leg, raised his front leg, his knee bent at his waistline. With his right foot bladed to one side, he stomped down violently on Billy Joe's right leg just above the bulky boy's knee cap. Billy Joe's knee snapped like a dry tree limb. Claxton High School's star linebacker collapsed on the pavement, his leg bent backwards grotesquely at the knee. He wailed in pain, unable to rise. Three of the cheerleaders began to scream and cry. The other two buried their faces in their boyfriends' chests, horrified by the brutal episode they'd just witnessed. Billy Joe's once aggressive and scornful teammates looked on distraught and sheepish. Mickey backed away and turned to Dirk Ballard. "Get an ambulance. He's going to need it."

Like robbers fleeing a crime scene, Dirk Ballard and Mike piled into the F-150 and sped away into the night. Lolita rushed over to Mickey. The two embraced.

"How on earth did you learn to fight like that?" she asked.

Mickey held her close and spoke softly into her ear. "Abe taught me."

CHAPTER SIXTEEN

By Monday morning talk of Billy Joe Speed's misfortune was churning around town like a pot of soup boiling on a hot stove. By the following Friday, news had reached every university that had offered him a football scholarship. Billy Joe lay in a bed at Baker County Hospital, his right leg in balanced traction with corrective hardware and stitches in his knee. Albert Speed signed two five-figure checks to cover special services rendered and travel expenses. One was issued to the leading orthopedic specialist of the Mayo Clinic, the other to the same caliber physician of Johns Hopkins. Both world-renowned doctors were in full agreement. Billy Joe Speed's football career was over. He'd walk with a limp the rest of his life.

. . .

Mickey followed the familiar man into the private room. Bookshelves lined three walls from floor to ceiling. Several of the shelves had gaps between the rows of books. Framed photos of the man accompanied by other black people occupied most of the gaps. Odd trinkets from Africa and other keepsakes took up the others. Most of the shelf spacing, however, was filled with books. A large, multi-colored rug covered most of the hardwood floor. A mahogany desk, far nicer than the one in Principal Williams' office, sat in the middle of the room. The wall behind it had no bookshelves. Instead, framed photos of the man and members of his family along with two stately diplomas adorned it. The largest words on one diploma read Wiley College. Dallas Theological Seminary was sprawled across the other.

The man raised a hand toward the armchairs that faced the desk. "Have a seat."

Mickey sat down.

"How are you doing, Son?"

Mickey shook his head. "Not too good, Reverend Washington. Can't get the scene out of my head. Can't sleep. Don't eat much. And, worst of all, I feel really guilty about the whole thing."

The pastor pressed his lips and peered at Mickey through narrowed eyelids. "And—why do you feel guilty?"

Mickey lowered his head. His torso began to quake. He wiped moisture from his eyes with a thumb and index finger. "Billy Joe, he'll—" Mickey's voice cracked, his throat feeling like it had a dagger stuck in it. He swallowed a hard lump.

"Take your time," Reverend Washington said. "We're not rushed for time."

Mickey adjusted himself in his seat and wrestled the reigns of his emotions. He sucked in a belly full of oxygen, then exhaled, his jaws rounded, his lips puckered. "He'll never walk normal again all because of me."

"You're wrong about that."

The holy man's frankness grabbed Mickey like an invisible hand. He shot his eyes open. "But I destroyed his knee."

"Uh huh. And just why did you do that?"

"Because he came charging at me."

"To do what?"

"He was going to drive me into the pavement and beat me up."

"And what did he do before that?"

"He tried to punch me in the face."

"And what did he do before that?"

"He said some bad stuff to Lolita and backhanded her across the face."

"Just when and where were you and Lolita when this happened?"

"It was last Friday night. We were at the golf course. About eight o'clock I'd say."

Reverend Washington leaned forward in his chair and folded his arms on the top of his desk. "Eight o'clock on a Friday night is an odd time to be being playing golf. Wouldn't you say?"

Mickey raised his opened palms over his lap. "We weren't playing golf. We didn't want to be there in the first place. Billy Joe and some of his friends tricked us and took us there. He said he wanted to fight me. I told him I didn't want to. They had Lolita gagged. Billy Joe started saying some really bad things to her, then he smacked her across her face." Mickey made a backhand motion in the air. "When he did that, I was ready to fight him . . . I wanted to fight him."

"Sounds like Billy Joe is an evil young man."

"You have no idea."

The pastor sighed. "Yes, I do. You just told me about him. He brought everything on himself. You did what you had to do. You did nothing wrong. As a matter of fact, you had a situation similar to the ones some of the disciples had to deal with after Jesus went back to heaven, no doubt."

The words hit Mickey like a hammer. Mickey pushed back against his chair, a look on his face like he'd just eaten something that tasted odd. "Really?"

"Really. And I can prove it to you."

Reverend Washington reached for the Bible on the side of his desk and slid it close to Mickey. "Open it to Luke chapter twenty-two. Verse thirty-six. Read it out loud."

Mickey took the Bible and opened it to the passage. He cleared his throat and began.

"And said he unto them. But now, he that hath a purse, let him take it, and likewise his scrip: and he that hath no sword, let him sell his garment, and buy one."

Mickey looked back up at the pastor.

"What would a man use a sword for?" Reverend Washington said.

Mickey narrowed his eyelids and moved his eyes back and forth a few times. "To defend himself?"

"Well, he sure wouldn't use it to catch fish or change a wagon wheel or slice a loaf of bread, now, would he?"

"No sir."

"And, Mickey, let's say he struck a man on the leg with it. You think it would affect that man for the rest of his life?"

Mickey nodded and returned a slight grin. "Most definitely."

"You're exactly right," the preacher said. "Now, let's talk about Lolita. Do you think Billy Joe would have hurt her?"

"Yessir. He had already. Said he would do even more."

"Think about that for a minute. A big strapping football player physically assaulting a young girl. That's not right. Is it?"

"No sir."

"She needed someone to rescue and protect her. Did she not?"

"Yes sir."

"Now turn to Genesis chapter fourteen. Start reading at verse fourteen and read down through verse sixteen."

Mickey flipped through the pages of the Bible and found the passage.

"And when Abram heard that his brother was taken captive, he armed his trained servants, born in his own house, three hundred and eighteen, and pursued them unto Dan. And he divided himself against them, he and his servants, by night, and smote them, and pursued them unto Hobah, which is on the left side of Damascus. And he brought back all the goods, and also brought again his brother, Lot, and his goods, and the women also, and the people."

Mickey looked up at the pastor. "What does smote mean?"

"It means he killed them." The reverend raised an index finger. "And remember, the Bible tells us that Abraham was the friend of God."

"Mm. That's amazing."

"It is. And that's not all. Now, turn to Psalms one hundred forty-four and read the very first verse."

Smiling and now re-invigorated by what he'd just read, Mickey turned enthusiastically to the book of Psalms. Found chapter one forty-four and read aloud again.

"Blessed be the LORD of my strength, which teacheth my hands to war, and my fingers to fight."

"Who wrote that Psalm?" the preacher said.

"David."

"Yup. David. The man after God's own heart. Said he was taught to fight by the LORD Himself. Isn't that what you just read?"

"Yessir."

"Now, let's talk about you. Abe taught you to fight. And the time came when you used those skills. Not because you wanted to, but because you had to. To defend yourself and protect someone important to you. Correct?"

"Correct."

"So, there's no need to feel guilty because you did nothing wrong. You did something that was necessary and good. Now, how do you feel?"

"I feel better. Like a big rock was taken off my back."

"Anything else you need to talk about?"

"No sir. I'm good."

Reverend Washington smiled, his eyes warm and caring. "Mind if I pray for you before you go?"

Mickey gave an affirming nod. "I'd like that."

The faithful pastor shut his eyes and bowed his head. Mickey did likewise. The minister spoke simple, fervent words. Mickey smiled as he listened. If Mickey hadn't known otherwise, he would have sworn Reverend Washington was sitting in a rocking chair next to the Creator on the front porch of heaven.

CHAPTER SEVENTEEN

The crowd consisted of just over seventy people. One white boy. Two white women. One white man. And a tan girl whose features were both Anglo and Hispanic. The rest were black. The girl sat beside the boy. The July mid-day sun waged a war of Fahrenheit on them all. They'd convened because of a metal, oblong chest. The chest measured twenty-four inches wide. Seventy inches long. A multi-colored floral spray covered it. The most dapper of the crowd stood at one end of the chest. He pulled a small, leather New Testament from the inside pocket of his black dress coat. He opened it and read from the First Epistle to the Thessalonians, then made remarks about a future resurrection and a certain hope regarding eternity. When he concluded, five of the onlookers stepped close to the chest and, with perfect pitch, sang *When The Roll is Called Up Yonder*. Acapella. The suited gentleman then announced the location for a meal that had been prepared and invited all to partake. He asked the gathering to bow for prayer. They did so and he thanked God for the brief life of Leslie Tucker.

Abe put an arm around Mickey and hugged him firmly. With watery eyes Mickey gazed at the casket. "It's just me now. I'm all alone."

"No. You're not all alone, Mick. I'm here," Abe said.

Mickey leaned his head against Abe's shoulder. "I don't know what I'd do without you."

Abe clapped his palm against the top of Mickey's arm. "Same goes for me."

One by one, each member of the Mount Pisgah Missionary Baptist Church offered Mickey their condolences. As did Big Ed and Erma. When the crowd thinned, Mickey stood to his feet, Lolita's hand in his. She gave him a caring embrace, as did her mother. Reverend Washington stepped up to Mickey and handed him a bulging clasp envelope. "Folks at the church want you to have this. You do as you please with it. You hear?"

Mickey wiped his eyes and sniffled. "Yessir."

"I'll see you all at the church," he said.

Mickey nodded as did Lolita and her mother.

Abe shook the pastor's hand. "Mickey and I have a matter to discuss and, then we'll be on our way."

"Take all the time you need," Reverend Washington said.

"We'll be waiting for you at the church," Lolita said, her mother affirming her daughter's statement.

The three of them began making their way to their vehicles. Abe returned his arm to Mickey's shoulders and the two of them stepped close to Leslie Tucker's casket. Abe placed his free hand on it. "Your mother and I had many private conversations as you know."

Mickey nodded and pinched the tears from his eyes again.

"We talked about several different things. But the thing we discussed most was this day, Mick. She knew she was dying and made some preparations."

Mickey's shoulders began to quake as he wept.

"She—," Abe's voice cracked. He gathered his emotions and continued. "She asked me if I'd take care of you . . . adopt you . . . you know, be like your father. I told her it would be a great honor to call you my son if it was agreeable to you."

Abe shook Mickey lovingly. "Most everything has been done. Papers have been drawn up. So, Mick. What do you say? Would you like for me to adopt you?"

Mickey turned and embraced Abe as if they'd just reunited after a long period of separation. "Oh yes, Abe. I'd love for you to. I feel like we've been family from the first day we met."

"I love you too, Mick. I'll call Dan tomorrow and start making plans to finalize everything."

Mickey wiped the wetness from his eyes and cheeks with one sleeve. He pushed back from Abe and looked up into his hero's compassionate eyes. Abe smiled and pulled him in tight again. After a few moments, they released each other. Mickey reached down and pulled a rose bud from the spray and gazed at the coffin. "Mama, I will ALWAYS love you. No boy ever had a better mama. Thank you for taking care of me. And thank you for wanting Abe to adopt me. He and I are as close as any father and son has ever been. So don't you worry. I'll be just fine. Until I see you again, I'll make you proud. I promise."

They turned and walked away from the casket. Arm in arm. They passed a man kneeling at a nearby grave as they made their way to the Blazer. Mickey felt as if his heart was the rope in a tug-of-war. Grief pulled him in one direction as he pondered the fact that he'd never hear his mother's voice again, never feel her affectionate palm against his face, never see her smile or her loving eyes. Joy pulled him in the opposite direction. Abe, his champion and mentor, would soon be his father. He'd be able to say things he'd never been able to say before. Things like "I'll have to ask my dad," and "My dad's picking me up." When other kids asked him about his nice clothes or his cool pair of shoes he could say, "My dad bought them for me." The book of Mickey's life now had a sad chapter, but it also had a happy chapter. In time, surely the happy one would numb the pain of the sad one. He opened the door of the Blazer and climbed in.

"Excuse me," came a voice.

The man who'd been kneeling at the grave just moments earlier, stood next to the passenger door, his attention fixed on Mickey.

"Yes. What can we do for you?" said Abe.

"Are you Mickey Tucker?"

"Yessir."

The man handed Mickey a light blue legal-sized envelope. "This is for you."

Mickey drew down his brow. "Do I know you?"

The man smiled and walked away.

Mickey and Abe looked at each other and shrugged. As they drove off, Mickey stuffed the blue envelope in the glove compartment and opened the thick one Reverend Washington had given him. "This is a lot of money. More than I've ever seen."

"Count it," Abe said.

Mickey pulled the bills from the envelope and began counting. "Twenty-eight hundred."

"What are you going to do with all that money?"

"I don't know. What do you think I should do with it?"

"I'd buy a car if I were you."

"A car, huh?"

"You'll be sixteen next month, won't you? So, why not?"

"What do you think I should get?"

"You can buy a pretty nice car with that much money. What kind do want?"

Mickey pressed his lips and rubbed his chin. "Let's see. Hm." He looked around inside the Blazer. "I'm used to driving this one because you've been letting me ever since I got my learner's permit. So, one like this would be nice."

Abe surveyed the inside of the truck. He rubbed a hand over the dash, then bumped a fist on the seat. "A truck like this one, huh?"

"Yeah. It doesn't have to be the same color or as new. But one similar. Think I can for the money I got?"

Abe turned the radio on, then off. He worked the driver's side sun visor up and down and pressed the horn a few times. "Yeah . . . yeah." Abe nodded. "I think you could get a truck like this one. And for less than twenty-eight hundred."

Mickey raised his eyebrows. "Really?"

"Really," Abe said.

"Where?"

"From me."

Mickey looked around at the inside of the Blazer. "You'd be willing to sell me this truck for less than twenty-eight?"

"Yup."

"Well, then, I definitely want to buy it. How much?"

Abe kept his attention on the road. He turned his head slightly toward Mickey and cut him a look through the corners of his eyes. "How does five dollars sound?"

"Five bucks? Are you crazy?"

"Yeah. I'd be willing to sell it to YOU for five bucks. Not anyone else." Abe reached out a hand for a shake. "What do you say? We gotta deal?"

Mickey grinned and shook Abe's hand. "Deal!" he said, the grief of his mother's death now temporarily dulled from his thoughts.

The ladies of the church prepared enough food to feed a sizable army regiment. Everything from pork chops to red velvet cake. Mickey and those who cared for him feasted even though the occasion was anything but festive. When it came time to go home, Abe handed Mickey the keys to the Blazer. "Here, you drive me home in YOUR new truck."

As they approached a railroad crossing, the bell began to ring, the red lights started flashing and the gates came down. Three locomotives rolled passed. It was going to be a long one. Mickey pushed the shifter into park and turned off the engine.

Abe pressed the release on the glove compartment latch and the door dropped down. "Let's see what we have here?"

He pulled out the mysterious blue envelope and ripped it open. The words of the letter inside hit him like ice in the face.

Dear Mr. Mickey Tucker,

You are hererby summoned to appear before the Baker County Magistrate Court at the Baker County Courthouse in courtroom number 214 on Wednesday, July 21st, 1999 at 10 AM in regard to the assault and battery complaint against you made by Mr. Albert Speed and Mr. Billy Joe Speed. Sincerely. The Honorable Thomas Hightower. District Judge.

CHAPTER EIGHTEEN

Thomas Hightower was the epitome of a small-town insider/power broker. A Claxton High School graduate. Did a six-year stint at the University of Alabama. Awarded a law degree. Returned to Claxton and began riding the coattails of Theodore Hopkins Hightower. His father. At the zenith of his litigating career, the elder Hightower, or "T.H." as he was both affectionately and unaffectionately known, was the most regarded legal mind in Central Alabama. The running joke was that if T.H. Hightower sued the Pope for child support, the jury would render a guilty verdict.

T.H. had big plans for Thomas, his only son, and . . . himself as well. Thomas would serve alongside his father for ten years. During that time T.H. would woo his A-list of clients to his son and gradually fade into the background. Thomas would grow to become the face and force of Hightower & Associates. T.H. would spend his remaining years providing guidance from the backseat. "Confidential consulting" as he termed it. He'd maintain a fifty-one percent controlling interest and a forty percent financial interest in the firm until the time of his death. A fine strategy. However, less than a year in, the gavel came down on the master plan. A stroke turned T.H. into a vegetable and within three months he was laid to rest.

Thomas, alone and inexperienced, put forth his best effort to maintain Hightower & Associates' client role. He assured and reassured the various politicians, entertainers and business owners that they would continue to receive the same level of legal expertise they'd grown accustom to from his father. Nevertheless, his words fell on deaf ears and Thomas soon found himself sitting in an impressive office with high overhead and no A-list clients. The amount of local business he drummed up wouldn't pay the bills. With this being his reality, he decided to run for public office. Being the son of T.H. Hightower may not have been enough to keep the big fish in the family firm's net, but it proved to be enough to get him elected district judge. And, for eighteen years he'd sat on the county bench.

The fact that Mickey was to appear before Thomas Hightower concerned Abe. The blue blood local judge was a founding member of the Claxton Country Club. Chaired the board of directors for the Chamber of Commerce and presided over the annual peach festival, the town's biggest sales tax revenue generating event. Everyone who was anyone played proverbial footsie under the table with Thomas Hightower. The man's lifestyle far exceeded his Baker County salary. Rumors and speculations were as plentiful as mosquitos in September as to how Hightower was able to afford the house he lived in and the cars he and his wife drove. He was frequently seen out in public with local money people. The one he hobnobbed with the most was none other than Albert Speed. No doubt the hearing was a ploy concocted by the two of them while lounging by Speed's swimming pool or sipping twenty-four-year-old scotch at the country club.

Abe scanned the cars as he and Mickey pulled onto the parking lot of the Baker County Courthouse. He raised an index finger. "There! Park close to that white Buick LeSabre."

Mickey eased the Blazer into the empty space nearby it. The car had a Georgia license plate. Abe and Mickey got out. The man behind the wheel of the LeSabre threw up a hand and grinned. Abe made a gun gesture with one hand, at the same time returning a big smile with a wink. The driver emerged from the car, a leather padfolio in one hand. He wore a blue suit with a red tie and matching pocket handkerchief. He and Abe shook hands, then embraced, each clapping his palms on the back of the other.

"It's good to see you, Abe," the man said.

"You too. It's been way too long."

The two men released one another.

"Thanks for coming," Abe said.

"Glad to."

"I called Everett and told him you were coming. Thought we'd drive up to Birmingham and catch up over a good steak."

"Sounds like a plan. I haven't seen him since Key West."

"He's got the fish hanging in his office." Abe said.

Mickey remembered the time Abe took him to see Doctor Smith. The doctor that cleaned all the wax out of Mickey's ears. He had all kinds of animal heads and fish mounted in his office. His name was Everett. Mickey wondered if he was the Everett they were talking about. Probably so. It's not every day you meet someone named Everett.

The man looked down at Mickey. "This must be Mickey."

Abe rested a hand on Mickey's back. "This is Mickey." He gripped the top of one of Mickey's shoulders and shook him gently. Mickey loved it when Abe did stuff like that. It made him feel special—really special.

The man reached out his right hand for a shake. "My name's Dan."

Mickey shook the man's hand firmly, careful to look him straight in the eyes just like Abe had taught him. "Nice to meet you, Dan. Are you a lawyer?"

Dan nodded. "I am," he said and leaned down to make eye contact with Mickey. "And not just any lawyer." He touched Mickey's chest with his pointing finger. "I'm your lawyer."

Wow! Abe knew some really cool people. First, a doctor. Now, a lawyer.

"Are you from Georgia?" Mickey said.

Dan shook his head. "Nope. I'm from Virginia. The car's a rental. I flew into Atlanta." He pushed up his left sleeve and looked at his watch. "We got five minutes. Better get going."

The three of them climbed the courthouse steps. Abe pulled opened one of the large glass doors and held it for Dan and Mickey. The place smelled different than other buildings Mickey had been in. It smelled clean. Kinda like a doctor's office but different. Dan and Abe's shoes clicked on the marble floors as they walked. Mickey's Converse One Stars didn't. He could've sneaked around without anyone hearing him if he'd wanted to.

They opened the door to Room 214. The inside reminded Mickey of Reverend Washington's church without the carpet or a pulpit. A pole with an American flag stood in one front corner. A large round disk with an outline of the state hung on the wall behind the judge's desk. The words *Seal of the Great State of Alabama* encircled the shape of the state. Two tables faced the judge's desk. Each had two chairs. The three of them walked to the front of the room. Dan laid his padfolio on one of the tables and sat down. He pulled out the chair next to his. "Here Mickey. You sit next to me."

Mickey did as he'd commanded. In the movies and on television, people always sat next to their lawyers in courtroom situations. Abe sat down in one of the spectator chairs behind Dan and Mickey. Dan turned in his seat, put a hand on Mickey's shoulder and looked him in the eyes. "Now, when the judge gets here, you don't say a word unless I tell you to. I'll do all the talking for you. That's my job."

Mickey nodded. The back door swung open. Mickey turned to look. A hefty man walked in. He wore a gray suit. Black necktie. No pocket handkerchief in his chest pocket like Dan. The Speeds' lawyer. Probably just as mean as them too. Billy Joe sat in a wheelchair, a dejected look on his face. His mother held the door open as Albert Speed pushed his boy into the room. The man in the gray suit walked to the vacant table and set his black attaché case down on it. The metal feet of the case made a loud tap against the wooden top of the table. Mickey bet the man had done it for the sake of drama. To make him, Abe and Dan feel small or nervous. Mickey knew the man was wasting his time if he thought he could get a space in Abe's head. Wasn't going to happen. As for Dan, Mickey had just met him. But since he was Abe's friend, Mickey guessed it didn't affect him either. Mickey, however, felt like a sheep in the presence of a wolf. The man pulled one of the chairs out from the table and moved it to one side leaving an empty space. Albert Speed rolled his son into the space and sat down in the chair the man had just moved. The man sat down in the chair next to Billy Joe. Mrs. Speed took her seat in one of the spectator chairs behind her husband and son. Noise bounced off the walls inside the room again as the man flipped the attaché down on its side. He released the case's brass latches with his thumbs, then cut a look at Dan and Mickey, a slight smirk on his face. What was up with this guy? Albert and Billy Joe kept their focus on the judge's bench. So did Mrs. Speed.

A slender black woman entered from a door at the front. Mickey guessed her to be about the same age his mama was before . . . before she died. Her hair was pulled back into a bun behind her head and emphasize the pleasant features of her smooth face. The hem of her brown skirt swayed back and forth against her knees as she walked. Her stiletto heels hammered the floor with each step she took. She stopped at the front of the judge's desk and faced the small gathering. "All rise for the Honorable Thomas Hightower." All except Billy Joe Speed stood to their feet. Like a secret door, a section of the wall behind the bench opened. Thomas Hightower entered and took his place in the large oxblood leather chair.

"Please be seated," he said.

The well-dressed woman exited the room.

Judge Hightower opened the folder he'd brought in. "I declare this hearing in session. The counsel for Mr. Billy Joe Speed will present his complaint, then the counsel for Mr. . . . uh—" Hightower looked down at the folder, then back up to those present. "For Mr. Mickey Tucker will present his rebuttal. Both of you state your names before you begin. You'll make remarks from your seats. I don't permit standing for a courtroom hearing. I would remind you that the purpose of this hearing is to decide if the complaint made by Mr. Speed against Mr. Tucker rises to a level that I deem worthy of litigation. If it does, then we'll all go to court. If it doesn't, then I'll dismiss the whole thing and you can go about your lives. Do we understand?"

Dan and the other lawyer responded with "Yes, Your Honor." Everyone else with an affirming nod. Thomas Hightower looked at Billy Joe's attorney. "Okay. You're first."

The gray-suited man cleared his throat and began. "Your Honor. My name is Clint Mims. I'm with Mims and Lockhart here in Claxton. My client, Mr. Billy Joe Speed, as you are aware, is an upstanding young man from one of Claxton's finest families."

"Mr. Mims, I don't need you to tell me what I'm aware of. And we are not here to evaluate your client's pedigree. So, get to the point."

Clint Mims smiled. "Of course, Your Honor. My client was assaulted and permanently injured by Mr. Tucker. Currently, he has accumulated more than a quarter of a million dollars in medical expenses. He will need more medical attention in the future, so the amount is sure to increase. Furthermore, my client was a promising football player and, as such, had scholarship offers from fourteen universities, nine of which were Division I schools including the University of Alabama and Auburn University. The brutal actions of Mr. Tucker have robbed my client of a collegiate athletic scholarship, a college football career and the potential of a professional football career which he certainly would have had. In addition, he has experienced and will continue to experience emotional pain and suffering because of the fact that Mr. Tucker assaulted him."

Mickey leaned over to Dan. "What does assaulted mean?"

"It means you physically attacked him."

"That's a lie. He attacked me."

Dan raised an open palm, his fingers spread apart. "Just sit tight."

"Do you have documentation regarding Mr. Speed's medical diagnoses?" Judge Hightower asked Clint Mims.

"I do indeed, Your Honor. May I approach the bench?"

"Yes, you may."

Clint Mims raised the top of his attaché case and pulled out a stack of papers as thick as a dictionary. He stood to his feet, walked up to the bench and handed them to Thomas Hightower. "Here are the medical bills and evaluations my client has gotten thus far. There'll certainly be more. Also copies of the numerous scholarships he was offered from esteemed universities. A breakdown of what my client could've earned as a professional football player if Mr. Tucker had not ruined his life and future earning potential. And a conservative estimate of what my client is entitled to due to pain and suffering."

Hightower looked over the rims of his eyeglasses at Clint Mims like a teacher at a student. "Mr. Mims, I'm only concerned with the medical bills and evaluations. This is a hearing. Not a trial. You can return to your seat."

"Yes, Your Honor." Mims turned and walked back to his chair. When he sat down, Albert Speed leaned toward him and said something Mickey couldn't hear. Hightower gave the papers a cursory browsing, mumbling throughout the process. Mickey looked back at Abe. The wink and tight smile from his hero leveled his nerves a bit. Mickey responded in like fashion.

Hightower held the papers in his hands and dropped the bottom of the stack on his desk a few times to straighten it, the walls reverberating the sound. He set the documents aside and looked at Dan.

"Ok. Your turn."

"Thank you, Your Honor. I'm Dan Thompson of Thompson, Rutherford and Whitcomb. We're a firm based in Alexandria, Virginia. I—"

Hightower raised an open palm to Dan. "Stop right there, Sir. Can you prove that you're licensed to practice law in the state of Alabama?"

Dan pressed his lips and nodded. It was obvious that he anticipated the question. He opened his padfolio and pulled out a sheet of paper. "Permission to approach the bench, Your Honor."

"You may."

Dan walked up to Thomas Hightower. "I have a signed letter from the Attorney General of the United States addressed to Your Honor stating my credentials."

Hightower's eyes shot open. He reached out a hand. Dan gave him the letter. Hightower pushed his glasses up on the bridge of his nose and began examining the piece of paper. "Department of Justice letterhead and all," he said.

"Yes, Your Honor," Dan said.

Hightower looked down at him. "This will suffice, Counselor. You may return to your seat and continue with your remarks."

"Thank you, Your Honor."

As Dan was making his way back to his seat, Hightower shot Clint Mims and Albert Speed an *Oh, Crap!* look. Mickey suddenly felt tall on the inside. He turned in his chair and looked back. Abe had a look on his face that said, *I told you everything was going to be fine.*

Dan resumed his place at the table. "Your Honor, as I was saying, I represent Mr. Tucker and we object to this complaint on the basis that the injuries suffered by Mr. Speed came because of Mr. Speed's own actions. He and some of his friends deceived my client to lure him to a predetermined location. Mr. Tucker was taken to the predetermined location under false pretenses. When he arrived, Mr. Speed attacked him. My client simply responded in self-defense to Mr. Speed's aggression. Furthermore, my client's friend, Lolita DeRosa was basically kidnapped and taken to the scene of the event in question."

Thomas Hightower removed his eyeglasses and exhaled. He placed his elbows on the top of his desk and interlocked his fingers. "It is clear, beyond question, that Mr. Speed suffered life-altering injuries whatever the circumstances. Furthermore, it is clear, based on the testimonies of both the plaintiff and the defendant that Mr. Tucker inflicted the injures. Whether those injuries were the result of Mr. Tucker assaulting Mr. Speed or Mr. Tucker defending himself against Mr. Speed is a matter that must ultimately be decided in a court of law. Therefore, my ruling is that the case must go to trial. We are done here."

Hightower rapped his gavel once, gathered the documents and exited out the door he'd entered by. Clint Mims and the Speeds huddled together and began whispering. Dan motioned with his head for Mickey and Abe to follow him out of the room. Once they were in the hallway, Dan turned to Abe. "That was an act if I've ever seen one. Those two probably vacation in the Bahamas together."

"Hightower's performance was worthy of an Oscar," Abe said.

"Yeah. And how about Mims for best supporting actor? No telling how much time they spent rehearsing. We have our work cut out for us."

As they exited the courthouse and descended the steps, Mickey wondered what Dan meant by *we have our work cut out for us.*

Chapter Nineteen

Harold Jones dropped out his senior year of high school. Book learning wasn't for him, so he said. He fired up a charcoal grill in his back yard and started cooking steaks. Something most any even half-competent man can do. But Harold Jones had something no other man had. A secret seasoning created by his grandfather, Rodeo Jones. At no extra cost, and within a five-mile radius of the double-wide he lived in, Harold would deliver a "Rodeo" steak along with two slices of white sandwich bread to anyone willing to pay. Twenty-three years later, the words *Let's go to Harold's* were borderline ecstasy to any steak lover in Central Alabama. Most of the big-name steakhouse chains had locations in the Birmingham metropolitan area, but not one of them packed in hungry customers like Harold's Rodeo Steakhouse. The place opened at 5 PM till 10 PM on Fridays and Saturdays only. Folks with a taste for beef started lining up at the doors at 3:30 PM. To be later than 4:30 meant running the risk of a two-hour wait at the least or not even getting in the building before closing at the most.

Mickey, Abe and Dan Thompson walked through the door of Harold Jones' establishment. Abe and Dan began scanning the large room of one hundred plus diners. In one of the back corners of the room a man stood and motioned with one arm. Dr. Everett Smith. He'd secured the four of them a prime table by arriving at 3:30. Mickey and his two champions made their way through the feasting crowd. Everett and Dan shook hands and embraced, both expressing how good the other looked and how it'd been too long since they'd last seen each other. After Abe and Mickey made their salutations to the good doctor, they all sat down.

"It's on me, fellas," Everett said. "Go with the ribeye."

Dan bumped the top of the table with hammer fists. "Alright, I'll take your word for it. Won't even look at the menu."

"They don't have menus, Squid," Abe said.

Mickey drew down his brow. Why did you call Dan a squid?

"That's right," Everett said. "It's either a sirloin, a T-bone or a ribeye. That's it. This, my friend, is a STEAK house."

He looked at Mickey. "We Navy brothers call each other Squid."

Mickey relaxed his expression. "Oh, okay."

By the time the steaks hit the table, Abe and his two friends were deep into stories of their military careers. Mickey soaked them in. He was sure that if some big shot Hollywood film producer was sitting at the table, he'd be chomping at the bit to make a movie. The things Abe, Dan and Everett had done were real. Not imaginary stuff like Keanu Reeves or Arnold Schwarzenegger or Mel Gibson.

A woman wearing a cowboy hat, jeans and a western shirt interrupted the storytelling. "Thanks for dining with us tonight. Can I get you anything else?"

Everette took inventory and looked up at the waitress. "I think we're fine. You can bring the check."

"The check has already been taken care of."

"What? You're kidding. Right?" Everett said.

"I'm dead serious."

The three men looked at one another, each one's face displaying amazement.

"Was it on the house?" Abe said.

"No sir. Complements of a customer." She pulled a slip of paper from a back pocket. "He asked me to give you this." She handed the paper to

Abe, then scanned the men's faces. "It has been a pleasure serving you gentlemen tonight. Be safe going home."

She turned and walked away. Abe unfolded the paper and read the words to his friends.

Envelope under the panther.

• • •

Abe knew exactly what the anonymous bill payer meant by "the panther." As would anyone else in Baker County. The Jamison Panthers were the Claxton's Tigers arch cross-county football rival. "The panther" was the black iron big cat attached to the Jamison High School sign. Most every Claxton High football player aspired to painting it pink during the week leading up to the annual "big game." Over the course of the two school's forty-nine-year rivalry, only a relatively few had succeeded. But one thing was sure to happen each year during the two teams' annual showdown—the Claxton marching band would give a rendering of *The Pink Panther* during halftime. For the citizens of Jamison "the panther" was a local landmark, every bit as endearing to them as *The Arch* was to the people of Saint Louis or *The Golden Gate Bridge* was to the folks of San Francisco.

Mickey pulled the Blazer up close to the panther, the truck's headlights on high beam. Abe got out and inspected the local icon. Taped under the cat's neck was a black envelope. Abe removed it and got back into the truck.

"Okay. Let's go."

"Awe, come on. Open it. I'm dying to know what's in it."

Abe switched on the dome light, the envelope clutched in his right hand as tight as if he were determined to keep someone from snatching it. He raised it up to Mickey. "This may be a set-up, Mick. Remember, back at the restaurant the note was anonymous. That's a REAL red flag."

"It could be legit though? Come on. Open it."

Abe cocked his head and looked at Mickey through the corners of his eyes. "I'm going to, but if it sounds like a scheme, that's it. We're not falling for it."

Mickey nodded. "Okay."

Abe opened the envelope, pulled out the piece of paper inside and unfolded it. The words were typed.

They underestimated your taste in lawyers. They're worried and they'll start flexing their muscles. Everyone who helps you will pay starting with William Fleming and Pamela Baldwin. Both will be fired tomorrow. Make no mistake. You're at war. I'll help you fight as best I can . . . from the shadows. When Tree Brand pocketknives are on sale, check the panther. One more thing. You have to find a way to get Hightower off the case. I'm pulling for you, Squid.

• • •

Abe pulled up to the house. A late model Ford Taurus was parked in the driveway, a mid-eighties 4WD pickup truck in the grass beside it. Dented license plate from trailer hookup miscalculations. Chrome toolbox across the front of the truck bed. Abe got out of his vehicle and walked up the steps. The front door opened before he could knock. William Fleming stood on the other side of the screen door. The blue, company-issued Dickie's work shirt and matching pants he wore were still clean. It was 10 AM. The axe had fallen as soon as his shift had started that morning.

William's expression was feelingless. "Morning."

Abe nodded. "Morning."

"So, Loomis, what brings you to my front door on this not-so-fine Thursday morning."

"A monetary proposition. Want to start a classic car business." Abe cocked his head and rolled an open hand. "You know. Restore barn finds, rollers and what have you and sell them." Market for them is good. Closest classic car store is nearly fifty miles away in Montgomery."

Fleming stared at Abe for a couple of seconds, sighed and pushed his top lip up with his bottom. "Believe it or not, I'm looking to sell a few."

Abe shook his head. "I'm not here to buy your cars. I'm here to ask you to be my partner. You got the inventory. I've got the working capital.

Figure we split the profit fifty-fifty on everything we sell." He reached in his pocket and pulled out a roll of Federal Reserve Notes. "I figure our company could rent your place till we can find a permanent shop." He offered the cash to Fleming. "Here's the first month's rent and a security deposit. I'll cover all business costs. Tools. Paint. Parts. All you gotta do is let me know. What do you say, Mr. Fleming?"

"Well, if that don't beat all." Fleming looked over his shoulder back into the house. "Audrey, put a pot of coffee on for me and Mr. Loomis. Would you, Honey? And cut us each a piece of your pecan pie. He's heard all about it." He pushed open the screen door. Abe stepped inside.

. . .

Abe sat in the corner. The clock on the wall said twelve forty-five. The lunch crowd had thinned out to a lingering half dozen. Abe watched Pamela wipe down tables and slide the loose change tips into the pocket of the apron she wore. As she worked her way closer, he continued to push the buttons on the pocket calculator, pausing now and again to write down numbers on a legal pad. He raised his cup. "Excuse me. Can I get a refill?"

Pamela looked up. "Sure," she said and walked over to his table. She looked at him with a squint and pointed an index finger. "You're Mickey's—"

"Stepdad. I'm Mickey's stepdad. The adoption papers were finalized about two weeks ago."

She shook her head, the tight smile of a pleasant surprise on her face. "God bless you. That kid's been through a lot."

She took his cup and headed to the front of the restaurant. In seconds, she returned, Abe's cup filled to the brim with cola and crushed ice. She glanced down at the pad of paper. "Don't mean to be nosey, but what are you working on?"

Abe took a drink and set the cup back down. "I'm crunching the numbers for a new business my partner and I have just started."

"What kind of business?"

"Restoring old cars. Thinking about calling it *Big Boy Toys*. How does that sound to you?"

"Sounds cool."

Abe snapped his fingers and pointed at her. "Actually, you might be able to help me."

Pamela drew down her brow. "How's that?"

"We're needing to hire an administrator." Abe rolled an open hand. "Someone to pick up parts. Pay bills. Set up files. Answer the phone . . . when we get one." He looked her in the eyes. "Full-time. Monday through Friday. Ten dollars an hour starting out. Opportunities for raises and bonuses. Do you know someone who might be interested?"

Pamela Baldwin lowered her chin and looked at Abe from under her eyebrows. "When do I start?"

Abe shot his eyes open. "You serious?"

"Dang right. I don't make ten an hour at this place AND I have to work two weekends a month.

Abe nodded. "Alright, then." He checked his watch and sighed. "I'm in a spot. It's almost one o'clock now and I got a list of stuff that needs to be picked up at Walmart, another list that needs to be picked up at paint warehouse up in Alabaster." He rubbed his chin. "I know it's asking a lot, but it'd really help me out if you could just walk out of here and start right now." He reached into his pocket, pulled out a wad of cash and peeled off four large bills. "If you'd be willing to do that, I'll pay you for a full week in cash right now."

Pamela's eyes bulged at the sight of the money. She looked back into Abe's eyes. "Let me grab my purse and I'm outta here." She turned to walk away but caught herself and turned back to Abe. "And Mr.—Uh."

"Call me Abe."

"Yeah . . . Abe . . . right." She brought a palm to her forehead. "Sorry. It was on the tip of my tongue."

Abe grinned. "Don't think twice about it."

Her emotions settled down a bit. "You REALLY don't have to pay me four hundred dollars for a day and half's work."

"Look Pamela. I'm asking you to burn a bridge by walking out without giving a two-week notice. That's a big deal. I really feel I should." Abe extended the money to her. "So, take the money."

CHAPTER TWENTY

Local consumers welcomed Walmart to Claxton with open wallets and open checkbooks in the late 1970s. For more than a few of the local merchants or "little guys" in town, the retail behemoth's presence was a dagger in the heart. Ira Cooper's Hardware and Farm Store, on the other hand, not so much as hiccupped in Sam Walton's retail shadow. Ira Cooper's establishment offered many things Walmart didn't. A full line of farm supplies including horse tack. Free popcorn, parched peanuts and fountain soft drinks on Fridays and Saturdays. Running tabs at no interest. Free delivery. And not the least of all . . . hometown, southern hospitality from the man who owned the place.

Abe and Mickey inhaled the aroma of freshly popped popcorn and roasted peanuts as they opened the door. Adorned in faded blue overalls, Ira Cooper sat on a stool behind a long glass display counter. "Morning. Ya'll just come right on in."

Mickey made a beeline to the soda fountain.

Abe stepped over to the counter. He studied the numerous pocketknives on display.

"Looking for anything in particular?" Ira said.

"What do you recommend?"

Ira stood to his feet and walked over to Abe. He slid open the back glass of the case and reached in for one of the knives. "This Case XX is a good knife." He pulled it out and set it on the counter in front of Abe. "This is a new color. Just came out this year."

Abe opened one of the blades and inspected it. "My daddy used to carry a Queen Steel."

Ira puckered his lips and blew a whistle. "Some kind of fine blade. High as a cat's back though. I don't have any, but I can order you one. I've got a catalogue in my office. Want to see it?"

Abe closed the knife and handed it back to Ira. "Naw. That's alright. How about a Tree Brand? Got any?"

"Sure do. You wanting a single blade? Two blade? Three blade?" Ira said as he returned the Case XX to its spot in the display.

"Probably a three blade."

Ira reached for another one. He pulled a thick, three-bladed knife from the case and handed it to Abe. "This is a Tree Brand. German steel blades. It's a dandy. And Tree Brands are on sale this week."

Abe cocked his head and narrowed his eyes. "That's good to hear. What's the sale price?"

"They're twenty percent off. That knife is normally fifty, but you can buy it today for forty."

Abe opened all three of the blades. "I tell you, Mr. Cooper. I really like it. Think I'll take it." He handed the knife back.

Ira put it back in its box. "Anything else for you today?"

"No. I think that'll do it."

"Okay, let's step over to the register and I'll ring you up."

Ira stepped from behind the glass display and over to the cash register. It was an old brass National made in the 1940s. The nostalgic machine dinged with each number Ira punched.

"That comes to forty-two dollars even."

Abe pulled his leather bifold from one of his back pockets. He flipped it straight, pulled out a fifty and handed it to Ira. Claxton's beloved merchant raised the back of the register's plastic cash drawer just enough to slip the bill under it. He dropped the drawer back in place, skinned four notes from inside the tray and shoved the drawer shut.

"Alright," he said and began laying the cash in Abe's open hand. "Five. Six. Seven. And eight." He looked up into Abe's eyes. "I sure appreciate your business and hope you'll come back."

Abe nodded. "Oh, I'll be back. Think I'll start collecting Tree Brands. I'll check back with you often and buy one every time they're on sale."

Ira extended his hand to Abe for a shake. Abe obliged, then called out across the store. "Okay, Mick, I'm ready! Are you?"

Mickey turned from the shelves of ammunition he'd been perusing, a large fountain drink in one hand, a bag of popcorn in the other. "They got plenty of thirty aught six . . . thirty-thirty too." He took a drink of his soda and kept chewing.

Abe pulled the front door open and held it. "We'll remember that come deer season." Mickey walked out and Abe followed. They climbed into the Blazer, Mickey at the wheel.

"Where're we headed?"

"I bought a Tree Brand. It was on sale."

"That means we're going to Jamison," Mickey said.

Abe pumped an open hand. "Let's wait till it gets dark. Head toward the high school. I want to show you something."

It was a typical Saturday in Claxton. Slow moving traffic. Crowded sidewalks. Busy stores. People shopping for everything from furniture to clothing. Jewelry to musical instruments. Mickey eased the Blazer down the main street of the teeming downtown, mindful of jaywalkers and brake lights. The traffic light at the south end of town turned red before Mickey could drive under it. Abe pointed an index finger. "When the light changes, turn in up there where the Curb Market used to be."

The Curb Market was once THE go-to place for fresh produce, live plants, and various yard maintenance supplies and décor. It even sold pumpkins and Christmas trees in the fall and winter months. Within a year of Walmart's arrival to town, however, the mom-and-pop operation's forty plus year legacy was blown away like dust in the wind. Locally grown couldn't compete with imports from third-world countries. Locally owned was no match for corporately run.

Mickey turned into the weathered parking lot. Weeds and grass had taken advantage of the roadmap of cracks in the asphalt.

Mickey raised one eyebrow and turned up one side of his top lip. "What are we doing in this old place? It's been closed for years,"

"Been is the key word, Mick. It's BEEN closed, but it's about to be open."

"What's it gonna be?"

"A new business called *Big Boy Toys*."

"What's *Big Boy Toys*?"

"The classic car lot Bobby Fleming's dad and I are opening."

"Are you kidding?"

"I'm not kidding. Got my dealer's license in the mail just the other day."

Mickey shook his head, a broad grin on his face. "Man, it'll be da bomb!"

"We think so. And Teresa Baldwin's mother is going to help us run it."

"It'll take some work to fix it up. Place looks like something out of a horror movie," Mickey said.

"I know. I've already met with the bank. They're giving me a second mortgage on the house. Construction guys will start Monday. Let's take a walk around the place and I'll fill you in on our plans."

By the time they got back in the Blazer, the sun was halved and dark orange on the horizon. Abe tucked his sunglasses over the passenger-side visor. "What do you say if we grab a bite to eat somewhere? By the time we're done, it'll be dark. Where you wanna go?"

"How about Super Burger?"

"Fine with me. You're driving."

The popular fast-food joint crawled with customers. Mickey and Abe sat down at the same table Abe had sat at when he persuaded Pamela Baldwin to tell the management to stick the job where the sun doesn't shine. Mickey shoved a crinkled fry in his mouth. It was time to find out.

"Abe, I can ask you anything. Right?"

"Of course. Fire away," Abe said and bit a plug out of his burger.

"Did you ever have a family? You know . . . before me and you."

Abe looked Mickey in the eyes and pressed his lips. He cleared his throat. "Yes. I did."

"Well . . . will you tell me about them?"

Abe inhaled and exhaled. "Victoria and I met my last year at the Naval Academy. She was attending the University of Maryland in the day and waiting tables at a seafood restaurant at night. I dropped in one evening and that's when I first saw her. It was oyster night. All you could eat. So, I ordered oysters."

"You like oysters?"

Abe shook his head. "Not at all."

"So, why did you order them?"

Abe grinned. "Because she was my waitress and them oysters was my excuse for staying there and watching her till closing. I just kept eating them and she'd just keep bringing them. All the while I was thinking how I could get her to give me her phone number. I knew that every man that had come through the doors of that place had asked her before, so I had to come across as—."

"Genuine," Mickey said, finishing his sentence for him.

"That's right. I knew if I came across like all those other clowns I'd leave there without her number just like they had."

"Did the oysters make you sick?"

"I tell you, Mick. She killed me the first time I laid eyes on her. I was too in love for them oysters to make me sick."

Abe and Mickey burst out into laughter.

"How did you get her number?"

"It was closing time and I was the only customer left. When she brought me the check she said, 'Here's your check, Oyster Lover.' And that was the opportunity I'd been waiting for."

Mickey sat up on the edge of his seat, his eyes large. "What did you say?"

"I said, 'I hate oysters. I came here tonight to eat crab legs. What makes you believe I love oysters?' She said, 'Because you haven't stopped eating them since you got here.' I said, 'The only reason I ordered them was so I could stay till closing and beg you to give me your phone number.'"

"Then, what did she say?"

"She said, 'I'm not giving you my phone number, but I WILL let you join me for a late-night dinner. . . unless you're too full.' I said, 'I can eat again if it means I get to sit across the table from you.' She said, 'Are you sure about that?' I said, 'I've never been more sure about anything in my life.' She said, 'Can I choose the place?' I said, 'Absolutely. I'm hungry for whatever you're hungry for.'"

"So, where did you guys go?"

"A place right down the street called *Frankie's Oyster Bar*."

"What did she order?"

"Oysters."

"And what did you order?"

A wide grin stretched out on Abe's face, his eyebrows raised. "I had crab legs."

"Crab legs? Why"

Abe lowered his chin and looked at Mickey from under his brow. "Because I hate oysters."

They burst out laughing again.

"When did ya'll get married?"

Abe's countenance turned somber. "Six months later. I graduated on a Friday. We got married the next day on Saturday."

"Then what?"

"Thirty days later I got assigned to a nuclear sub. Nine months after that I got a message telling me—" Abe's voice cracked; his eyes welled. "That she and my son had died while she was giving birth."

Abe sniffled and pinched the water from his eyes with an index finger and thumb. Mickey paused to allow Abe to gather his emotions.

"Then what did you do?" Mickey said.

"I became a SEAL."

"Is that when you met Dan and Dr. Smith?"

Abe nodded. "That's when I met Dan and Dr. Smith."

"Never got married again?"

"No."

"Why not?"

"Because I could never love anyone but Victoria."

"Is that when the drinking started?"

Abe pulled his head back and wrenched one side of his face. "I don't drink."

"You don't now, but you used to. I saw three empty whiskey bottles in your garbage can the first day we met?"

Abe relaxed his expression and started nodding. "Alright. Alright. No secrets." He pushed back in his chair and interlocked his fingers on the table. "That's when I started drinking. And the day we met was the day I quit."

"Just like that?"

"Just like that."

"Why?"

"Because God sent you to me."

"What do you mean God sent me to you?"

"When I retired from the Navy, I had lots of free time on my hands and no one to spend it with. The drinking got worse. I felt like I had no reason to keep living. By the time we met, I was at the end of my rope. Do you remember what I had with me that day?"

"A gun."

"A hunting rifle to be exact and I wasn't hunting. It was springtime. Remember?"

Mickey nodded slightly; his eyes locked onto Abe's.

"My plan was to do it at the pond. Just kneel down, put the end of the gun in my mouth and pull the trigger. As I walked from the house I prayed and asked God to show me a sign. To give me a reason to keep living. When you told me that you were fishing so you and your mother could eat, I knew you were God's answer to my prayer. I went back home and poured out EVERY bottle of liquor in the house. I haven't had a drop since."

"Could I get you refills?" said a waitress.

Abe and Mickey snapped back to reality.

"I think we're fine," Abe said. "We were just about to leave."

They finished off their drinks and rose from their seats.

"Can I drive your truck?" Abe said.

"Of course," Mickey said and handed him the keys.

The Blazer was parked near the front of the restaurant.

"Hey!" came a gruff voice as they were pulling open their doors.

They paused and turned to see.

A thick, muscled man leaned on his elbows against the roof of a white Cadillac CTS. Butterfly.

Mickey rolled his eyes and shook his head. "It's that guy again."

"Nice truck," Butterfly said and raised his chin, adding emphasis to his condescending expression.

Chapter Twenty-One

From the ice cream parlor across the street Abe and Mickey sat staring through the windshield. 9 PM. The outline of the panther was barely visible.

"You'd think they would've gotten a call by now or gone for donuts and coffee somewhere," Mickey said.

Abe checked his watch. "We've only been sitting here for eighteen minutes.

"Seems like it's been longer than that. I wish they'd just go somewhere already."

As if they'd been listening to Mickey's impatient words, the two Jamison Police officers turned on their headlights and drove away from Jamison High School.

"Looks like your wish was granted," Abe said and pulled the shifter down into drive. He eased the Blazer up next to the school's sign and got out. He ran one hand under the panther's neck. Like before, the taped envelope was there. He pulled it free and got back into the vehicle. He and Mickey drove back across the street and parked. Abe turned on the light inside the cab of the truck and opened the envelope.

Big Boy Toys is a great name. I wish you great success. William Fleming knows his stuff when it comes to old cars. They're still scratching their heads about Pamela Baldwin quitting the day she was going to be fired. Good job! Hightower and Speed are more than friends. The Lucky Mermaid docks at

Garcon Point every other Tuesday between 2 and 3 AM. Odd time. Don't you think?

• • •

The light of the full moon reflected off the surface of the turquoise water. The surf crashed against the beach as the tropical storm churning off the coast of Cuba began extending its influence along the Florida panhandle. Warm wind from the south jostled the tops of the palms and pine trees of the sleepy coastal town. Abe and Mickey watched the pier from the Chrysler Sebring Abe had rented for the down and back trip. Mickey had picked out the car. It was his first road trip in a convertible. Actually, his first trip in a convertible . . . period. They'd arrived in Pensacola in the early afternoon. Eaten dinner at a seaside restaurant. Neither had ordered oysters. They'd caught a matinee showing of Star Wars I, then hit a bowling alley for a few hours before taking I-10 over Escambia Bay, then the southbound of Highway 281 to Garcon Point. It was like a mini vacation for Mickey who'd never been out of the state of Alabama before. It had been a great day. Before they left Claxton, Abe and William Fleming closed their first deal. *Big Boy Toys* had successfully renovated and sold a 1970 GTO Judge. Orbit orange. 400 Ram Air engine. Numbers matching. Firestone Wide Oval Tires. Profit: $8800. William Fleming's cut was more than he was used to making for a month's work at the paving company that had fired him. Abe wrote Pamela Baldwin a bonus check for two hundred dollars from the deal. The first bonus the single mom had ever received.

At 1:05 AM, about a half mile from the end of the pier, a light flashed on and off three times.

"That must be a signal," Mickey said.

"I'd say so," Abe said.

A black panel van tooled up the narrow road along the edge of the beach and came to a stop close to the pier's landing. The sound of the boat's engine grew louder in the darkness as the vessel drew closer. It reached the end of the pier. Another signal light. This time it stayed on for a few seconds, just time enough for Abe and Mickey to read the words painted on the side of the boat near its bow. *The Lucky Mermaid.* Two men got out of the van and walked to where the boat had docked. They were greeted by three crew members. Words were exchanged and the five of them began transporting plastic containers from the boat to the van. Abe and Mickey counted forty-eight. When the last one was loaded, the driver handed one of the crewmen a manilla envelope. He inspected its contents, then he and his two cohorts started walking back to the boat. The two men got back into the van and drove away. Without turning on the car's headlights Abe pulled onto the street and followed the van. He and Mickey kept a distance. Just south of the I-10 overpass Abe switched on the lights and sped up to get closer. The van turned north on Highway 89 and crossed the state line into Alabama. On the north side of the small town of Brewton, the van turned off the road and passed through an opened chain-link gate. The gate closed behind it and the van continued on toward the raised roll-up doors of a warehouse. As he and Mickey cruised by, the door of the large metal building began creeping down as the van came to a stop inside.

When they arrived back in Claxton, the sun was beginning its climb on the horizon. Abe nudged Mickey. "Wake up, Mick."

Mickey yawned, stretched as best he could and rubbed his eyes. "What time is it?"

"Almost six."

"Let's go get in the bed."

"I can't sleep when the sun's up," Abe said. "I'll take you home and come back to the car lot."

"Cool. I'll sleep three or four hours, then come to the lot when I wake up."

Abe flipped open his cell phone and pressed a button.

"Who you calling?"

"Dan," Abe said, holding the phone to his right ear. "Hey, Squid. You up and at'em yet?" Abe paused for Dan's response. "Hey, listen. Mickey and I just took a recon trip down to a little coastal town close to Pensacola called Garcon Point. You ever heard of it?" Abe paused again. "I got a tip about a fishing boat named *The Lucky Mermaid*. Turns out the tip was legit. Something suspicious is DEFINITELY going on. You got a connection at Customs and Border Patrol?" Abe listened for a few seconds. "Good. Be interesting to find out what's going on. I'll catch you later."

Abe closed the phone and turned into the driveway. Mickey got out of the car. He was beat. Couldn't wait to collapse on the bed.

• • •

Mickey walked out the door, revived thanks to a three-hour nap and shower. He'd be at the car lot right at noon. Perfect. His stomach sounded like it had an angry grizzly bear in it. He and Abe hadn't eaten at *Casa Amigos* in over two weeks. Perhaps that would change today. Mickey could already taste the nachos and cheese sauce. He climbed into the Blazer, fired up the engine and turned on the radio. Gregg Allman was mid-way into the first verse of *Whipping Post*. Mickey cranked it up and lowered the driver's side window. Rocking with The Brothers, he backed out of the driveway and headed up the road, his left arm resting on the driver door. School would be starting back in two weeks. Mickey looked forward to it. Now that he had his driver's license the days of riding the school bus were over. He'd be quite the man on campus driving a 4WD. Not to mention having Lolita riding shotgun every day. It was the end of the summer, and she was looking good.

He made a right on Highway 31 and kicked in the big V8. The sound of the dual exhaust was therapeutic. The wind felt good blowing in his damp hair as it circulated inside the truck. Wait. What was that? A slick place in the road, perhaps. Something made a loud pop and the front right side of the Blazer dropped down against the pavement. The truck veered hard to the right. Mickey white-knuckled the steering wheel. In his peripheral, he saw the front wheel bolt across the field next to the road. He stomped on the brakes. The Blazer flipped off the road and rolled down the embankment. Darkness.

Mickey sensed pressure applied to his left hand. He felt fingers combing through his hair. His eyelid hurt as he eased open his right eye. He couldn't open his left.

"Mickey," came a familiar female voice.

His vision cleared. Her face was as pretty as ever. His nose felt strange. Like one of his nostrils had something stuck in it. And his throat . . . his throat ached, but he was determined to say her name.

"Lolita?"

"Yes. It's me."

"I'm here too, Mick," came the voice of his champion.

Mickey turned his head toward him. "What happened?"

"You're in the hospital. You had an accident. Luckily you were wearing your seatbelt."

"The Blazer?"

"We'll get you another one," Abe said.

"I loved that truck."

"It was just a truck. You're okay. That's all that matters"

"I don't know what happened. I was just driving like normal and all the sudden . . ."

Abe pulled his face close to Mickey's. "It was rigged to crash, Son. They thought I'd be driving it."

"What do we do now?"

Abe shook his head. "WE don't do anything. I'll get to the bottom of it. You just rest and get well."

Mickey felt like something was pulling the energy out of him. He tried to keep his eye open, but it was too heavy. Lolita's voice started fading as if they were drifting apart from each other. Sleep won.

Chapter Twenty-Two

The brunette behind the desk pushed the hair back from her face. "Mr. Loomis, Chief Davenport will see you now." She pointed an index finger to the corridor. "Down the hallway. Last door on the right."

Luther Davenport's position as the Claxton police chief was as safe as ice in a new deep freezer. Unlike the county sheriff, the portly law enforcement boss was immune to the four-year election cycle. Davenport served at the will of the town board. And to maintain his salary, retirement, benefits, and insurance, the head of Claxton's finest needed only to stay in the good graces of five of the nine aldermen. A feat he'd faithfully accomplished for more than nineteen years.

Abe walked into Davenport's office and sat down. He didn't wait for permission, offer a handshake or thank the chief for seeing him. He didn't smile or say hello. His expression was solemn. His purpose was to get a straight answer.

"Chief Davenport, you know who I am, so let me get straight to the point. Why has the investigation of my son's accident been closed?"

Luther Davenport placed his elbows on top of his desk and interlocked his fingers. "Lack of evidence. Plain and simple. There were no prints anywhere on the truck other than yours and your sons. We couldn't conclude with any measure of certainty that the vehicle had been tampered with in any way. We've talked to every neighbor within a half mile of your house. Not one of them can testify that they saw the man you suspect at, or even near, your house. Furthermore, he has credible references who can testify of his whereabouts the day before and the day of the accident." Davenport spread his hands apart, his palms turned upward. "There's no reason to continue the investigation. Might as well be looking for seashells in a desert. It was just a freak accident."

Abe folded his arms. "Chief Davenport, before I get up and walk out the door, I want to make sure I understand you clearly." Abe cocked his head and looked at Davenport, one eyebrow drawn down. "So, you're telling me a vehicle is traveling down the road at a speed of sixty plus miles an hour. One front wheel strips all fives lug studs and flies off and your experience as a law enforcement officer leads you to conclude that it was a freak accident with no reason to suspect foul play? Is that what you're telling me?"

Davenport adjusted himself and sat up straight in his chair. He picked up the stray pencil that lay next to his coffee mug and tapped the eraser end a few times on the top of his desk. "Look, Mr. Loomis. Your son was lucky. He's going to fully recover. Your insurance company will replace the totaled vehicle. Count your blessings and move on with life."

"Move on with life, huh?"

"Sure. Sure. For your own sake. For the kid's. For everyone's."

Abe paused for a few moments and found his words. "Okay. I'll move on, then."

• • •

Abe dropped four quarters in the slot and turned the knob. The commercial grade clothes dryer began to toss the clothes behind the glass door. Toward the back of the laundry mat a lady huffed as she banged a red plastic container against the rim of a washing machine.

Abe turned his attention to her. "Ma'am, I got plenty of detergent. You're welcome to it."

She looked up at him, "I thought I had enough, but I don't. And I'm out of money. I just need to wash these. I can hang them out to dry on the line at home."

Abe picked up a blue plastic bottle and walked it over to her. "Here, help yourself."

She responded with a smile in dire need of dental work. "Thank you so much, sir."

"Glad to. Why don't you just keep it. I have more at home."

"You sure?"

"Of course." He pulled his wallet from his back pocket and took out a twenty.

The lady's face reddened as he offered it to her. "Sir, you don't need to do that."

"I know. But I want to. If you don't take it, you'll be robbing me of blessing."

The woman took the bill from his hand. "You must be an angel."

Abe shook his head. "No, I'm just a regular guy trying to get along in this world like everybody else." He turned and started back to the dryer. The lady said something he couldn't make out. He looked back.

"I beg your pardon."

"You ain't regular, Mister."

Abe could have done his laundry at home. His washer and dryer were in fine working order. He was at *Washed Up Coin Laundry* because of its location. Directly across the road from Albert Speed's dealership. Abe had been watching the office building of the sprawling dealership for more than an hour. The white Cadillac CTS hadn't moved. It was getting close to noon. Surely, Butterfly would be going to lunch soon. Abe's cell rang. He flipped it open. Dan. Abe pushed the answer button.

"Hey, Squid."

Abe kept his eyes on the Cadillac as he listened to Dan. "Well, well. I'll make sure I'm in front of the television at five when the news airs. Mickey's doing fine now. Doctor says he'll probably release him from the hospital in the next couple of days."

Abe watched as Butterfly walked to his car and got in. "I need to go. Something just came up."

Abe hung up the phone and turned back to the woman. "I have to step out for a few minutes. Would you mind keeping an eye on my clothes till I get back?"

"Absolutely. Is that your basket on the table?"

"Yes," Abe said and walked out the door. He got into the 1995 Silverado Extended Cab he'd picked up at the Birmingham auction the week before. Butterfly pulled onto the road and headed north. Abe followed him two cars behind. Seven miles north of Claxton in the bedroom community of Thornsby, Butterfly turned off the highway into the parking lot of a grain warehouse turned restaurant. *The Feed Mill* was a hotspot at lunch time for men who worked with their hands. The locally owned eatery offered an all-you-can eat food bar consisting of three meat options, a wide variety of vegetables and a homemade dessert that varied depending on the day of the week.

Abe waited ten minutes before he entered to make sure Butterfly was settled into his mid-day meal. As he ascended the steps, a man with a John Deere cap stepped out from inside the restaurant. He held the door open as Abe entered.

"Thank you, sir," Abe said.

The man smiled and picked his teeth with a wooden toothpick. "You better hurry before all the pot roast is gone."

"It's that good, huh?"

"Yes, indeed."

Abe walked in. He heard the door shut behind him. The aroma of country cooking filled his nostrils. A waitress hustled by him. The tray she balanced on one hand bore witness that banana pudding was the dessert of the day. Abe looked around the room. Butterfly sat at a table in the back of the large dining hall. The man he dined with sat with his back to the front of the room. Abe couldn't tell who he was. To one side of them was an available table. Abe hoped it still would be when he finished his run of the food bar. He took his place in line wondering if he'd so much as taste the pot roast before the stuff hit the fan. By the time he got to the end of the buffet, his plate was well-stocked with piping hot food and a sizable brick of cornbread. He drew off a glass of sweet tea from the beverage dispenser and headed toward his target. The table was still unoccupied. He grinned on the inside. He was about to "move on with life."

He set his plate and glass of tea on the table and took his seat. From the corner of one eye, he could see Butterfly glaring at him. He lowered his head and shut his eyes. He thanked God for the meal and asked that the command to be *shrewd as serpents and innocent as doves* would be his reality in the turn of events he knew was soon to take place.

"Amen," he whispered and opened his eyes.

"Well, that was touching," Butterfly said, his words dripping with venom.

Yup. Everything was going as planned.

Abe looked the jacked man in the eyes. "Well, I'm glad your heart was moved. But my concern was with someone much bigger and stronger than you . . . Butterfly."

Butterfly pushed away from the table and stood to his feet, fire in his eyes.

"You listen to me, you nig—"

"Now, now," the man sitting with Butterfly said. "No need for any trouble." Abe cut a glance at the man. Thomas Hightower.

Abe looked up at Butterfly and smiled, "That's right, Butterfly. I'm not looking to start any trouble."

"Well, that's too bad. Because I'm going to break your neck. Now, get up!"

Oh, what wonderful words! Thank you, Lord.

Hightower raised a trembling hand. "Robert, this is not the way to handle this. Now, please just sit back down and finish your lunch."

The big man looked down at Hightower. "Nobody calls me names and gets away with it. I mean nobody." He walked over to Abe's table, picked up his glass of tea and poured it out on Abe's head. "Get up! You nigger!"

Numerous customers ceased their eating and focused on the scene. Abe pressed his lips together and wiped the tea from his face with a napkin. He looked up at Butterfly. "This is not the place to have this kind of conversation." Abe fanned an open hand around the room. "Look how uncomfortable you're making all these good people. Surely, we could discuss this another time, Butterfly."

"I'll either bust you up in here or I'll bust you up outside. You decide."

"Robert, listen to me!" Hightower said.

"Shut up, Judge. I'll handle this. It's been a long time coming."

Hightower put a palm to his forehead and shook his head.

Abe eased his chair back and stood to his feet. He raised his opened hands chest level. "Well, if there's no other option, I say outside."

"Let's go," Butterfly said.

Abe turned and started towards the door. Butterfly shoved him from behind. Several men, dirtied from manual labor, got up from their tables and followed them. Abe exited the restaurant and descended the steps. He walked to a broad, open space in the parking lot, Butterfly matching him step for step, spouting out threats and racial slurs all the while. Abe turned and faced the steroid hothead. The working men drew in and looked on. Abe shrugged his shoulders. "So, why are we out here, Butterfly? What's the problem?"

Butterfly made fists and assumed a boxing stance.

Abe bladed his torso and raised his opened hands. "Whoa! Whoa! Whoa! I thought we came out here to have a man-to-man conversation."

Butterfly threw a right haymaker. Abe let the punch through. It connected just above his left eye. Abe fell to his all fours. A drop of blood splashed on the pavement.

Butterfly looked around at the men who were observing. Some were excited. Others seemed saddened like they wanted to intervene but lacked the courage. Butterfly grinned, his adrenaline fueled by the fact that he had an audience. He turned his attention back to Abe. "Get up, Nigger. You're gonna wish you'd never called me Butterfly."

Abe kept his head down and smiled. Butterfly had drawn the first blood. It was on, now. Abe thanked God again and stood to his feet. The muscled man jabbed with his left. Abe blocked the punch. And, in the same motion, gripped the top of the man's wrist and wrenched it downward. The unnatural movement forced Butterfly to lower his shoulder. While maintaining pressure on the big man's arm with his left hand, Abe shot a reverse palm-heel strike with his right. It connected with the back of Butterfly's left elbow. The force of Abe's strike hyperextended the elbow, snapping it like a dry twig. Butterfly cried out in pain and fell to his knees. Abe kept his tight grip on the man's left wrist. He raised his right fist high in the air. He dropped all his weight with his arm bent at a right angle. The triceps of Abe's muscular right arm slammed against Butterfly's already damaged elbow. The force of the impact further severed the tendons and cartilage. Butterfly wailed in agony as his arm, from elbow to hand, dangled like a cheap earring. Abe jumped behind him and seized him in a chokehold around the neck. Butterfly heaved and grunted in a useless effort to breathe. Abe leaned down next to his ear. "The only reason you're still alive is because I know you rigged the truck thinking I'D be driving it. Otherwise, I'd snap your neck. You'll never use the arm again. Leave town or I'll kill you." Abe released his grip and shoved Butterfly forward. The big man's face smashed hard against the asphalt. Abe turned to walk away. Police sirens sounded in the distance.

"Knife!" one of the onlookers yelled.

Abe spun around and jerked back barely avoiding the blade slicing through the air. Butterfly lunged forward, the blade of the knife aimed at Abe's throat. Abe jumped back into a strong stance, his feet firmly planted. Butterfly flipped the knife in his hand and raised it high. As he brought it down to stab, Abe crossed his fisted hands just above his wrist and x-blocked Butterfly's arm. He gripped the man's right wrists and violently twisted the man's hand. Butterfly dropped the knife. Abe raised his right foot and stomped down hard just above the man's kneecap. Butterfly lashed out in agony. Abe grabbed Butterfly's hair, pulled his head back and thrusted a fist into his throat. Butterfly fell to the ground. Motionless.

Two Thornsby squad cars barreled into the parking lot. The doors swung open and four officers bailed out, two from each car. Abe raised his hands over his head and got down on his knees. One officer rushed over, pulled Abe's arms down behind his back and handcuffed him.

A man stepped forward from the observers. He wore a green work uniform. The patch on his right side just below his shoulder read *Porter*

Transmission Service. The patch on his left side read *Herb.* "It was all self-defense, officer," he said.

"That's right. Self-defense," a tall, bearded man affirmed.

One officer turned to the bystanders. "How many of you saw the whole thing?" They all raised their hands. "Would you be willing to issue written statements?" All answered in the affirmative.

Abe looked at them, a *thank you* smile on his face. He had been as shrewd as a serpent and as innocent as a dove. He watched as a Lincoln Town Car drove away from the restaurant. Thomas Hightower.

The police officer removed the handcuffs. Abe stood to his feet. The officer focused on Abe's bleeding eye. "You should have a doctor look at that," he said.

CHAPTER TWENTY-THREE

"There, that ought to do it," she said as she tied off the last stitch and cut the thread with medical scissors. "Your eye may be swollen for a few days. I'll give you a prescription for some pain medicine." She applied a salve to the suture and covered it with an adhesive bandage. "Stitches should be ready to come out in ten days. Won't leave much of a scar . . . if any. You can go to your family physician or any clinic to get them removed."

Abe raised up from the exam table and stood to his feet. He touched the top of the bandage with his fingertips. "Thank you, Dr. Patel. Am I good to go now?"

"Yes."

Abe exited the room and headed down the hallway. He didn't know what the status was for Butterfly. An ambulance came and hauled him away. To a hospital in Birmingham no doubt. Was he still alive? Abe didn't know. Didn't care.

Abe pushed open the door and entered the room. Mickey had his bed inclined, Reverend Washington sitting on the couch.

Mickey turned and looked at Abe. "Hey."

"Hey, Son. How you feeling?"

Abe walked over and stood at the foot of the bed.

"I'm fine. Doctor should be in any minute to take the bandage off my head. Least that's what the nurse said. What happened to your eye?"

"Ah . . . just a scratch. It'll be fine."

Reverend Washington rose from the couch and shook Abe's hand.

"Thanks for sitting with him," Abe said.

The faithful minister flashed his white smile. "Anytime."

The door swung open and in walked a man dressed in scrubs and a knee-length white, cotton jacket. A stethoscope hung from his neck. His name badge read *Dr. Jacob Benning*. He focused his attention on Mickey. "You ready to get that bandage off?"

"I sure am."

Dr. Benning removed a few pieces of medical tape and began unwrapping the gauze. When he finished, he tossed the soiled bandage in the waste can next to the bed, then gently removed the patch from Mickey's eye. Mickey opened it and wrestled the light in the room with a squint until his pupils adjusted. Dr. Benning placed the earpieces of the stethoscope in his ears and held the chestpiece over Mickey's heart.

"Sounds good. Have you been having any headaches or dizziness?"

"No sir."

"Appetite been good? Bowels been moving like they should?"

"Yessir."

"Let me see you get up and walk."

Mickey stood to his feet and held the back of his gown closed as he walked to the door and back.

"How do you feel?"

"I feel fine. I wanna go home."

"I tell you what. You stay here tonight. I'll come around first thing in the morning. If everything is still good, I'll let you go home. Deal?"

"Deal."

Dr. Benning turned to Abe and drew down his brow. "What happened to your eye?"

"Oh, just a little cut. No big deal."

The doctor relaxed his expression and nodded slightly. "Do you have any questions for me?"

"No sir. I appreciate all you've done."

"Glad to. Mickey's a strong boy. He should be able to start school next week. No problem."

"That's good news," Abe said.

Dr. Benning shook hands with Abe and Reverend Washington. He turned and cupped a hand on Mickey's shoulder. "Okay, Mickey. I'll see you in the morning."

"Okay."

Dr. Benning exited the room. Abe looked at his watch. "Click on the television, Mick. News should be about to come on."

Mickey reached for the remote and pushed the "ON" button. The television sprang into action. The closing credits of the Andy Griffith Show were making their changes as the familiar whistling tune of the Fishin' Hole played.

"Switch it over to ABC," Abe said.

Mickey pushed a button. The opening announcement of WBRC Channel 6 Birmingham was coming to a close. Abe, Mickey and Reverend Washington watched as a man dressed in a coat and tie and a woman dressed in ladies' business attire introduced themselves. The camera then gave the full screen to the woman and she began with the breaking story of the day.

"We have a story breaking near Pensacola, Florida. WBRC journalist, Larry Oliver, is on the scene. We turn there now for a full report. Larry"

The camera cut to a man in his mid-twenties. Lean build. Blonde hair. He held a microphone. "Thanks, Dana. Earlier today, US Customs and Border Patrol officials seized forty-eight containers of exotic animals off the coast of Garcon Point, Florida. The containers contained yellow-naped parrots, scarlet macaws and poison dart frogs. Authorities say the animals were being illegally smuggled into the US in order to be sold at numerous underground pet sales throughout the US. The animals are said to have a value of well over two hundred thousand dollars on the black market. Officials took five men into custody. They also seized guns, an undisclosed amount of cash, a cargo van and the fishing boat that was used to transport the animals. The boat in question is *The Lucky Mermaid*. It was being chartered at the time by two of the men that were arrested by US Customs and Border Patrol officials. However, the boat is owned by two men from Claxton, Alabama. Albert Speed, an automobile dealer and Thomas Hightower, a district judge. It is uncertain at this point if either

Speed or Hightower had any knowledge of the smuggling operation. The matter is currently under further investigation. Back to you, Dana."

The camera cut back to the Birmingham studio. The female news anchor made no comments about the report. Instead, she started talking about a potential worker strike at Delta Airlines.

"Okay, Mick. You can turn it off now." Abe said.

Mickey turned off the television. "Wow! So, that's what was going on."

"It'll be interesting to read the local newspapers for the next week or so," Abe said.

"The love of money," Reverend Washington said.

"Is the root of all evil," Abe said.

Reverend Washington shook hands with Mickey and then with Abe. "Well, I'm gonna be on my way. I've still got to get by the nursing home to see Mrs. Earlene Rogers. And Sunday's coming and my sermon is still in the oven."

"What are you preaching on?" Mickey said.

"Proverbs fourteen and verse twelve. There is a way which seemeth right unto a man, but the end thereof is the way of death."

"Sounds like a good one," Abe said.

"I'll be looking forward to it," Mickey said.

"Alright. I'll be expecting to see you gentlemen Sunday."

The minister turned to Abe. "You know to call me if you need anything."

"Yessir."

Reverend Washington walked out of the room.

• • •

Dan Thompson took his seat in Judge Thomas Hightower's chamber. He was dressed in dapper fashion. Navy blue double-breasted Calvin Klein suit. Bright red silk necktie with matching pocket handkerchief. Allen Edmond black wingtips.

Hightower's light brown dress coat draped from one of the wooden pegs of the coat rack near the door along with a green and beige paisley tie. The judicial figure leaned forward in his chair, his arms folded on the top of his stately mahogany desk. Several dark hairs, like sprigs of untrimmed grass, stuck out from his open collared oxford shirt.

"Mr. Thompson, it is rather unusual for the counsel for the defense to meet with a judge without the counsel for the plaintiff being present. So, why this peculiar change in protocol?"

"It's a matter of professional courtesy, Your Honor."

Hightower drew down his brow and narrowed his eyes. "I don't follow you. You'll have to explain."

Dan Thompson tugged at one of the cuff links of his French sleeves, his eyes fixed on Hightower's. "Well, Your Honor, given the fact that you have a personal as well as a business relationship with the plaintiff, we think it would be best if you recused yourself. Better yet, dismiss the case altogether."

Hightower huffed. "Are you insinuating that I'm unfit to preside over this case?"

"Exactly, Your Honor. We don't feel that we could get an unbiased ruling."

"That's nonsense. The law's the law. Plain and simple. Regardless of personal or business matters outside the courtroom."

"We'd hoped that Your Honor would have responded differently. But with things as they are, we will file a formal motion stating our concern and request. After all, it is our right and the proper formal procedure. Now, when might Your Honor's schedule allow for our motion?" Dan pulled a planner from his attaché case and opened it.

Hightower tightened his jaw, a look of contempt on his face. "It'll be at least six months."

Dan nodded. "That's fine. We're in no real rush." He flipped a few pages. "So . . . that would put us in the month of February." Dan pulled a Mont Blanc from inside his lapel and looked back down at the planner. "What day are we looking at?"

"I'll have to let you know."

Dan looked up and pushed up his bottom lip. "No problem. We'll wait to hear from you, then."

"Counselor, I hope we're done here. I have court in an hour."

Dan closed the planner, stuffed it back in his attache´ and stood to his feet. "That's all I have. Good day, Judge."

Dan exited the room and walked to his car where Abe was waiting. He opened the driver door and got in.

"Well, how did that go?" Abe said.

Dan tossed the attache´ into the back seat. "Just like we thought. Took it personal. Won't budge. We'll have to wait and see when he grants an audience for our motion. The longer, the better. Time is our friend."

CHAPTER TWENTY-FOUR

The totaled black Blazer was replaced. Just like Abe had said. Mickey rolled into the student parking lot of Claxton High School driving a blue early 1990s version of the same model. Big tires. Fog lights. Chrome bumper. Lolita in the passenger's seat. Was there ever a question?

Whispers and rumors about the fight at the golf course circulated throughout the student body. Everyone knew that Mickey Tucker was no kid to mess with. A humiliated, scholarship-stricken Billy Joe Speed was living proof. Every day his mother delivered him to school in their newly acquired handicap van. He attended classes in his wheelchair up until the Christmas break. When school started back after the new year, Albert Speed's boy did return to campus without the wheelchair . . . but with a crutch under each arm, nonetheless.

In mid-February, Dan Thompson received a letter from Thomas Hightower. It notified him of the date that had been set for the formal motion to be entered. When the day arrived, Dan, Abe and Mickey entered Hightower's courtroom. Clint Mims, Albert Speed and Billy Joe were already seated. Hightower emerged from his chamber and took his seat on the bench. He made a few introductory remarks, then recognized Dan.

Dan stood to his feet.

"Your Honor, the defense makes the motion that the case be dismissed as we do not see a path to a fair and just ruling given the nature of your close personal relationship with the plaintiff. And, if you do not dismiss the case, that you show your high regard for jurisprudence by recusing yourself from it."

Hightower looked down at Dan, his expression cool. "The motion must be formally entered. Do you have a written motion to present?"

"Permission to approach the bench, Your Honor."

"Permission granted."

Dan stepped to the bench and handed the document to Hightower.

"Motion received and duly noted. You may return to your seat, counselor."

Dan returned to his seat.

Clint Mims raised his hand. "Permission to speak, Your Honor."

"Permission granted."

"Your Honor, in order for the case to be dismissed on the basis the defense has requested, it must be proven that the bench is jaded to the point that a clear, unbiased judgment cannot be rendered. The defense has done nothing more than present a formal motion. It is incumbent upon the defense to present here the necessary evidence proving such relationships exist."

"Point well-taken."

Hightower turned his attention back to Dan. "Do you have evidence to present?"

"Yes, Your Honor. Permission to approach the bench again."

"Permission granted."

Dan walked back to the bench and handed Hightower a stack of papers.

"Your Honor, what you have is a list of the members of the Claxton Country Club. Please note that you and Albert Speed, Billy Joe Speed's father, are both members. You also have a copy of the title as well as the bill of sale for a commercial fishing boat. The Hull Identification Number or HIN for short, matches that of the boat known as *The Lucky Mermaid*, the very boat that was seized last year for being used to smuggle exotic animals into the US illegally. The boat is titled to Your Honor and Albert Speed jointly."

"Your Honor, permission to speak," Clint Mims interrupted.

Hightower, without expression or emotion, raised his hand signaling Dan to pause. He turned to Mims. "Permission granted."

"Thank you, Your Honor. A thorough police investigation was conducted last year, and it was discovered that the boat in question was chartered by two of the individuals who were arrested at the time of the crime. Neither you nor Mr. Speed had any knowledge of their smuggling activities. As a matter of fact, the lease agreement states that the boat was to be used for commercial fishing purposes only."

Dan raised his hand. "Your Honor, if I may."

With a tight smile on his face, Hightower turned to Dan. "Yes, Counselor. Go ahead."

"Your Honor, the reason I bring this up is not to suggest wrongdoing on your and Mr. Speed's part, but simply to show that you owned the boat jointly as business partners."

"Your Honor," Mims interrupted again.

Hightower turned to him.

"Yes, Mr. Mims."

"Thank you, Your Honor. It should be noted that just because two people have a business partnership does not always mean they have a personal relationship. As a matter of fact, many business partners have animosity toward one another. For example, it is common knowledge that band members of several world-famous music groups, though they travel and perform together, actually have great conflict with one another as well as hard feelings toward each another. Groups like The Eagles and Creedence Clearwater Revival. Also, it is public record that some of James Brown's band members filed suit against him for not paying them properly. So, business partnerships are not sufficient evidence to establish that those partners are personal friends. Neither does an organization's membership role give evidence of personal relationships among its members. I'm a member of my neighborhood homeowner's association, but I don't really even know the neighbors who live three houses down from me on my street."

Mims stopped talking.

"Mr. Mims are you finished?" Hightower said.

"Yes, Your Honor."

Hightower looked at Dan. "Mr. Thompson, do you have any other evidence you wish to present?"

"No, Your Honor."

Hightower picked up the papers, pushed back in his chair and studied them for a few seconds, then cleared his throat. "I see no reason why the case shouldn't move forward to litigation. Furthermore, after listening to both the counsel for the defense and the counsel for the plaintiff I see no reason why I should recuse myself. Therefore, I will see both of you in court. Gentlemen, consider this matter settled."

Hightower rapped his gavel twice, rose from his seat and exited the courtroom. Dan leaned over to Abe and Mickey. "Another award-winning performance. We have our work cut out for us."

Clint Mims and Albert Speed engaged in jovial talk, laughing and shaking hands. Billy Joe kept his head down, a blank stare on his face. They all rose from their seats and began making their way out of the courtroom. As they did, Albert Speed approached Abe. "Mr. Loomis, could you and I have a personal word with one another?"

Clint Mims kept walking. Abe looked to Dan for advice. Dan shrugged and nodded. "You can talk to him if you want to. I'll be just outside the door."

Dan and Mickey walked out and into the hallway.

Albert Speed faced Abe squarely. "I'd like for you and I to have a good gentleman's understanding."

"And just what might that understanding be?"

"I realize that I'll never be able to match you in a physical confrontation. You maimed my personal bodyguard for the rest of his life. And he was a former professional boxer. He moved back home to Louisiana. He's pretty much useless. But I just want you to know something." He looked Abe in the eyes like a serpent at its prey. "For years, I've had my way in this town. I don't intend for that to change. You're just a bump in the road. A pea gravel in my shoe. Because of you, my boy will never achieve his dreams. So, I'm going to hit you where it hurts. That welfare brat you've adopted, he's going to pay. And I'm going do everything in my power to send you to hell in the process."

Abe flared his nostrils and drew in close to Albert Speed's face. "Well, from one gentleman to another, get ready." He raised his chin a bit and curled his upper lip.

Dan pushed the door of the courtroom open and leaned inside. "Abe, is everything alright here?"

Abe kept eyes fixed on Albert Speed's. "Yeah. We were just finishing our friendly conversation."

Albert Speed gave a tight, devilish grin. Abe turned and headed toward Dan.

CHAPTER TWENTY-FIVE

The scheduled trial date was three weeks away. Abe thought it might be a good time to add a new pocketknife to his collection. The bell dinged as pushed the door open. He and Mickey walked inside, instantly greeted by the pleasant aroma of parched peanuts and freshly popped popcorn. Mickey headed to the source of the appetizing smells, Abe to the familiar glass display case. As usual, Ira Cooper sat on a stool, his knees bent, his feet resting on one of the stool's leg supports. The adjuster on one of his Overall galluses was an inch higher than the other. A Cattleman's Association cap was pushed up on high on his forehead. The slogan on it read *Eat More Beef.*

"Well, well. You knife shopping today?" Ira Cooper said.

"I am if my favorite brand is on sale."

The beloved business owner shot Abe a big southern grin. "You're timing is perfect. All Tree Brands are thirty percent off today only." He got up from the stool and walked to one side of the display case. "I got a new one in I've been wanting to show you." He slid open one of the back glass doors and reached inside. He fisted a large pocketknife and handed it to Abe. "Ain't it a beauty?"

Abe pulled open one of the blades.

"It's a 2000 commemorative. Limited production," Ira Cooper said.

"I'll take it."

"Ain't cheap. Even with the discount, it'll run you close to a hundred dollars."

"Ring it up, Mr. Cooper. It's perfect."

. . .

Mickey sat in his truck with the motor running as Abe locked the doors. *Big Boy Toys* had another good day. A couple had driven into town from Macon, Georgia. When they started on their journey back to the peach state, the man sat behind the wheel of the pickup truck they'd arrived in. His wife, on the other hand, sat behind the wheel of a 1969 Dodge Super Bee. Purple. Her favorite color. The transaction had netted an eleven-thousand-dollar profit. William Fleming pulled out of the parking lot, eager to get home and tell his wife and son they'd be leaving the next morning for The Smoky Mountains. It'd be their first time—ever. Before Pamela Baldwin left for the day Abe handed her an envelope containing three Benjamin Franklin's. They'd come in handy, no doubt, as she and her daughter, Teresa, were still settling into their starter home south of town.

Abe climbed in and Mickey pulled onto the main drag of Claxton. As they rode by the Country Club, Abe noticed Albert Speed, Thomas Hightower and Probate Judge Willard Logan walking along a fairway, each with his bag of clubs slung over one shoulder. No personal relationship huh? What a crock of crap.

They rolled through the last traffic light on the north side of town and Mickey kicked up the speed to fifty-five. "I think this truck runs better than the one I wrecked."

Abe continued gazing out the passenger window. Unresponsive.

Mickey turned to him. "Don't you think?"

Abe snapped back to awareness. "I'm sorry, Son. What did you say?"

"I said, 'I think this truck runs better than the one I wrecked.'"

"I'm sure. I had William go through it from bumper to bumper. Take care of it. Keep the oil changed and I bet it'll last you a long time."

"I'll be a junior this year."

"A junior. Wow. That means your first prom is coming up. Ought to be fun. You're a good dancer." Abe bumped Mickey on the shoulder with the back on his hand and smiled. "Who you gonna ask?"

"You already know."

"Lolita?"

"Yup. She's the only girl for me. I sure hope she says 'yes.'"

"I don't think you have anything to worry about. That girl wouldn't give another boy the time of day."

The evening was wrestling the daylight into submission when Mickey and Abe pulled up next to the panther. Abe got out, snatched the envelope from under the mascot statue's neck and was back in the truck in under thirty seconds. Mickey pulled away as Abe tore it open. He slid out the sheet of paper, unfolded it and began to read.

Time to play hardball. If Hightower resides over the case Mickey will go to prison. Hightower has a BAR exam secret. It's what killed the old man. Expose it and half the battle will be won. Your lawyer needs to talk to Wyatt Edmonds. Marshall County Correctional Facility. Holly Springs, MS. I'm probably a dead man for telling you this.

• • •

Dan Thompson pushed his driver's license and business card under the opening at the bottom of the bullet proof plexiglass. The lady seated behind it reviewed them, then passed them back to him along with a photo ID badge that had been prepared ahead of time. As Dan approached the metal detector an armed security guard patted him down, had him take off his shoes, socks and belt and inspected his attache´ case. Dan walked through the device with his hands raised over his head. Once on the other side, his belongings were given back to him. Dan put his shoes and socks back on. A buzzer sounded and iron bars slid to one side allowing entrance into the belly of the facility. "This way," the officer said. Dan picked up his brief case and followed. Prisoners, dressed in one of four color-striped scrubs, passed him by as he walked through the hallway.

Dan knew the protocol. Green. The most trusted inmates. Black. Those for whom early parole was not an option. Red. The most violent offenders. Yellow. Men under discipline for bad behavior.

The security officer led Dan into the cafeteria. He pointed to a heavy door at the far end of the large room. "He'll be coming in from over there. Sit wherever you prefer."

Dan walked to a long table near the door. Set his attache´ on the table and took a seat at the end of the bench. A buzzer sounded. The door slid open to one side. In walked a man in his late fifties. A fresh haircut that was far from subtle. Clean-shaven face. Green striped bottoms and a crisp, white top. All of which were the state penal system's attempts at making good impressions on visitors. Especially when those visitors were lawyers.

The man walked over to the table and sat down. Dan offered him a handshake across the table. The man obliged.

"Thank you, Mr. Edmonds, for agreeing to meet with me. I'm Dan Thompson. I'm a lawyer and I represent a teenage boy. He beat up an older boy in self-defense and the prosecution is bent and determined on sending him to prison."

Wyatt Edmonds nodded. "Okay. So, how do you think I can be of assistance?" He lifted his hands and cut his eyes to one side and then the other. "Look around. I'm not exactly in a position to be a part of your defense team."

"You can be a big part of my team."

"How's that?"

"Thomas Hightower is the judge presiding over the case. I understand you might know something about his BAR exam."

Edmonds shook his head and sighed. "So, Hightower is a judge now. Didn't get to follow in his dad's footsteps after all. Huh?"

"Do you know something about his BAR exam?"

Edmonds leaned forward. "I'm due to get out in eighteen months and nine days. My plan is to keep my nose clean and my mouth shut. I'll never be able practice law again, but I can have some semblance of a normal life. Maybe even get married again. I ain't that old."

"So, you do know something. Something that is so significant that you fear it could cause you trouble."

Edmonds raised his eyebrows and shrugged his shoulders.

"What if I could get you immunity if you help me? Maybe even get your sentence commuted."

Edmonds huffed. "You'd have to have friends in REALLY high places for that. I'll stick to my plan." He put his hand up to his lips and made a motion like he was turning an imaginary key.

"I'd say the US Attorney General is high enough. Wouldn't you?"

Edmonds cocked his head and looked at Dan from the corners of his eyes. "You serious?"

"He attended my wedding."

Edmonds stared into Dan's eyes and sighed again. "Yeah, and Elvis works at a car wash in Tupelo."

Dan opened his brief case and pulled out a photograph of two couples. He held the photo up for Edmonds to see. The two ladies wore sleek dresses and outlandish fancy hats. The two men wore seersucker suits and fedoras. "This was taken at this year's Kentucky Derby. Fusaichi Pegasus won by a length and a half."

Dan returned the picture to the briefcase. He pulled out a sheet of paper and slid it over to Edmonds. "This is a signed letter from the US Attorney General himself. Notice the official letterhead. You don't see it every day. It states that you will have immunity if you help me. Read it."

Wyatt Edmonds eyes moved back and forth as he read.

"Edmonds, you're in here because you tried to bribe a judge. Problem was the judge was honest. Now, I'm not so sure about Hightower. If you know something that could help get this kid out of his courtroom the attorney general and I would really appreciate it. What do you say?"

Edmonds handed the letter back to Dan.

"Alright, Counselor. Let's play ball."

Dan pushed the letter to one side and pulled a legal pad from the case. "I'm all ears."

"I used to be an attorney in Dothan, Alabama. For four years I served on the examination board for the state. The board grades the BAR exams.

We got paid 2 grand for every section we graded. I graded essay portions dealing with criminal and constitutional law. One day I'm at the greyhound track down in Pensacola with another board member. We are having some drinks and betting on the dogs. The guy was hitting the Jim Beam hard. Before long it started loosening him up and he started talking about. T.H. Hightower. You ever heard of him?"

Dan shook his head. "No."

"T.H. Hightower was a legend in the state of Alabama. I mean the man was a lawyer par excellent. Invincible. Owned the courtroom. Well, this guy starts telling me that Hightower has a son who will never pass the BAR. Says the kid will fly through the multiple choice no problem. But will crumble when it comes to the essays. Then, he tells me he has been approached by someone about helping the kid out. Says it would be worth fifty grand for the kid to get a passing grade. Mind you, the guy that's talking to me grades the BAR too. Civil and property essays. I asked him, 'How can you help someone pass the BAR?' You know. You're a lawyer. You have to show your ID every time you sit. You have to have an NCBE number. You're observed the whole time. It's impossible. This guy tells me that we can get some of the kid's handwriting samples so we know which essays are his. He says the kid can pretend to be sick on the scheduled test days and the state BAR will permit him to take it in an alternative location. So, he and I agree to be graders for the alternative location where Hightower's kid is going to be. Turns out, Thomas Hightower's not the only one. There're two other applicants at the alternate location, but that's not a problem for us because we know the kid's handwriting. When the papers are turned in we made sure we got his. Sure enough, the kid's essays were bad. And I don't mean just bad. I mean terrible. I don't know how he passed undergraduate English. We scored his essays just high enough for him to make the points he needed. A week later, after the grades are released, we go back to the dog track because that's where we were to get paid. A guy shows up and pays us twenty-five grand a piece."

"Was it Thomas Hightower?"

"No, it was someone else."

Dan pulled out a newspaper clipping that pictured the members of the Claxton Country Club and slid it across the table to Wyatt Edmonds. Is the man who gave you the money in this picture?"

Edmonds studied it, then put a finger on Albert Speed. "That's him."

"You sure?"

"A man hands you twenty-five grand and you never forget his face."

Dan returned the clipping to his brief case.

"What about the other grader," he said. "Did you keep up with him after that?"

"Off and on till the Mob killed him."

"What for?"

"Gambling debt. It got so bad that he once blackmailed T.H. Hightower. Told him about his son's BAR exam. Said he'd spill the goods unless he coughed up a hundred grand. I don't know if the old man ever paid it. He had a heart attack and died shortly after. I don't know for sure, but I've always believed it was because of the news of his kid's BAR."

CHAPTER TWENTY-SIX

Two weeks after Dan's visit with Wyatt Edmonds, local media outlets broke the story. The Alabama Attorney General suspended Thomas Hightower from the bench. A federal investigation followed. Nine months later, when the investigation concluded, Hightower cut a plea deal with the Feds in exchange for a reduced sentence. A nine-year holiday at The Bullock County Correctional Facility. He'd never darken a courtroom again.

Albert Speed was never questioned as the "supposed" cash transaction could not be substantiated. Hightower, in his confession, never mentioned Albert Speed. Edmonds' accomplice couldn't corroborate the story because he was six feet under. And Edmonds' story was just that and nothing else—a story. No sane prosecutor would drag a man to court over just one man's word alone, especially if that man was a disgraced, corrupt attorney serving out his sentence in a Mississippi prison.

• • •

Lolita said yes when Mickey asked her to the junior/senior prom. His reputation and dance skills, coupled with her inner and outer beauty, made them quite the item. Billy Joe Speed attended, accompanied by the daughter of one of his father's country club associates. The two of them spent the evening talking to those of "their kind." They never once took to the dance floor. It would have been awkward, even embarrassing perhaps, if Billy Joe would've tripped over his cane in front of an audience consisting of nearly half the student body and most of the faculty.

. . .

Abe and William Fleming continued to bring classic automobiles back from the dead and sell them for handsome profits. Pamela Baldwin grew into a formidable business manager for them. In addition to her hourly wages, Abe saw to it that she received a bonus with every car *Big Boy Toys* sold.

. . .

It was the first Friday night since school had adjourned for the summer. *Casa Amigos* teemed with customers, many of which were students celebrating their upcoming three months of freedom. Abe and Mickey sat at a booth along the front wall of the restaurant. They curbed their appetites with chips and salsa as they waited for Dahlia to bring them their meal.

Abe scooped out a small pile of salsa with a tortilla chip and shoved it in his mouth. "I brought you here tonight for two reasons."

Mickey took a long drink of his soda. "Okay. What are they?"

"First of all, I know you like this place. So, we came to celebrate a little. You had a great junior year. Made good grades. I'm proud of you, Son."

Mickey smiled. "I love it when you say that."

"Say what?"

"That you're proud of me. Mama used to always say that. It never gets old."

"Well, it's true."

"What's the second reason?"

"I want us to talk about your future . . . you know, your career."

Dahlia walked up, full plates in both hands. "Hot plates. Hot plates."

She set a plate of burritos with rice and beans down in front of Abe, a plate of tacos with rice and beans down in front of Mickey. "Can I get you anything else? Refills?"

Abe looked up at Dahlia. "I think we're good for now."

"Okay. Enjoy. I'll be back to check on you later."

She turned and walked off. Abe and Mickey looked at each other and bowed their heads. Abe prayed a brief prayer and they dug in.

Mickey picked up one of the tacos. "I've been thinking a lot about that lately." He took a bite and chewed till he could speak again. "I really like business. Remember when we first met, and you taught me how to make money selling candy bars?"

"So, you remember that little experiment, huh?" Abe said and bit a big chunk out of one of the burritos.

"It was great. It really helped me to see how business works. And now I see you and Mr. Fleming doing so well. I really think I want to start a business. Don't get me wrong. College is cool. I mean, how can someone be a doctor or teacher if they don't go to college? But you don't necessarily have to go to college to make money."

Abe nodded. "Think you want to go in the direction of an entrepreneur?"

Mickey shoved some more food in his mouth. "I really do. Look how well you and Mr. Fleming are doing selling classic cars and trucks. I bet he's never been to college."

A loud explosion made the table tremble. Everyone in the restaurant paused from their eating and discussions, jolted by the commotion. Mickey looked at Abe, his eyes open wide. "What was that?"

Abe cocked his head. "I don't know, but I'd say it caused some damage. Whatever it was. Sounded pretty close."

Sirens began sounding. Abe rose from his seat. "Let's step outside and see if we can tell."

Mickey got up and they exited the restaurant. People were beginning to stop and stare at the ball of fire and smoke that rolled in the distance.

"Looks like it's in Peachtree Corners Subdivision," Abe said.

"I wonder if anybody got hurt," Mickey said.

Abe looked around, then back up at the fireball. "We could jump in the truck and go check it out, but we'd probably just be in the way."

A police car sped by, lights flashing, siren sounding. Then, a firetruck. The sirens of other emergency vehicles sounded from different directions.

"We might as well go finish our dinner. We'll find out soon enough," Abe said.

By the end of the evening word had spread throughout Claxton that the explosion had occurred at the home of Probate Judge Willard Logan. His wife and son, Brad, were not at home at the time, but the judge's charred remains were found in the rubble.

The next morning Abe roused Mickey from his sleep.

"I'm going into town. If you want to sleep in, that's fine. But if you want to go, you need to get up."

Mickey turned in his bed, stretched and rubbed his eyes. He rose from his slumber, pulled on a shirt and a pair of gym shorts.

"There's a pan of biscuits on the stove. You can grab a couple on the way out. I'll be waiting in the truck."

Abe walked out of the room. Mickey slipped his bare feet into his Sperry Topsiders and walked to the bathroom. After brushing the morning breath out of his mouth and urinating, he grabbed two biscuits from the pan on the stove, an orange soda from the fridge and headed out the door. He climbed into the passenger seat of the truck and Abe backed out of the driveway.

In less than ten minutes they were pulling up to the curb at Ira Cooper's Hardware and Farm Store. Abe got out of the truck and hustled through the door. Ira sat in his usual spot. The stool behind the glass display counter. He wore his typical attire. Faded Liberty Overalls. A Cattleman's Association cap. Abe walked over to him. He did not greet Abe. Nor did he smile. His chin quivered as he uttered his words. "Tree Brands are not on sale today and never will be again." His eyes welled. He pulled a handkerchief from his back pocket and wiped the moisture away. Abe leaned down. He propped his elbows on the top of the glass and covered his face with both hands. Ira Cooper sniffled. "You know who did it, Mr. Loomis. This town needs to be rid of that man."

Abe raised his head and looked Cooper in the eyes. "Yes, it certainly does."

• • •

The eighteen-wheeler pulled into the parking lot of *Big Boy Toys*. Mickey walked outside and gazed at the vehicles in the car hauler the big rig towed. All were Chevrolets. The driver jumped down from the tractor cab and walked around the front of his truck. "Where do you want them?"

Mickey raised a hand toward the back of the parking lot. "Just put them back there."

"When I get them unloaded, I'll need to pick up a check for the delivery charge."

"See Pamela inside. She'll take care of you."

The trucker adjusted the Georgia Bulldogs cap on his head. "10-4. I'll be done in about thirty minutes."

True to his word, in less than thirty minutes, the car hauler was an empty giant steel frame on wheels. Seven sedans and two pickup trucks, purchased earlier in the week from the *Atlanta Auto Auction*, lined the back of the parking lot of *Big Boy Toys*. The driver walked into the sales office and stepped up to the counter. He handed Pamela a receipt. She pulled open a filing cabinet drawer and produced a large, hardback checkbook. It made a thud on the surface of the counter when she opened it. Abe emerged from his office and greeted the driver with a handshake. "I'm Abe."

"Carl," the man replied.

Mickey walked in from outside. "That's my son, Mickey. You'll be seeing a lot of him."

The driver nodded and reached out a hand for a shake. Mickey responded in like fashion.

"When will the other nine be here?" Abe said.

"I'm driving straight back to Atlanta. I'll have them here by lunch tomorrow. No problem. You gain an hour when you cross the state line into Alabama."

Pamela handed him the check she'd just written. The man smiled as he took the check. He glanced down at her ringless left hand, then looked back into her face. "Thank you, ma'am. Will you be here tomorrow?"

Abe looked at Mickey, winked, then turned his attention back to the man. "She's here every day," Abe said and smiled. "She runs the place."

Pamela blushed and grinned.

The man folded the check and slid it into his shirt pocket. "Well, I better get back on the road." He raised an open palm as he backed up a few steps. "I'll see ya'll tomorrow." He looked at Pamela, touched the brim of his cap and turned and walked out the door.

Abe raised his eyebrows to Pamela. "I bet he'll be here way before lunchtime tomorrow."

Pamela blushed again. "Awe, cut it out now. He was just being polite."

"Oh yeah. He was being polite. No doubt about that."

Pamela shook her head, a broad grin stretched on her face.

Abe's expression turned serious. He looked at Mickey. "Alright, Mr. Businessman, you got nine cars out there you gotta move. Clean'em up. Check'em out. Oil. Antifreeze. Brakes. You know what to do."

Mickey started toward the front door. "I'll get on them."

Abe turned to Pamela. "Remember. We have a strategy. Two hundred dollars over cost. No more. We're going to war with Speed. He's got too much overhead and too much pride to sell used cars that cheap. Before long, people all over the county will know where to find the best used Chevrolets at the best prices."

"Got it," Pamela said. "This is gonna be fun."

Abe clicked his tongue. "I don't know about fun, but it'll be dramatic. I'm sure."

Within an hour Mickey had one of the sedans and one of the pickups prepped and lined up next to the road. He wrote the prices on the windshields with a thick, white dealer marker. A mid-eighties Ford F-150 pulled into the parking lot, smoke blowing from its exhaust, all four hubcaps missing. The back right quarter panel made a statement. A fender bender sometime in the past. The driver stopped near the front of the sales office. The truck coughed and backfired when he turned off the ignition. The man got out and walked to the Chevy truck. Mickey tossed his rag in the bucket of soapy water and joined the man.

The man took a tour around the truck.

"Is the price on the windshield right?"

"Yessir."

The man pulled open the driver door and looked inside. "Clean as a whistle too."

"We just got it in. Wanna hear it run?"

"Yes, Son. I believe I do."

Mickey trotted to the office, then trotted back holding the keys. "Here you go."

The man slid into the driver's seat, put the key in the ignition and turned it. The engine fired up. The man revved it several times and released the hood. Mickey raised it and the man joined him in front of the engine.

"Got a five point three liter V8 in it," Mickey said as the man pulled the dip stick to check the oil. "

"Looks and runs good," the man said. "I've been a Ford man since I was a kid. But for your price I could be a Chevy man."

"Wanna take it for a test-drive?"

The man shut the hood down hard. "Son, I believe I will."

The man climbed back under the steering wheel of the truck and pulled onto the road. In less than an hour he was sitting in the office across from Pamela, signing paperwork and counting out the cash.

At 11:30 the next day, Carl rolled back into *Big Boy Toys*, his car hauler loaded with nine more Chevrolets. With the same efficiency as the day before, he unloaded the automobiles and parked them. By the end of the day, Mickey had three pickups, two SUVs and ten sedans lined close to the road. Each gleaming in the sunshine with bold, white numbers written on their windshields. It would have been twelve sedans, but two had sold earlier in the day.

A late model Impala pulled into the dealership. A man got out of the car, a clip board in his hand. He pulled a pen from the pocket of his silk, Hawaiian shirt and began walking between the inventory, making notes as he went. Mickey greeted him with a cheerful hello and handshake.

"Are you the boss around here?" the man said.

"Not hardly. Would you like for me to go get him?"

"Yes, I'd like to speak to him."

Mickey walked away and returned, Abe accompanying him. "What can I do for you today, Sir?" Abe said.

"You're a new dealer in town. Aren't you?"

Abe released his smile. "Been selling restored classics for several months. Just started selling newer used cars."

"Um Hm. You got SOME kinda sharp prices" The man ran one hand along the trunk of a Monte Carlo. "About the best I've ever seen."

Abe nodded. "Yessir. We aim to offer the best used cars at the best prices around."

"All you have is Chevrolets. No Fords. No Toyotas or Nissans."

"No sir, I only sell Chevrolets."

The man scratched the scalp of his head with an index finger. "That's odd. Why Chevrolets only?"

Mickey piped in. "We plan to—" Abe put his hand on Mickey's shoulder. Mickey got the message. It was time for him to stay quiet.

"It's just our strategy," Abe said. "We're just about to close for the day. Are you in the market for a used car?"

"Not just one. All of them."

Mickey glanced up at Abe, his eyebrows peaked. He mouthed the word "awesome." Abe maintained a cool expression.

"All of them?" he said

"Yes," the man said.

Abe wrinkled his brow. "All fifteen?"

"Yes. I'm a wholesaler. I buy for dealers."

"Uh huh. I see. And which dealers do you buy for?"

The man continued to walk and look at the cars. Abe and Mickey followed him.

"Oh, some here. Some there."

Abe looked down at Mickey and half winked. He looked back at the man. "Really just for Albert Speed's dealership. Correct."

The man grinned and sighed as if he'd been caught scheming. "Nothing gets past you. Does it, Mr.—?"

"Loomis. But you already knew that."

The man shrugged his shoulders. "Hey. Money's money. Right? Whether it comes out of different pockets or just one."

"If that one pocket is Albert Speed's, then it makes a big difference."

"So, how about we finalize the sale first thing tomorrow morning? Say nine o'clock?"

Abe paused, then nodded. "We'll plan on seeing you then."

The man reached out his hand. Abe obliged and shook his in return but said nothing, any semblance of southern hospitality washed from his face.

By the time the man arrived the next morning, Mickey had all the numbers washed from the windshields of the Chevrolets. The man got out of his car, the same clip board in his hand. He walked into the sales office. Abe met him at the counter. The man pulled a checkbook from the inside pocket of his blue sport coat. "Alright, I added up the numbers and the total is—"

"Incorrect," Abe said.

The man looked at Abe as if he'd been stumped by a hard question. "Beg your pardon? I ran them three times before I got here."

"The prices you wrote down are for retail customers."

The man slapped the top of the counter. "I see. You have a wholesale price since Mr. Speed is buying all of them." He rapped his knuckles a few times. "Now, that's good business."

Abe smiled. "Glad you think so."

The man held his pen on the check he intended to write. "Okay, what's the total?"

"The total is eighteen hundred dollars more per unit. So just add twenty-seven thousand to the number you have."

The man slammed the pen down on the counter. He looked at Abe through fiery eyes. "Why, that's ludicrous. What are you trying to pull?"

"I'm saying that for Albert Speed to buy those cars he's gonna have to pay twenty-seven thousand dollars more than what you told him."

"Mr. Speed can't pay you that kind of money for the cars."

"Then, he'll need to buy his cars somewhere else."

The man closed the check book and returned it to the inside of his jacket. "Mr. Speed's not going to like this. He's a man who's used to getting his way." The man turned on his heels and headed to the door.

"You tell Mr. Speed I said hello," Abe said as the man reached for the door handle.

The man waved him off with one hand without looking back, then flung open the door and walked out.

Chapter Twenty-Seven

Mickey handed the husband the keys to the car. The man turned to his wife. "Do you want to drive it first?"

"No. You go ahead," she said.

The man took his place behind the wheel, his wife the passenger seat. The man cranked the car.

"Good Lord, this thing sounds like a race car," she said.

The man shook his head, his face grimacing with disappointment. He looked up at Mickey. "Something's wrong with it. We can't buy it like this."

"It was running perfect yesterday. I don't know why it's running so loud all the sudden," Mickey said.

The man turned to his wife. "Why don't we drive the first one we looked at. It cost a little more, but it's two years newer and has leather seats."

The lady agreed, and they got out of the car.

"I'll get the keys," Mickey said. He fast walked to the office and pulled open the door. "Something's wrong with the Impala. Sounds terrible."

Abe shot Mickey a confused look. "I thought it was running fine yesterday."

"It was. But it's not now."

Mickey pulled a set of keys from a nail on the wall. "They want to drive the Malibu now."

As he headed out the door, Abe fell in behind him. Mickey rejoined the couple at the second car. He handed the keys to the husband. "Here you go."

The couple opened the front doors and got in. The man inserted the key into the ignition and turned it. The engine roared. The lady put her hands over her ears. "This one's louder than the first one. I guess that's why the prices are so cheap."

Abe shook his head and dropped down to his belly. He inspected the car's under carriage, then stood back up. "Someone cut the catalytic converter off. Must have done it in the night." He began inspecting the other vehicles.

"If you want to come back in a few days I'm sure we'll have them fixed," Mickey said to the man and his wife. "I promise you they're good cars. We don't sell any junk."

The couple got out of the car. "Okay, we'll come back in a few days," the man said. He and his wife returned to the car they'd arrived in and drove away.

"The cats have been cut off every one of them," Abe said, walking back to Mickey.

"Who do you think did it?"

Abe raised his open hands at his sides. "Who do you think?"

"Albert Speed?"

"Exactly."

Pamela opened the front door of the sales office and leaned her head out. "Abe, you got a phone call."

"Let me go answer this. Go get William. All the cats will have to be replaced."

Abe walked toward the front door. Mickey headed to the shop area where he found William Fleming under the hood of a 71 Firebird. He and Abe's next flipping project.

"Mr. Fleming, we got a problem."

Fleming strained as he tried to loosen a bolt with a socket and breaking bar. "What's that, Mick?"

"Someone cut the catalytic converters off of every one of the cars we brought in from Atlanta."

Fleming turned and looked at Mickey. "You've got to be kidding."

"No sir. Did it last night."

The seasoned grease monkey laid the breaking bar down on the top of the car's breather cover, pulled the rag from his back pocket and wiped his hands. "Come on, let's go check it out."

William Fleming was under a Silverado 1500 when Abe returned from taking the phone call. "William, can you believe this?"

"The cuts are all fresh. Someone took a reciprocating saw to them last night."

"Have Pamela order the replacements," Abe said. "I'll pay you to put them on. How long you think it'll take you?"

"I can probably do them all in a day and half once we get the parts."

"Alright. Mickey and I are about to leave. We have to take a trip. Won't be back till tomorrow night, probably."

"No problem. I'll get'em taken care of. Don't worry."

"Where we going?" Mickey said.

"I'll tell you on the way home. Got a long drive. We'll have to pack a bag."

. . .

Abe and Mickey parked in the midst of charter buses, church vans and other out-of-state vehicles. *Lambert's Restaurant* in Sikeston, Missouri was jumping with business. As usual. Abe and Mickey walked in to the sight of a line of hungry patrons waiting to be seated.

Abe put a hand on Mickey's shoulder. "Come on. She said she'd be waiting for us."

They worked their way to the hostess counter where they were greeted by a young girl wearing blue jeans and a red and black plaid short-sleeve shirt.

"Mam, we are meeting a party who's already seated," Abe said.

"You must be Mr. Loomis."

"Yes, I am."

"Your party said we could expect you. Follow me"

Abe and Mickey followed the girl through the crowded dining hall to a booth where a lady sat alone, a troubled look on her face. She rose to her feet when they arrived at the table.

"Please. No need to get up," Abe said and sat down across from her. Mickey flanked him on one side.

"Mrs. Logan, thank you for calling. This is my son, Mickey."

Mickey loved it when Abe introduced him as his son.

"Nice to meet you," Mickey said.

The lady nodded. "Brad's told me all about you."

Who was this lady? What all had Brad told her? How was Mickey supposed to respond? Heck, he and Brad hardly ever spoke to one another at school. And it was all Brad's fault. Because of that whole skeleton hand fiasco.

She turned her attention to Abe. "Mr. Loomis, is it okay for me to speak with Mickey here?"

"Perfectly," Abe said.

"What may I get you to drink?" a female voice said. Abe and Mickey turned to look. A middle-aged husky lady stood at the edge of the table.

"I'll have sweet tea," Abe said.

"I'll have the same," Mickey said.

A large plastic cup filled with water sat on the table in front of the mysterious woman. She must have ordered it before Abe and Mickey arrived.

"I'll bring your drinks and, then take your orders," the waitress said and walked away.

"Hot rolls," a man bellowed out from the other side of the room.

Abe held up his hand and the man threw him one of the large, warm pieces of bread. Mickey held up a hand and the man launched one to him.

Abe looked at the woman. "You want one?"

She shook her head. "No, I'm not really hungry. I'm just having something to drink."

The waitress returned with two large, plastic cups filled with sweet tea. She set one down in front of Mickey, the other in front of Abe. "What can I get you to eat?"

"Catfish," Abe said.

"Chicken tenders," Mickey said.

"Coming right up." She turned and walked away again.

The lady leaned forward. "Mr. Loomis, like I told you on the phone, my husband told me to contact you should anything ever happen to him. And as you know—" Her voice cracked. Her eyes welled. She tore a paper towel from the roll on the table and dabbed her eyes and sniffled. "Our house exploding was no accident."

Okay. So, the woman was Judge Willard Logan's widow. Brad Logan's mama. Why did Mickey and Abe have to drive all the way to Missouri to meet her? Couldn't they have met in Claxton somewhere? Jeez.

"Albert Speed did it. He and some of his minions."

"Why do you think so?" Abe said.

"Because my husband knew things about him and Thomas Hightower. I knew Willard was giving you information. He told me. When it came out about Thomas' BAR exam, they killed him because they figured he leaked information to the Feds."

"Why did he do it? Why did he help me and Mickey?"

"Because of Brad."

"What do you mean?"

"Here you go," the waitress said and placed Abe and Mickey's plates on the table.

Abe looked up at her. "Thank you."

Mickey followed suit.

Abe turned back to Mrs. Logan. "What does your son have to do with all this?"

"We have been friends with the Hightowers for years. Thomas and Willard played little league together. Graduated high school together. Went to college and law school together. Our kids were raised together. When all that happened with the skeleton hand a few years ago, Billy Joe just cut Brad off. Wouldn't have anything to do with him. They were best friends, and then, just like that, Brad was nothing to Billy Joe."

She looked at Mickey. "I'm sorry that my son lied about you. Billy Joe put him up to it. Billy Joe took the hand and had Brad put it in your backpack. When the principal called Brad into his office, Brad broke down and told the truth. Billy Joe told him their friendship was over. He and the other kids that Brad used to hang around with just cut him off. Treated him like he was a leper or something."

"Mrs. Logan, kids do stuff like that, especially spoiled kids. I'm still not seeing how this ties together."

"When Billy Joe and the other kids shunned Brad, it affected him. The doctor says the rejection has caused Brad to have acute traumatic grief. He hardly ever says anything. Keeps to himself. Stays in his room. Willard talked to Albert and Thomas about it. He hoped they'd talk to their boys. Billy Joe especially because he is kind of like the leader. Well, he used to be before Mickey—" She caught herself. "Before Billy Joe brought everything on himself. Anyway, when Albert and Thomas ignored Willard, that did it. He was through with them. Brad is our only child." Her voice quaked again and she wept. She took a moment and gathered her emotions. "He's my only child. But he was OUR only child before they killed my husband." She broke down again, then recovered. "As I said Willard told me that if anything should happen to him for me to give you this." She took a brass key from her purse and slid it across the table to Abe.

"What is this?" Abe said.

"It's the key to a safe deposit box at the First Covenant Bank in Alabaster. You'll find everything you need to bring down Albert Speed."

"Alright," Abe said and slipped the key into his pocket.

"You need to be very careful. Albert Speed is dark and wicked. The man has no soul. That's why I left Claxton and moved up here. I'm scared of the man. He'll kill you if you get in his way. He'll kill Mickey too. He hates both of you. Mickey would be in prison right now if Thomas was still on the bench. Your exposing Thomas REALLY complicated things for Albert. He doesn't know it was you, but he'll figure it out before long. When he does, he'll come after you."

"He better bring an army."

"He will. His family's tied to the Mafia in Louisiana. His father was a hitman for Carlos Marcello."

"How did your husband and Thomas Hightower get mixed up with Albert Speed?'

"It's all in the box the key goes to." She checked her watch. "I have to get going." She looked back into Abe's eyes. "Mr. Loomis, before I leave I want you to know that my husband was a good man. He wasn't like them. When the money started rolling in, he had a change of heart. His only fault was that he knew what all they were doing and didn't tell anyone. And it bothered him his whole life. I know he died at peace with himself. I saw the look in his eyes when he would sit down and type a message for you. He helped you because he knew it was the right thing to do." She looked at her watch again. "I really have to go."

She pulled the strap of her purse up on her shoulder and left them at the table.

CHAPTER TWENTY-EIGHT

Abe watched in the side mirror as the car pulled over to the curb of the street. It had been following them since Sikeston, Missouri.

"What are we doing here?" Mickey said.

"I need to speak with Everett. You stay in the truck. Lock the doors. I'll only be a few minutes."

Abe exited the truck and hurried through the front door of Everett Smith's clinic. He returned in less than five minutes. They'd be in Claxton by dusk.

•   •   •

"Why are we taking the backroads?" Mickey said.

Abe glanced up at the rearview mirror. No sign of the car. "A car was following us. Must've lost them."

His cell phone chimed. He flipped it open. A Claxton number Abe didn't recognize. He pushed a button and answered. "Hello."

"Abe . . . help me," a frantic young female voice said. She began to cry. Abe could hear the phone shifting to another person. "You've got something I want. I've got something you want," the man said.

"Speed, you so much as mess up her hair and I'll chop you up a little piece at a time. You hear me."

"Who's he got?" Mickey said.

Abe raised an open hand to Mickey.

"The old cotton mill. I'm on my way," Abe said. "Listen, Speed . . . hello . . . hello."

Abe flipped his phone closed and turned to Mickey. "He's got Lolita."

Mickey's complexion paled. He lowered his chin to his chest. "I love her."

Abe placed a hand on Mickey's shoulder. "I know, Son. We'll get her. Don't worry."

The machines of the Claxton Cotton Mill first started spinning and weaving in 1929. By the 1950s an entire residential community had sprung up within walking distance of the facility. Most of the homeowners paid their mortgages and other household expenses from the paychecks they earned at the thriving factory. In its heyday it boasted of over one hundred employees. In the1970s the American textile industry started losing the battle to low-cost, sweatshop-labor countries like China and Vietnam. And by the 1990s the old mill was little more than a deteriorating brick structure with foundation deficiencies and broken windows.

The rusty iron double doors squeaked as Abe and Mickey pulled them open. Before they could take a step inside both felt the pressure of cold steel to the backs of their necks.

"Make one wrong move and we'll blow your heads off," said the man behind Abe.

They walked in. With the sound of a click the inside of the retired building turned from black dark to dim. A gopher rat scurried across the littered floor and into a crack in the corner. Lolita sat in a metal folding chair at the far end of the room. A single bulb lamp shone directly into her horrified face. "Abe! Mickey! Is that you?"

"Lolita, listen to me." Abe said. "Don't worry. Everything is going to be alright."

Albert Speed stepped from the darkness and put a gun to her head. "Glad you could make it, Mr. Loomis," he said with a sarcastic emphasis on Abe's name. "Come, come. Don't be so shy."

The men shoved Abe and Mickey forward with their guns. The doors squeaked again as two more men pulled them closed.

Abe and Mickey walked closer to Lolita. Speed pushed the gun harder against her head. "That's far enough." Abe and Mickey stopped.

"As I said on the phone, I have something you want." Speed ran his free hand through her hair. Mickey lunged forward. Abe grabbed him. "Uh, uh, uh," Speed said, looking Mickey in the eyes. "That'll get her killed for sure." He turned his attention back to Abe. "And you have something I want."

"And just what might that be?"

Speed laughed mockingly. "Don't play games with me, Loomis. I know you have a very important key in your pocket."

"I'm sorry to disappoint you." Abe reached into his front pockets and reversed them. "But I don't have anything in my pockets."

The look of a devil flashed on Speed's face. He signaled with a nod to the men holding the guns. They smashed Abe and Mickey in the backs of their heads and they fell to the ground. Lights out.

The water felt like needles in their faces. Abe and Mickey shook the fog out of their heads and opened their eyes. Chains bound their hands above them and held them suspended six inches above the floor. Ten feet away, Lolita faced them, bound and hanging in the same fashion.

Albert Speed walked up to Abe. "Throwed rolls. That's a brilliant marketing strategy don't you think?" He pulled his cell phone from his pocket, pushed a few buttons, then held it up to Abe's face. "Look what we have here."

Abe opened and closed his eyes a few times to focus. A picture of Abe sitting across from Willard Logan's widow, the key on the table between them. "The bigger tip you leave, the better service you get," Speed said. He turned the phone so he could see the picture. He gazed at it for a few seconds, then turned it back to Abe. "And I left your waitress a BIG tip." He grinned at Abe like he was inspired by hell. "Before you ever arrived."

"You can have me. I'm who you really want," Abe said. "But let them go."

Speed returned the phone to his pocket and patted the side of Abe's face with an open hand. "You're right. I do want you. My boy's lame for life because of you."

"It was me. I did it. Not him. Let him go." Mickey said.

Speed drew in close to Mickey's face and peered into his eyes. "Courage, boy. I like that."

Speed turned back to Abe. "Two for two, Loomis. You and the key for the boy and the girl. That's the deal."

"You'll have to settle for me. I don't have the key."

Speed turned his head to one side. He closed his eyes and grit his teeth. He looked back at Abe. "Okay. Perhaps something else will persuade you." He walked over to Lolita, pulled a knife from his pocket and, with a flick of his wrist, flipped it open. He rubbed the flat side of the blade against one of her cheeks and then the other.

He looked back at Abe. "You ever dressed a deer, Loomis?"

Abe raised his upper lip in scorn but said nothing.

"What you do is you kill the deer first, THEN you gut it. But I'm going to gut her first, then kill her."

"No, please," Lolita cried out.

Speed moved the knife down to her midsection and cut away the front of her shirt exposing her stomach."

He looked back at Abe again. "Last chance. The key or we're going to see what she had for dinner."

A loud crack from a broken window and the man standing behind Abe fell to the ground. Another loud crack and the man standing behind Mickey fell to the ground. The men at the back of the warehouse pulled their guns but couldn't get their shots off before bullets from the broken window penetrated their foreheads. Another shot sent a bullet through Speed's hand, knocking the knife to the floor. One of the back doors flung open and in walked Everett Smith, a .45 caliber 1911 in his right hand. He walked over and began freeing the three of them.

"I was beginning to worry," Abe said.

"Oh, come on, Squid," Everett said. "Why be early when you can be fashionably late?"

Mickey rubbed the soreness out of his wrists. "How did you know where we were?"

"Tracking device," Everett said.

"What?"

Abe raised his shirt, exposing the small electronic device taped to his chest.

"So, that's why you had to speak to him today."

"That's it," Abe said. He walked over to a cowering Albert Speed. The rich thug cradled his bloody, mangled hand.

Speed looked up at him. "I'm unarmed."

Abe reached down and jerked him to his feet. He placed his hands on each side of Speed's head, his thumbs over his eyes. Abe began applying pressure. Speed wailed in pain as Abe crushed his eyeballs. He released him and Speed fell to his knees, seething in pain. Abe grabbed his scalp and pulled his head back, exposing his bare throat. He drew back a knife hand.

"Stop, Abe! Don't do it!" Everett commanded.

"He deserves to die," Abe said, his fiery eyes fixed on Speed, his upper lip raised. "You saw what he was about to do to Lolita. He would have killed Mickey too."

"It'd be murder. You'd go to the state pen for life." Everett said and tossed the key on the concrete near Abe's feet. "We got everything we need. It's over for him."

Abe glanced down at the key, then shot Everett a look. "I don't care what happens to me. This animal needs to be eradicated."

"He doesn't deserve a quick death. Blind, rotting in prison is better. Besides, think about Mickey, Abe. He needs you."

Mickey stepped up behind Abe. "He's right . . . Dad."

Abe turned and looked at Mickey and relaxed his expression. He shoved Speed's head forward causing him to collapse on the floor. Mickey rushed to Abe's embrace.

Police cars barreled onto the scene, blue lights flashing. Chief Luther Davenport and three of his officers rushed through the doors, weapons brandished.

Chapter Twenty-Nine

Chief Luther Davenport stepped up to the mounted cluster of microphones and gripped each side of the rostrum. Cameras flashed. Reporters sat ready with pens and notepads.

Davenport began. "Last night, we responded to a report of shots fired at the old cotton mill. When we arrived on the scene, we found Mr. Albert Speed in need of medical attention. His injuries were not life-threatening. He is currently hospitalized at Baker Regional Hospital. We are currently questioning four individuals who were at the scene. The bodies of four armed gunmen have been transported to the local morgue. I will take a few questions."

Davenport raised his hand to one of the reporters.

"Chief Davenport, what can you tell us about the four individuals you're questioning, and do you suspect they are responsible for Mr. Speed's injuries?"

"Their identities are being withheld for the time being. Two of the individuals are minors. That's all I'm at liberty to say about them at this time."

Davenport looked to the back of the room and motioned to another reporter.

"Chief Davenport, did the four gunmen open fire on you and your men when you arrived?"

"They were neutralized before they were even able to fire their guns. Our officers undergo rigorous training to prepare them for situations such as this. They responded according to their training. I'm glad to report that the four gunmen were the only fatalities. We credit this to fine police work. That'll be all for now."

Other reporters began raising their hands and shouting questions. Luther Davenport turned and walked away.

One week later

Two well-dressed individuals sat behind a desk. A man and a woman. The woman launched into the story.

"We have an earth-shattering development coming out of Baker County in the town of Claxton. We turn now to our own Larry Oliver who is in Claxton."

Larry stood in front of Albert Speed's dealership, a large microphone held just below his chin. "Dana, behind me is the Chevrolet dealership currently owned and operated by Mr. Albert Speed. Several months ago, questions arose about Mr. Speed's business dealings when a fishing boat he owned was discovered close to Pensacola loaded with illegal exotic animals from Central America. That fades in comparison to the recent information that has surfaced. Authorities have acquired a treasure trove of evidence dating back to the mid 1980s linking Speed to offshore money laundering, drug trafficking, illegal importing, bribery, blackmail, and even murder. If convicted, Speed faces up to life in prison and possibly the death penalty. He is currently hospitalized for injuries he sustained in a showdown with local authorities that left four people dead of gunshot wounds. Once released from the hospital, he'll be placed in the Claxton City Jail where he'll be held without bond. We reached out to Speed's attorney, but our calls were not immediately returned. In light of these recent revelations, executives at Chevrolet's Detroit headquarters have permanently suspended Speed's franchise agreement. It is uncertain what will become of Claxton's largest automobile dealership. Workers here are on edge as to what their future holds. Dana, back to you."

Six months later

Mickey gazed up at the building. Above the glass awning three flags hung down from their tilted poles and frolicked in the New York breeze. The etched address 20 Rockefeller Plaza separated the two sets of brass entrance doors on one side from the two sets on the other. Centered above them in large letters the possessive word *Christie's*.

Abe stepped into a section of one of the revolving entrance doors and pushed himself inside. Mickey followed his lead. They took their places in the line of people awaiting service from the welcome desk. When their turns came, the lady seated behind the counter greeted them with a wide, white smile. "Welcome to Christie's. Are you here for today's auction?"

"Yes," Abe said.

"Will you be needing a bidder number today?"

"No, we're not here to buy. We have some items being sold today."

"Great. We appreciate you entrusting us with your treasures. Take the elevator up to the second floor. We'll be getting under way shortly."

The elevator dinged and the door slid open. Abe and Mickey followed the crowd and migrated into a large room. They sat down near the back. A man wearing a royal blue suit and pink tie stood at a podium at the front of the room. He checked the microphone. After a couple of "one-twos" he welcomed the crowd and announced the first item up for bid. A French vase from the 1840s. After a round of bids, he dropped the hammer and announced, "Sold for twelve thousand five hundred."

Mickey watched in amazement as items he considered a little above worthless sell for thousands, some even for tens of thousands.

"Now, we have three items from a first-time seller we think you'll find especially exciting," the auctioneer said.

A lady wearing white gloves positioned a book on an easel next to him.

"This is a first edition of F. Scott Fitzgerald's *The Great Gatsby*. No flossing. No loose pages. No markings. Who'll start the bid at sixty thousand?"

Bidders throughout the room jumped into the action. In less than two minutes the auctioneer made his declaration. "Sold for ninety-six thousand."

The gloved lady removed the book and replaced it with another.

"The second item from the collection is this first edition of Ernest Hemingway's *The Sun Also Rises*. It is in near mint condition and signed by the author. We have verified that the signature is authentic." A lady seated in front of Abe and Mickey nudged the man seated next to her. She leaned over to him. "There it is. Don't let it get away."

The man nodded. Abe smiled, his attention fixed on the front of the room.

"Who'll give me eighty thousand?"

The man raised his paddle and the war ensued. When the shark fest ended the man had successfully concurred with the woman's wishes. At a price of one hundred and twenty-three thousand dollars.

The lady nudged the man again and he turned to her. "Thanks, Honey," she said and kissed him on the mouth.

The auctioneer's assistant removed the book and placed a photograph on the easel.

Mickey shot his eyes open and gaped his mouth. He turned to Abe. "Hey, that's the picture from the kitchen. The one of your great grandfather and the guitar player."

Abe nodded. "Yup."

"But why—?"

Abe raised his index finger to his lips. "Shh. I'll explain later."

The auctioneer began his opening remarks. "This is a remarkable piece of music history. The man with the guitar is renowned Mississippi Delta bluesman Robert Johnson. Johnson is regarded as the most influential blues musician of all time. His life is cloaked in mystery. Legend says he sold his soul to the devil in exchange for musical fame and fortune. This is only the third picture known to be in existence and the only one where he's accompanied by another musician. The man with the harmonica is an ancestor of the person offering the photo up for auction today. The photo has been authenticated by the Mississippi Delta Blues Museum. Now, who'll give me five hundred thousand?"

Three paddles shot up. The auctioneer pointed to one bidder. "I saw yours first." He looked out over the rest of the room. "Can I get six hundred thousand?"

"Six hundred thousand," a woman said. She stood behind a counter along one wall of the room and held a telephone receiver to one ear.

Abe and Mickey looked on as bidders drove the price higher and higher. When the auctioneer finally rapped his gavel, the photo had garnered a price of one million three hundred twenty thousand dollars.

· · ·

The sun had been up long enough to warm the water at the pond's dam side. Bream would be schooling close to the bank. They'd hit almost as soon as the worms splashed into the water. The catfish . . . well, to land some of them, they'd have to cast out twenty feet or so from the bank and fish deep. Probably three feet. Maybe even bottom fish them.

Abe lowered his cane pole. The worm on the hook went for a swim and the bobber kept it ten inches below the water's surface. An ideal scheme to entice the bream. Mickey flicked his fiberglass Shakespeare. The monofilament line made a zinging sound as it unwound from inside the Zebco Spincast reel. The hooked chicken liver plopped on the murky surface and plunged under. Mickey turned the handle a half turn to set the drag. Three or four more turns to tighten the line. Then, he sat down in his chair.

"You regret selling the books and the picture?" he said.

"Not at all," Abe said.

"I still can't believe you sold them. Especially the picture."

"The way I look at it, I didn't really sell them. I just traded them for a dream."

Abe raised the cane pole, lifting a hand-sized blue gill from the water. He swung the flopping fish in close and caught the line above its mouth. With the diligence of a surgeon, he began freeing the hook from the fish's mouth.

"Think we'll get it?" Mickey said.

Abe sewed the nylon cord through the fish's mouth and gills. He eased it in the water and pushed the metal needle of the stringer into ground. "I plan for us to. The question's going to be how much we have to pay. I'm sure we're not the only ones interested in it."

Mickey reeled in his line, then recast his bait to a more desired spot in the pond.

"When did you buy THIS place?"

"I didn't."

Mickey looked at Abe, his face scrunched like he'd caught the scent of something foul. "What do you mean you didn't?"

Abe dropped his rebaited hook back in the water and rubbed his hands on the legs of his pants. "I mean just that—I didn't pay for this place."

"What about the house?"

"Didn't pay for it either."

"Then, how did you get it all?"

"I've never told you the story?"

"Nope."

"Well, I guess it's time to tell you, then."

Abe lifted his bait out of the water and laid the cane pole on the bank. Mickey reeled his line in. If Abe stopped fishing to tell the story, Mickey thought it best to stop fishing to listen to it.

"I'm looking forward to hearing this," Mickey said.

When the bobber reached the top eyelet of his rod, Mickey laid the rig on the ground. Abe began.

"My great, great, great grandfather was born a slave. His name was Napoleon Loomis. He was the most famous horse trainer in all of Alabama. One spring a massive ice storm hit. As the plantation's horse trainer, he was responsible for taking care of the master's horses. So, he got up early in the morning and went out to the barn to feed them. Ice was covering everything. While he was in the barn, a big tree limb snapped and fell on the roof. The impact made the barn collapse. Napoleon was trapped under the rubble. But somehow, he was able to free himself. As soon as he did, he heard his master calling his little girl's name. Turned out that his daughter had gone to the barn to feed her pony and she was penned under a big timber. Napoleon managed to free the little girl and save her life. Shortly after, his master called him to his office. Napoleon was afraid that his master was going to sell him or sell some of his family. Instead, the master set him free and gave him one hundred acres of land."

Abe spread his opened hands and looked toward the horizon. "This one hundred acres that you and I live on today." He lowered his hands and put them on his hips. "Been in my family ever since."

"Whatever happened to the little girl?"

Abe looked at Mickey. "Her name was Rose. And she loved Napoleon and his family. Taught them how to read and write. In fact, the reason the master set Napoleon free was because the little girl asked her daddy to."

"So, a little white girl changed his life."

Abe nodded. "Yup. And not just his, but in a real sense, the lives of his descendants too. All the way down to me. Of course, God and good decision-making played their parts too."

"You completed the circle."

"What do you mean, Son?"

"Think about it. A little white girl changed a black man's life. And you, a black man, changed a little white boy's life." Mickey put a thumb to his chest. "Mine."

Abe's eyes moistened. He stood from his chair and spread his arms. Mickey jumped to his feet and into Abe's embrace.

CHAPTER THIRTY

Mickey thought more people would have been there. But then again, it was an odd thing. Big. Empty. Boring. Most people didn't need it. Wouldn't know how to use it if they had it. And definitely couldn't afford it. No one in the small crowd was even close to Mickey's age.

"What's a kid doing here?" several were thinking. No doubt. People stood in groups of two or three. Like they were teams or cliques. They talked amongst themselves as if they had secrets or were planning or scheming.

A man stepped up on a platform made of three wooden pallets covered with a piece of plywood. Evidently, he had expected a larger crowd and thought he'd need it so everyone could see him. Boy, was he wrong. Two other men and a woman stood in front of the platform. The man's helpers, Mickey guessed.

"Alright folks, it's ten thirty. Time to start. This is an absolute sale. In other words, the highest bidder, regardless of the amount, buys the property. The rules have been publicized, but let me cover them again to avoid any misunderstanding. The sale is final. The property is being sold as is. You signed a bidder agreement acknowledging this before you were issued a bidder badge. If you are the high bidder, you must put down a fifty-thousand-dollar deposit immediately. The deposit is non-refundable and must be in the form of cash or a bank check. It cannot be a personal check. If you cannot pay the deposit immediately, the next highest bidder will have the option to buy the property at the price of his or her bid.

Once the deposit is received, the bidder will have until 5 PM today to pay the balance. If the balance is not paid by the deadline, a new auction date will be set, and we'll do this all over again. Now, are there any questions?"

The man scanned the gathering. "Alright, since there are no questions, we'll begin. Who'll start us out at four hundred thousand?"

The two men and the lady began scanning the crowd. Mickey nudged Abe. "Aren't you going to bid?"

Abe shook his head. "Not first. We'll let someone else start it off."

That made sense. Why pay more than you have to?

"Come on, folks. This is a prime piece of commercial real estate. Three hundred thousand so everyone can get in."

"Yup!" the lady called out with an extended inflection, her hand raised over her head.

"Three fifty," the auctioneer said.

"Yup!" one of the men yelled.

"Four hundred."

Abe nodded.

"Yup!" the lady called out again, acknowledging his bid.

Within seconds, a man in the crowd bid five hundred fifty thousand.

·   ·   ·

The rooster wore a top hat and a necktie. His wings and tail blinked. As did the large ice cream cone he stood over. To draw even more attention an arrowhead the same size as the ice cream cone flickered on and off. The iconic metal sign was unavoidable to passersby. For more than thirty years the *Dari Delite* had served its fast-food selections and frozen treats to hungry customers.

The two of them sat at a concrete table as they waited for their food to be delivered.

"How are your therapy sessions going? Mickey said.

"Good . . . real good actually. Counselor's cutting our session schedule back from weekly to monthly. You doing okay still?" Lolita said.

"Yeah. Dad has really helped me. We talk about it often. I haven't had a nightmare in over two months now. It's one thing to watch it in a movie. It's altogether different when you see it in real life."

"Definitely. Even though they were evil people and had to be killed, it's still tough thinking about it sometimes. I'd never experienced anything even remotely like that before." She shook her head. "I really thought Albert Speed was going to use that knife on me."

"Good thing Everett showed up just in time."

"For sure. I never felt so helpless in all my life."

Mickey reached across the table and placed his hand on top of one of Lolita's. He squeezed it gently. "You were great through all of it."

Lolita looked into Mickey's eyes and smiled.

"I was SO proud of you," Mickey said.

"Those men just grabbed me and threw me in the trunk of their car. I might not have even been at that mill if I knew how to defend myself. Think Abe would teach me how to fight?"

"I'm sure he would. How to shoot too."

"Lunch is served," Abe said and set two trays of food and drinks down on the table. "Lolita, did Mickey tell you the news?"

"I didn't know there was any news. I thought we were just having lunch."

"Oh no. Uh uh. We're celebrating," Abe said.

Lolita drew down her brow. "Celebrating what?"

Abe sat down on the bench next to Mickey. He reached for one of the tall cups of soda and a straw. "Well, are you going to tell her or do you want me to?"

"I will," Mickey said, taking one of the wrapped burgers from the tray. He fixed his attention on Lolita once again. "You know the property where Albert Speed's car dealership was?"

"Yeah," Lolita said.

"We bought it today."

"What?"

She cut her eyes to Abe's. He raised his brow and nodded. "That's right. We bought it today," he said with a confident smile.

"That's incredible. What are you going to do with it?"

"Dad's been talking to Chevrolet's home office."

Lolita shot her eyes open wide. "And?"

Abe took a drink of his soda and set the cup down. "We still have a few things to iron out, but once we do and I pay them three hundred thousand dollars, we'll be the county's authorized Chevy dealer. Should be opening just as the two of you are graduating."

"What will you call it?"

Abe nudged Mickey with his elbow. "This is where you come in."

Mickey smiled and tilted his head a bit to one side, his eyebrows raised. "Well, we discussed a few options. Claxton Chevrolet. Loomis & Son Chevrolet. A&M Chevrolet."

"A&M?"

"Abe and Mickey."

Lolita bumped her forehead with the pad of one of her palms. "Well, duh. How could I not get that?"

"But we decided on something totally different," Mickey said and looked at Abe. "Drum roll, please."

"Sorry. Can't do a drum roll on a concrete surface," Abe said.

"Right," Mickey said and turned back to Lolita. "Oh well, imagine a drum roll."

"Come on. Give it up already," Lolita said.

Mickey gave a tight grin. "The name of the dealership will be Leslie Chevrolet."

Lolita brought her hand to her mouth. "After your mom?"

"Yup," Mickey said.

Lolita removed her hand from her mouth and placed it on top of Mickey's. "Oh my gosh, that is SO sweet."

The train rolling on the track below sounded its horn. It snaked along the rails, its two yellow cabooses in tow.

THE END

ACKNOWLEDGMENTS

Special thanks to my first readers: Jayne Vinzetta, Jenny Cooper, Clay Miller, Bill Bolton, Monica King, Kelley Hafner, Dawn Story, and Rebekah Olsen.

Thank you to my friend, Stephen Bittick, for his tech assistance.

My sincerest appreciation to Jim McGarrh, Rhonda Hardesty and Ryan Baker for their helpful input on Bar Exam and courtroom protocol.

And a big shout out to Reagan Rothe and all the team at Black Rose Writing in bringing the story of Abe and Mickey to the marketplace. Thank you very much!

About The Author

Levi Bronze is an Alabama native and resides in the Memphis, Tennessee area with his wife and son. He is the author of the young adult fantasy, *The Red Brick Road*. He is currently working on his next novel. Follow Levi on his website at: levibronze.com and on Instagram: @authorlevibronze.

Note From The Author

Word-of-mouth is crucial for any author to succeed. If you enjoyed *Two Yellow Cabooses*, please leave a review online—anywhere you are able. Even if it's just a sentence or two. It would make all the difference and would be very much appreciated.

Thanks!
Levi Bronze